MEN DJINN & ANGELS

Men Djinn & Angels

Awakening

ANTON D. MORRIS

MEN DJINN & ANGELS
AWAKENING

This is a work of fiction. All of the characters, names, incidents, organizations, and dialogue in this novel are either the products of the author's imagination or are used fictitiously.

iUniverse books may be ordered through booksellers or by contacting:

iUniverse
1663 Liberty Drive
Bloomington, IN 47403
www.iuniverse.com
1-800-Authors (1-800-288-4677)

ISBN: 978-1-5320-3899-0 (sc)
ISBN: 978-1-5320-3900-3 (e)

Library of Congress Control Number: 2017918855

Print information available on the last page.

iUniverse rev. date: 12/28/2017

www.mendjinnandangels.com

THE JOURNEY

Talib had a nightmare. It was the second consecutive night that he dreamt of Gorgo, the red-haired giant whose large hands were strong enough to hold a horned sheep while he bit into the beast's jugular with his jagged teeth. Talib was not as frightened by the savage brutality as he was by the golden eyes that seemed to illuminate from the giant when he lifted his head from the animal's lifeless body. Raw flesh from the sheep's throat dangled from Gorgo's broken teeth as blood spilled down his chin. The giant's head was disproportionately elongated at the crown, making him appear even more horrific, and although he was only an adolescent, Gorgo had become a vicious and remarkably proficient killer.

A short time later, Talib had been startled from his dream. He realized that his transportation had come to a stop. He did not know how long he was asleep, but the sound of moving feet across a wooden floor reminded him that he was inside the cargo area of a train that transported him from Beersheba, and he hoped he had already arrived at Ashqelon. When the door to the cargo area opened and a man who was perhaps six years Talib's senior entered, Talib knew that he had arrived.

"Is this Ashqelon?" he inquired.

"Yes," the young man confirmed. He was dressed in a uniform and red cap. He approached the corner where Talib had made himself comfortable. "Hurry."

Talib reached for a velvet sack with a drawstring. He opened the bag and took from it a small stack of cash. After counting it out, he handed the bills to the porter and stood. The porter walked away from Talib in a direction opposite from where he came. "Come this way," he said and led Talib to a door on the side of the train car—one that Talib never even knew was there. The porter opened the door and waited for Talib, who walked cautiously carrying a duffel bag tossed over his shoulder.

"You have to jump," the porter directed.

There were no steps by which to descend, and Talib was nowhere near a platform. The door turned out to be a rear one that was located on the opposite side of the station platform. Talib looked over the threshold to see how far the drop was. It was more of a drop than the length of his sixteen-year-old body.

"Hurry," the porter said again.

Talib tossed the duffel bag first, and then he followed. The ground was cemented and hard, and the bottoms of his feet burned from the landing. He looked up as the porter was closing the door and gently gave thanks. The porter never responded; he only shut the door. Now, under the shadows of a pre-sun-lit sky, Talib sighed. He had made it this far and was relieved, but it was still a long way to Cairo. He was afraid that escaping Israel by seaport would be more difficult than it was to sneak inside. He was hungry and low on cash, but there was no turning back—and nothing awaited him if he did.

The walk to the seaport was not long, but he was disappointed to learn that, after standing in a long line, he did not have enough cash to purchase the ticket and his age was insufficient. Saddened by the rejection at the ticket counter, Talib stepped out of line and considered visiting the nearby fruit stand to relieve the tightening of his stomach around his spine. He tried to convince himself that he could endure the hunger in much the same way that he did during the Ramadan fasting period—only now, it was not Ramadan, and he was neither fasting nor praying. The last time Talib tried to make prayer he closed his eyes and saw Baruch Goldstein turning toward him, holding an automatic rifle that spat deadly ammunition that whistled past him. The image was so shocking and appalling he was unable to pray. Furthermore, Talib could not bury his anger long enough to pray.

As he entered the fruit market, Talib cautioned himself against spending too much, as he imagined he would need to pay one of the dock workers for a chance to ride the boat to Alexandria, just as he did with the train ride from Beersheba. It was right then he noticed the pale-faced European man for the second time. The exact same man had stood behind him when he attempted to purchase a ticket. The thought of being followed frightened Talib. The man was rather large, built like a wrestler. He was clean-shaven with a military haircut. Talib imagined that this guy was perhaps in his mid-thirties, and he had a disposition that resembled more of a merchant than someone dangerous. Their eyes met, and Talib felt the stranger was indeed watching him, studying him as if he suspected Talib to be a thief. Swiftly, Talib purchased his fruit and exited the market. For a split second it seemed as though he was clear of the stranger, until ten paces later the man called to him. He spoke in near-perfect Arabic pronunciation—something that startled Talib. Turning, he saw the lad exiting the market at a swift pace. Whoever he was, he wanted to speak to Talib, but Talib was not interested in anything he had to say. Talib turned to run, but in his panic, he tripped over a woman who was walking near him.

It was then that he realized any attempt to escape through a crowded space between the dock and the market while holding onto a duffel bag was not a good idea. He tried to stand, but the man was already upon him and had taken him by the arm. His grip was strong, but gentle.

"Why do you run?" the man asked.

"What do you want with me?"

The man helped Talib to his feet; his eyes were gentle. He placed his hand on Talib's chest. Talib's heart raced.

"Relax. I won't hurt you."

Talib took a deep breath to slow his breathing. This man stood taller than Talib, and he smelled of expensive cologne. He also wore a gold ring with a strange symbol that looked like an owl and an astrolabe. His fingernails were clean and manicured. Talib hadn't had many experiences with foreigners but met enough wealthy men to know that such manicured hands were a sign of wealth. Just as Talib realized that he had taken a few moments to make observations of the man in front of him, the man had done the same. His brown eyes dropped to the charm around Talib's neck. It was uncovered from the fall. The charm hung from a silver chain and was made of brass. In it were thirteen small stones—a diamond in the center surrounded by twelve other jewels. The charm was no larger than three square centimeters and was shaped like a square. Centered toward the bottom was an extension shaped like the letter Y. Talib covered the charm, hiding it behind his shirt.

The stranger spoke first. "You look like you're searching for something." He then released Talib's arm.

"Were you just behind me at the ticket counter?" Talib countered.

"Yes."

"So you already know that I'm trying to get a ticket."

The man noticed that Talib had dropped his fruit. "Come. I'll buy you another one."

Talib followed him into the market. The man introduced himself as Theodore and insisted that Talib take as much fruit as he wanted. When they left the market together, Theodore inquired about Talib's destination.

"Cairo," Talib answered.

"I'm going to Alexandria. I'll get you on this boat."

"Why?" Talib asked, suspicious of Theodore's generosity.

"I want someone to talk to, and if I have to pay for it, I will. Furthermore, you look like a boy who's traveled for days without a bath or a decent night's sleep."

Theodore was convincing if nothing else, but Talib remained

suspicious. It took several hours before his suspicions melted away. Theodore proved to be an honest man. He purchased a ticket for Talib that came with a cabin, a bed, and a place to wash. Talib was grateful and obliged to give Theodore the only thing in return that he sought—conversation.

The two of them sat on deck and looked out across the water as the shore faded away. The sky and sea merged at the horizon until only a hint of sunset shown as the waters sloshed against the sides of the boat as it sailed the Mediterranean. Theodore disclosed that he was a sociologist by trade but had an affinity for astrology, theology, and, above all else, archeology. His love for archeology had lured him to Israel in the first place.

"There was some talk about ancient scrolls being found here. I work for a family," he explained. "Well, it is actually my family, but they will pay a lot of money for certain artifacts."

Talib nodded his head. He neither understood nor passed judgment. "So they like to collect things?"

"Yes and no," Theodore explained. "We are just fascinated with the power of some things. You may find it strange, but people do the oddest things to obtain certain artifacts. Then there are artifacts that have a certain power to them. Take, for example, a diamond ring. Now think about the influence it has. It will make a woman smile for days, and it will make a man commit murder, but in the end, it is just a rock." He laughed. "Isn't that odd?"

Talib nodded his head. He felt his eyes growing heavy. It had been days since he'd had a good rest, and the swaying, rising, and falling of the boat on the waves seemed to cradle him as the cool air caressed his face, soothing him, luring him to sleep. Despite his efforts to remain polite, Talib succumbed to the weight in his eyelids, and before he knew anything at all, he was fast asleep.

But sleep did not bring him comfort or relaxation. In fact, sleep brought him terror in the form of a figure that was made of light, but shaped like a man.

The figure carried a javelin and walked with the stride and

sternness of a soldier whose intent was destruction. His target was a medieval Mongolian army that lay siege to a walled city. It was from the wall that Talib witnessed the aggression of the lighted man. His target was not men, but the horses. He attacked them with his javelin, using the point to stab some and the handle to crush the skulls of others. His orange hue had become brighter, and his rage seemed to grow from his core and rise toward his head. It was as if this fiery figure had summoned an incredible amount of energy; he seemed to possess a vivaciousness that empowered him to move with incredible speed throughout the Mongol camp. He spared no horse, and when they were all dead, he took their bodies and arranged them in a perfect spiral shape that Talib thought resembled a seashell.

When the orange-hued man completed his design, he turned and spied Talib watching atop the wall. Talib understood that the creature had identified him and watched as the figure's eyes brightened and a pair of wings opening from behind and stretched out on either side of his body. Then he lifted his javelin and threw it in Talib's direction. Talib was transfixed in his position on the wall. He was too frightened to move, so he simply watched as the javelin struck the wall just below his feet. The collision caused an explosion, making the wall crumble. Talib felt himself falling with the debris. He screamed in terror as he awoke from his dream.

Theodore remained at his side. They had not moved from their seats on the deck of the boat.

"Bad dream?" Theodore asked.

"Yes," Talib answered.

"Have you had many nightmares?"

"Yes. It seems I can't sleep at all."

Theodore nodded his head as if he understood something that Talib did not. He pointed to the charm that Talib hid under his shirt. "Before you started to wear that piece, or after?"

Talib hesitated. He admitted that strange dreams were not new to him. He often dreamt of being in strange places with people he had never seen. But it was true, however, that the intensity of his nightmares had become stronger since he was given the charm by his older brother.

"If I were a betting man," Theodore said, "I would wager that your nightmares and that charm are connected."

Talib made no reply. He was lost in his thoughts.

"I know someone who could help you. Are you interested?"

"Help me to do what?"

"Help you to sleep. I have a niece, actually two of them. We can stop to see them when we reach Athens, no?"

"Athens?" Talib stood and ran to the railing of the boat as if he thought that he could escape. He turned to Theodore. "I need to get to Cairo."

"Relax." Theodore tried to sooth him. "The only way I could have gotten you out of Israel was to put you on this boat for Athens. From there, we can get to Cairo. We can see my nieces when we get there. If they can help you, great! If they cannot, then you will be on your way. Does that sound all right?"

Talib had no choice. He was on a boat somewhere in the Mediterranean Sea.

THE PSYCHIC

Talib was immersed in another dream. He dreamt of what he took
to be a party. In fact, it was a ceremony of some sort, held in an
open field with an overcast night sky and a mountainous horizon
in the near distance. There was a gentle rumble of thunder, but it
was barely audible over the loud drums and singing. There were
perhaps a hundred people with dark skin basking in celebration.
Talib supposed that they were African, although there were
few occasions in his life when he'd been within eyeshot of an
Ethiopian. The people in his dream, however, seemed nothing
of the kind. Their bodies had wider frames, incredibly muscular
backs, and skin that seemed darker than the nighttime sky. One
of them stood noticeably taller than the others. Talib had seen him
before in other dreams. His jaws were wide, and he had a flat nose
that seemed to swell over his thin black mustache. His eyes were
bright and golden like an afternoon sun that was soon to set. He
stood face-to-face with a woman; she was as dark as the others.
Her teeth were remarkably straight and set with perfection behind
elegant lips that moved back when she smiled. She had green eyes
that were more delightful and hypnotizing than frightening. Her
hair was braided into locks that stretched beyond her shoulders.
She had a regal decorum, yet she was mysterious. In one hand, she
held the bleeding heart of an animal, perhaps a pig – he could not
be certain – but it hung from the branch of a tree where she stood.
She extended her thin, black, blood-covered hands upward to the
tall man with golden eyes.

He moved slowly, but he was in no way cautious or afraid. He ceremoniously moved to a silent rhythm that was heard, despite the drums, by only him and the woman. He took the heart from her hand, put it to his lips, and sank his teeth into the tough flesh. Rain started to fall. It was light and misty at first, making the many people around him cheer as they circled the tree, dancing and singing. When he had taken in a portion of the heart, he returned it to her, and she lifted it high above her head; there were more cheers. Then came along another man dressed in military decorations and markings, moving through the crowd toward the tree where the animal hung. He stopped for a moment to make eye contact with the woman. She smiled approvingly, and he lowered his head until it was under the animal, letting blood from its opened chest spill over the back of his head. There were more cheers, and those who danced mimicked the actions, each person one behind the other, men and women both, bathing in the animal's blood.

The rain fell faster and came in larger drops that seemed to have no effect on the burning fires or the drumming and singing. Coincidentally, the celebration seemed to grow more intense. As the crowd celebrated, Talib could see past them and noticed what appeared to be a large group of men approaching from the mountains. They carried no torches for light, but there seemed to be an aura of brightness surrounding them.

They came by the hundreds, walking in formation as if they were an army. Talib's eyes shifted upon seeing another mysterious woman in the crowd of dancers and blood bathers. She was dressed in a long blue garment that resembled more of a robe than a dress. Her head was covered in a silky, sky-blue material that caressed her shoulders. At the very top of her head was a golden ornament, like a crown worn by a princess. Her eyes were greener and brighter than the woman who held the animal's heart overhead. Talib had seen her eyes before and recognized their shape. She seemed focused on him. Her eyes were magnetic, and he was held captive by them, unable to look away. She walked elegantly through the crowd as if it weren't there. When she was no more than three paces away, she stopped, her eyes crawling over Talib's body from head to shoulders, arms, hips, and feet.

Then she spoke to him. "*Weshi akupo.*"

Talib had never heard those words before, but somehow he understood her to say, "I see you." He made no reply. Talib felt his heart racing.

"*Mega war fi adema.*" She spoke again, shifting her eyes to the tall man who, at that time, had embraced the woman. Talib knew that the mysterious woman wanted him to keep track of the man. He was important, or at least something he carried was utterly important.

"I promised to seek his parts wherever they hide, and I will not stop doing so," Talib answered as he shifted his eyes to the man who had taken the woman's hand and followed her away from the crowd. When he shifted his eyes again, the mysterious princess was no longer there. Instead, the marching army of men from the mountains had arrived.

In their hands they each carried machetes. They were small in height, but each had broad shoulders, dense chest cavities, and dull, olive-colored eyes. They were warriors and had come, as it seemed, to attack the celebrating people. But they did not attack them violently. Instead, they seemed to seek out only those men or women who used the animal's blood for ablution. When the warriors made contact with the chosen ones, they approached from behind and ran their bodies into their seeming victims. It was then that Talib realized the warriors were not people at all; they were spirits who merged their energies with the men and women who participated in the blood bath. Talib saw the people's expressions change after the merger of energies. One man stood erect, while his chest seemed to swell and his eyes took on a brighter hue. The mysterious woman's voice seemed to come from nowhere. Talib received her words as if she spoke through his heart.

"*Tutamira du*," she said.

Her words caused him to shiver and awaken. She promised to kill them all, but Talib did not know of whom she spoke. Her voice carried the rage and hatred of a million people and a hundred years of fury. The bed on which he lay was cool and wet from perspiration, and his breath was heavy. As Talib slid to a seated position on the edge of the bed, his feet barely touching the floor, he remembered that he was far away from home. Theodore had taken him to an incredibly luxurious mansion on a small island in Greece. He had been given a room in which to sleep with the promise of help from a set of sisters who would rid him of these cursed nightmares, so Talib expected a night of rest. However, the dreams seemed more intense. This time, Talib felt as if he was part of the ceremony. He also shared a connection with the mysterious woman in blue, as if he knew her and her abilities. She was a beautiful lady, but her fury was deadly. Her spirit was loved by some but should have been feared by all.

Talib would do anything to stop the dreams. He did not know how these sisters could or would help him at all, but he was more than ready to hear what they had to say.

Two hours later, Talib showered and dressed in new clothes that fit him perfectly, save the looseness in the waist. He was then given the chance to meet the sisters. He was offered breakfast inside of a sunlit day room at a table set for three with a white cloth, porcelain plates, silver forks, and crystal glasses.

Talib was joined by three strangers who happened to be standing a few paces from him in the doorway. He expected Theodore, but he was not there. Realizing that he would not see Theodore, he was immediately uncomfortable, feeling as though he had done something wrong.

One of the strangers was a man who stood tall and erect, like a military captain. He was clean-shaven and had his hands placed on the shoulders of the two girls who stood in front of him. The girls wore different expressions. The smaller one seemed afraid, while the older, slightly more attractive one seemed to look at him critically, almost analytically. Her gaze made Talib squirm in his seat.

The trio spoke in hushed whispers that Talib could not hear. The elder sister took the younger sister by the hand, encouraging her to come along. Talib could see that the younger girl was as apprehensive as he was. The man behind them patted their shoulders and ushered them forward. Talib felt his heart accelerating as they approached.

"*As-salamu Alaykum*, Talib," the older one greeted him. She spoke Arabic to Talib's surprise.

"*Waalaikum asalam*," he returned the greeting. "Are you Muslim?"

She smiled. "No," she admitted.

Talib shifted his eyes to the younger sister who looked away as if intentionally refusing to make eye contact with him. Despite that, Talib saw that her eyes were gray, as gray as his. When he turned his attention to the older sister, he saw that her eyes were a different shade—brown and much darker.

"I apologize for having you wait. My name is Kate, and this is my sister, Fiona." She took a seat and gently touched her sister's arm, inviting her to sit.

"I do not believe this is really happening." Fiona spoke softly using a Katharevousa dialect that Talib did not understand.

"We will only speak to him, nothing more," Kate responded using the same words. She then focused her attention on Talib and smiled.

"I don't have to speak to him. I can feel him." Fiona's voice was soft and mystical. She eyed the plate in front of her, contemplating. "There is so much pain, so much anger."

Talib had no way of knowing what was said, but he could tell Fiona was dolorous. He wondered if she had been forced to see him. She had dark hair and a rather pale face for a fifteen-year-old. Her frame was thin, but the fullness of her cheeks indicated that she was well fed and healthy. Talib felt an ironic closeness to her, as if she were a distant relative—someone he had not seen since his toddler days.

Kate gently took her sister's hand. "Don't be afraid," she said. "I'm here with you." She turned attention to Talib again. "Do you know why you are here?" Kate asked.

"No. I'm not sure."

"You are here because you want help. Am I correct?"

"Yes."

"And you're afraid?"

"No."

"He lies," Fiona mumbled.

"We can help you. We will help you," Kate promised. "But first I believe I owe you an apology. I feel responsible for the many things that brought you here."

"He is the one," Fiona said. Her voice shook from fear. "His father was one they killed."

Kate stroked her sister's hand gently while locking eyes with Talib. "I'm sorry about your father."

Talib held back his tears. It had not occurred to him that he had not spoken of his father's murder to anyone. His melancholy overshadowed his curiosity concerning Kate's knowledge of his father's death.

"We know only a little about you," Kate noted. "It is only fair that I tell you a little about us."

"He likes stories," Fiona's voice was suddenly calmer.

Kate stared into his bewildered eyes. Talib's curiosity was growing. He suddenly needed to know how Kate came to speak Arabic. When he asked, she explained that her grandfather, who had recently passed away, was born in Egypt. His name was Umar, and he had a very special gift—one that had been in the family for more than two centuries. That gift was now in Fiona's possession.

"I believe that you have a similar gift," she said. "When I tell you about it, you will have a million questions, each having a very complicated answer. Because you happen to like stories, I will start from the beginning."

Fiona sipped her orange juice, and Talib did the same. Then she related the story of the Enlightened Titans to him.

The Enlightened Titans was an organization founded by an ancestor named Joseph Konstantinos who was young, wealthy, and ambitious; he ventured out to purchase land and build a city. He would call it Konstantinos. The dream was a lofty one, but when investors joined, it became an incredible reality. The designated location was a plot of land situated within a mountainous range that straddled the border between Syria and Lebanon called the Herman Mountains. The purchase of this land came under high protest by religious leaders from both Islamic and Christian sects. The religious locals believed the land was cursed by a group of highly supernatural forces who met there to form a pact. Muslims never spoke of this supernatural meeting, but Christians insisted with violent passion that the curse was real.

The city's establishment would prove to be rife with exploitation that involved the construction of elaborate churches and overcharging clergy for the work they performed. Joseph and his businessmen, however, would not pass up the opportunity of cashing in on construction. They believed that the publicly charged sentiments about paranormal activity would guarantee successful sale of the property. Joseph also believed that local fears and legends should in no way stand in the way of logical, financial decisions. Political pressures persisted, however, and eventually Joseph Konstantinos agreed that any relics found during excavation and land development would be considered property belonging to the local government for the sake of preservation. This consensus seemed to be a reasonable balance between businessmen and religious fanatics.

In the moment of truth, Joseph and his team failed to surrender the relics. When artifacts were discovered, he was summoned to the dig site, but it was already blocked off and four of his personally hired guards stood watch. Just barely jutting from the earth were two boxes—one large, and the second was half the size of the first. There were also three scrolls wrapped in silk cloth and secured with a wax sealant; each was engraved with patterns of interlocking circles.

When Joseph spied the artifacts, intrigue compelled him to open the boxes. He pulled the latch of the larger box, but it did not budge. Then he tried the smaller box to no avail.

"Maybe we should pry it a little," he suggested.

"I would advise otherwise, sir," said William. He was the eldest son of Rudolf Thornton, one of the investors. Up until that moment, William had what was thought to be a wasted education in archeology. His training had suddenly become important, as he was the first person called upon to meet Joseph at the dig site. "There were times when people in this part of the world hid secrets in boxes like this, and if opened improperly, the contents would be destroyed."

Joseph took one of the scrolls in his hand, pondering the advisement. He studied the wax symbol and held it up for William to see the arrangement of circles. "It's an ancient symbol; the seed of life."

With hands covered in tight vinyl gloves, Joseph pulled gently at the wax seal until it gave way. He was careful not to damage the precious relic. Because it had been rolled for centuries, it would not open easily. One of his assistants gave a helping hand. Together, they managed to extricate the parchment to find strange letters written upon it. Joseph was well versed in Greek and Latin script. He was also adept at deciphering Egyptian hieroglyphics, as well as the language of ancient Babylon, but this scroll told a story in a language that was foreign to him and his team of experts.

Joseph's next charge was to keep the discovery secret. He ordered his excavation team on vacation to keep away questions and snooping. The only people allowed to stay included his four security staffers who were assigned the task of guarding the artifacts with their lives. A third priority was to decipher the narratives written in the scrolls. William hand copied various lines and promised to ask around until he found someone with enough expertise to identify the characters.

A full month went by before Joseph learned about William's invitation to speak with an Irishman who claimed to have been inclined with the skill to speak the angel's language. It was suspected that the scrolls were inscribed, not by members from some Assyrian or Sumerian society, but from an angel of God. Joseph accepted the invitation, and both he and William traveled to the Irish island to meet the mysterious Edward Kelly.

Edward had a large home. The structure was composed of a wood frame surrounded by stone—the first of its kind, so he claimed. At any rate, the sound construction protected him well against the bitter cold. Over dinner, also attended by Celtic apprentices, Joseph and William were regaled by Edward's testimony of an incredible dream he had prior to a session where he attempted to summon Proteil—an angel that modulates communication between men and animals. In his dream, Joseph learned that Proteil was one of Solomon's many instructors. He compelled Solomon to capture and enslave the demon Barbatos, who taught the King of Israel to master the art of animal communication.

Edward admitted to not having a direct encounter with the angel, but he felt as though he was mentally transported to a mountain where he found alphabetic letters burning in the mountainside. He compared the experience to Moses's acquisition of the commandments and stone tablets. When he awoke from his dream, Edward made a written copy of the letters and stored them in a back room of the house.

"May I see the letters?" William asked.

Edward did not hesitate. He stood from the table and invited his guests to follow. They entered a small room with a wooden table and chair. He lit an oil lamp that cast a glow on the table revealing his work. There were twelve pieces of parchment spread across the table; each bore letters that represented nine different languages, including Arabic, Latin, Greek, and Hebrew. Angelic letters were printed at the tops of each page. Joseph prodded William, who pulled out his sample of the script copied from the scroll and shared it with Edward. Edward affirmed that these same letters resembled the ones from his dream. He believed that given time he could decipher the words and make sense of them. Promises of secrecy were made between the men, and Joseph handsomely compensated Edward for both his service and his discretion.

By the time Kate finished speaking of Joseph's visit to the Irish mystic, Talib had completed his meal of fruit, pastry, and juice.

"That was nearly five hundred years ago," she said, astonished. "Can you believe that we still have those scrolls?"

Talib made no reply. He did not share her excitement. He did not understand how the scrolls might help him or were responsible for his presence in their mansion. More importantly, he could not see how they would help end his nightmares.

"Would you like to see them?"

Unsure of what to say, Talib answered out of sheer politeness. "Yes," he said. His eyes turned to see Fiona. She looked away, lowering her gaze again.

Kate stood and asked Talib to follow. "We'll take a shortcut through the garden." She led the way.

Talib and Fiona were close behind. She and Kate continued to speak in their native tongue so that Talib could not understand.

"You should not do this," Fiona said.

"We must test him," Kate answered.

"I don't need to test him to know. I need more time."

"We don't have time. What if he decides to leave tonight? How will we convince him to help us if he leaves?"

"I don't want to feel him anymore," Fiona noted. "He frightens me."

17

"You have nothing to fear," Kate said, reassuring her sister. "I won't leave your side. You are ready for this; you've trained and prepared for this. It will be all right. Trust me."

The garden was situated within the walls of the mansion. It was beautifully adorned as four men worked diligently in preparation for spring.

Through the garden was a walkway that provided passage to a separate wing of the estate. They entered a set of white wooden doors and followed a long hallway to a set of carpeted stairs that led down to what appeared to be a lobby. It was furnished with antique chairs, and sculptured busts of men mounted on marble pedestals circled the center.

Kate stopped and pointed to one of the sculptures. "This is Joseph," she informed.

Talib was at a loss of words. His religious teaching forbade such forms of art. It was a Mosaic Law that he was taught to respect like a direct order from the Supreme One himself. He did not know if he should flee with great haste from the sculptures or simply ignore them. It was the first time he had been so close to a sculpted figure; in his own experiences, most art forms were geometric shapes and Arabic words creatively designed to send messages. Now, within the first days of his visit, he not only witnessed various forms of art that replicated butterflies and owls, but he was also seeing real-life sculptures of a man, and in this room, there were twelve.

"We keep them here to honor them," Fiona spoke. "We do not worship them."

She answered the very thought that circulated around Talib's mind. He paid no mind to the fact that she could sense his thoughts and internalize them; the suspicion had not occurred to him just yet.

Kate stood in front of the bust and reached out to it. She gently ran her fingers over the details of his face—the thin nose, the firm jaw, and the beard. "When he arrived home from Ireland,

Joseph was disappointed to discover that he had been robbed."
She continued with the story. "Rudolph, one of the investors,
was in charge of hiring security. Instead of using locals, he hired
foreigners. They were Africans. He trusted them because they
spoke good Greek, but they were traitors and thieves. They stole
one of the scrolls and two other objects."

She turned away from the sculptures. Behind her was another
room with glass walls and a single glass door. This one seemed
very bland in comparison to the rest of the well-furnished and
decorated rooms in the mansion. The hardwood floors begged
for varnish. Its naked walls were painted white. Above were dim
lights that shone softly on the faces of seven tables that were placed
in a sort of square. The center table was completely covered with
black silk cloth. Spread over the others were books and parchment
that seemed as ancient as time itself. A slim opening allowed
movement between the tables to the center.

"I have to warn you," Kate said. "In case you start to feel light-
headed, it is because the atmosphere in this room is regulated.
We cannot allow moisture, bright lights, or too much air inside."

It was then that Talib noticed Fiona had left them. She returned
with three pairs of latex gloves and medical masks to cover their
mouths and noses. Without a word, she offered a mask and pair
of gloves to Talib. He hesitantly accepted and followed the sisters'
lead.

They entered the room. It was cool and smelled like rubbing
alcohol.

"The scrolls were written in sequence. We have the first and the
third. It was the second that was taken by thieves," Kate explained.

They approached the table. Fiona moved inside the square and
eyed Talib as if expecting a reaction. He followed Kate around
the tables. She stopped at a book that was thick and heavy, bound
between two leather covers. On the front cover was an image of a
cross staff. Fiona continued to watch Talib for his reaction.

"That's a Jacob's staff," Fiona explained. "It is what they used to navigate their ships and find angles."

"It reminds us that we have a mission to navigate humanity to a better world," Kate added as she opened the book. "Can you just imagine a world better than this one? A world without war and free from sickness and unnatural death? That is what we are doing here."

Talib's eyes fell upon the opened book. He saw markings— letters that he had never seen before.

"This," Kate said, "is the letter from the scroll. This is the same letter written in our language. It took more than three hundred years to achieve a complete translation." She flipped the pages and came to a word. "*Gabamnoteh*," she said. "This word describes a slaughtered soul, one that was cut into pieces. There are others— some lost forever, and others whose energy lives among us. The slaughtered ones attach to and share their energy with living souls. When someone is fortunate enough to have a *gabamnoteh* attached to them, they are capable of doing remarkable things."

Talib doubted her. His religious teachings never mentioned the possibility of splitting a soul and attaching its pieces to other people. "I guess it's like lifting an automobile?" He was being sarcastic.

"He doesn't believe you," Fiona said.

"No." Kate was patient. "It is nothing as remarkable as that. But a single person has a different outlook on the world. He may view the world differently, and because of his vision, he is able to make inventions or create medicines for the sick. When was the last time you were ill, Talib?"

Talib smiled, proudly. "Not since three years old. I don't remember, but my mother told me. I had a fever. My mother took good care of us. If you eat the right foods, you should not get sick."

"Sounds like you have a smart mother," Kate replied as she moved toward the table covered with silk cloth.

"So, here are the scrolls." Kate pulled back the material and uncovered the parchment that stretched the entire length of the table.

Talib felt his heart flutter, and his breath became suddenly short. Then there was darkness.

The Giant and the Lyre

Talib had never heard of or knew what a nymph was, but now he dreamt that he was one of them, living among others in the mountains of an island chain somewhere in the Mediterranean. Attached to his back were wings that resembled those found on a honeybee. They were strong and lifted him from the ground, permitting him to fly with fascinating speed. There were nine nymphs in all, and he knew that they were somehow all related—brothers and sisters. Still, he favored one above them all. He felt a closeness to her that was not shared with the others; she was his twin sister. She had eyes like clouds before the rain fell from them. When she looked at Talib, he understood that she saw more than his physical features; she could see his thoughts and intentions. No words were needed between the two; all it took was a mere thought, and she reacted to him in kind.

At that moment, Talib's thought was fixated on flying as fast as his wings could take him, and his sister followed him closely. He did not want to make it easy for her to keep up, so he flew close to the mountains and through the vegetation within them. She was, however, as talented as he was. Perhaps having the advantage of being tuned into his thoughts, the twin knew to expect the sharp turns to avoid a collision against a massive rock or to take a sudden nosedive in lieu of ramming into a tree branch. Together they circled, dove, and climbed the humid air above mountain peaks in competition and joyous laughter.

Curiosity overwhelmed him when he noticed a large ship docked near the island. It bore white sails, and to his surprise, he saw someone standing on the prow and knew at once that it was not a man.

"Belphegor," she said to him as she hovered beside him.

"If that is Belphegor, then ..."

"It is true." She completed his sentence for him.

Belphegor was not a nymph. He was stronger and had abilities that were far more developed than theirs. When Belphegor sensed he was seen, he came to the pair in a flash—faster than the blink of an eye. Talib saw that in comparison to Belphegor, he was no larger than a humming bird. Belphegor's wings were white and shaped like those one might find on a flamingo. His eyes had a dull daffodil hue. From his brow rose four spiked horns the size and shape of those on a rhinoceros.

"Kabeir and Idoth," he greeted. "I've brought him to you." His voice was like the whisper of the ocean striking rocks along the shore. It was the first time that someone or something called him by a different name. He did not correct the spirit; in fact, he seemed to own the name as an alias.

The twins looked to the beach past Belphegor and saw a gathering of three dozen female warriors. Twelve were archers waiting to release their arrows. Twelve were sword bearers, their weapons sheathed, and hands prepared to draw. Twelve more held spears aimed and ready to thrust. The swordswomen and spearmen carried iron shields painted with the mark of the island's queen. Shoulder to shoulder, they circled the men from the ship, their shields connected like a brick wall. Behind them stood archers, their arrows ready to fly. Moving into the center of the circle, the army captain—a tall, muscular woman held a sword low as if daring any of the men to launch an attack. Aside from the giant standing among them, the men, from all appearances, were formidable warriors dressed in ancient attire that seemed to originate from nearby Mediterranean states.

Kabeir was thunderstruck at the giant's youthful appearance. It was a Nephilim—one part man, two parts immortal. "Is this what Asmodeus predicted?" Kabeir asked. "There are many things in his book, as you already know," Belphegor said. "As such, I can no longer guide him. You must look after him, and do not allow him near Jerusalem; the king makes many prisoners of our kind. Keep him safe at all costs—he may be our last hope."

With those words, Belphegor vanished, leaving them in awe of the legendary giant. He was only a boy and already the size of one and a half men. He carried no weapons or shield. His sole possession was a lyre with golden handles and strings of silver.

One man exchanged words with the captain of the female army. The twins could not hear what was said, but the captain seemed pleased. She then gave a signal and led the men away with her army marching on either side of the male visitors.

Idoth was first to fly toward the giant. Kabeir followed. When they reached him, they flew circles around his head. Kabeir had questions and wanted answers. "Can you hear me?"

The giant continued walking in line with the others and made no response to Kabeir's question.

"Yes, he can hear you," Idoth informed. "His name is Yaron."

"I can hear you, and I can see you," said the giant. "What do you want from me?"

"So, is it true? You are the son of Beelzebub? Have you seen the book?"

"I will not answer your questions."

"I've seen the book," Kabeir said. "I know what will come to pass."

"We are here to help," Idoth assured.

"The book is not certain. Asmodeus can write no more." The giant spoke in a low voice. He was aware that only he could see the small winged figures. The same was true with Belphegor. He was special—not simply by his size and strength, but by his birth, and Kabeir admired him.

"You have to save him," Idoth said.

"He doesn't need my help. His jailor is only human."

They spoke no more words to each other. The twins simply followed the giant and his mates into the courtyard and eventually to the judgment room of the warrior queen. She was dressed in long, silk garments of red and gold. To the right of her throne were five spears, mounted for easy access, the arrows pointing upward to the wooden ceiling where twelve chandeliers hung, each with twenty-four candles. The light from the flames illuminated the room, and the smoke stretched upward to the ventilation ducts above.

But not all the smoke escaped the room; some of it hung in the air and took the shape and appearance of a winged spirit that Idoth knew to be Ashtaroth, who gently descended from the ceiling and landed behind the queen's throne. Everything about her appeared human—from her movements to the shape of her body. Her hands and feet, however, resembled something scalier and reptilian. She hid behind the queen's throne and whispered into her ear.

"These men are in danger," Idoth said to her brother.

Kabeir moved close to the giant's ear on the left side and spoke to him. "Do you see her, behind the throne?"

"Yes," he responded.

"She is Ashtaroth. Her daughters will infect you with lust. This will allow the queen and all the other women to seduce you into an orgy. You will all be kept here until every woman is with child. At that time, they will kill all of you. Then, only the daughters will live. Those sons who are birthed will be killed."

"You should leave this place at once," Idoth informed.

Yaron, the giant, so attuned to the whispers from Kabeir and Idoth, did not hear the queen calling to him.

"Yaron," called the leader of their crew.

Yaron's face changed.

"The queen would like to hear you play," the leader noted.

Yaron turned his attention to the queen. She gazed back,

her eyes sinking into his golden, hypnotic stare. He had copper-toned skin, black hair, and a Phoenician bone structure that gave a gentle slope to his brow and a firm, masculine jaw. His shoulders were broad and his hands large, yet his voice was as elegant as a Seraphim.

Yaron sang of a djinni that fell in love with a Watcher—one who was sworn to abstinence and loyal to the Powers. But even though the Watchers resisted love from their own kind, they aptly fell in love with the flesh of women. They fell for the spells placed on them by Ashtaroth. As a result, the Watchers were banished to the prison Tartarus, from which there was no escape.

As Yaron told his story through song, the queen stood from her throne and danced. She was slow and seductive. Her hips and breasts told their own stories of lust and irresistible lasciviousness. As she danced slowly and stole the glares of all men, Kabeir saw a puff of air emerge beside the queen, taking on a smoky form. It was Ishtar, the daughter of lust. She was physically invisible to the men, but it was clear that their third eyes were fixed upon her. She moved in perfect synchronization with the queen, compelling the men's eyes to lust upon her thighs and hips. As the queen smiled and danced, the look in her eyes made each man believe she danced especially for him.

As the seduction went on, Kabeir noticed smoke emanating from the floor, with arms and elbows reaching out as if climbing out from underneath. He was hoping Yaron could see the figures crawling from the earth. They were ifrits, and with them, at least a hundred succumbi.

"Yaron," Idoth called to him. "They will take your men. You will not be spared either."

Yaron's song came to a sudden halt, and the queen turned toward him. Her enchantment had not completely taken over them, because she had not completed her dance. The other women in the throne room had already removed their clothes and were circulating among the men, singling them out for their anticipated sexual bacchanal. Yaron apologized for the abrupt ending to his song and promised to play another—one given to him by his mother.

"You are a lovely queen, and I wish to honor you with a song that is very dear to me," he said.

The queen approved, and Yaron again began to play his lyre. He performed a slower tune this time and crooned foreign lyrics. The queen continued her dance, but Ishtar, the smoked figure, stood there, unmoving. She seemed disturbed as she turned to Ashtaroth, her mother, who was then sitting in the queen's throne.

"Make him stop," Ishtar demanded.

Ashtaroth, however, did nothing of the kind. "Be patient," she replied before she departed, fading away into the air.

In her anger, Ishtar became human in form, and Yaron could clearly see how beautiful she was. It was understandable how she wielded power over men. She turned left and right, surveying the entire area around them and grew furious from what she saw. She was alone. The smoke had dissipated, and the hideous spirits were nowhere to be seen. The men, women, and even the queen had all fallen to the floor asleep, victims to Yaron's spell.

"You are supposed to help us!" the spirit yelled at him in anger. Then, she vanished.

When Talib awoke from that dream, he felt discombobulated and delirious. Kate was with him in the bedroom and cautioned him against sudden movements. Fiona sat quietly in a chair in the corner where she saw him unobstructed. He saw concern in Kate's eyes and detected it in her voice. He lay flat on the bed after a failed attempt to rise. He had no memory of how he got there or of leaving the room where he saw the scrolls. In fact, he could remember nothing at all, from the time Kate revealed the parchment and the letters to him.

"What happened?" he asked.

"Just relax," Kate said and touched his chest. "You need food."

At that moment, a young Ethiopian servant girl with braided hair and dark-brown eyes entered the room carrying a silver tray of food. He was served hot grained cereal, croissants, eggs, and fruit. Talib slowly sat up and rested his back on pillows sandwiched between him and the headboard. He noticed that he had not changed clothes and assumed he was carried to the bed. Kate invited him to eat, and he did.

"Did I faint?" he asked.

"Do you remember when I advised you about feeling light-headed?"

"Yes."

"Why didn't you tell me?"

"I didn't feel light-headed. I don't know what happened."

Kate watched him eat and turned to her sister. Fiona made no movement and spoke no words. Kate turned to Talib again. "You saw him, didn't you?" she asked.

Talib was unsure.

"You saw the giant in your dream?"

Talib was suddenly thunderstruck. "How do you know?"

"Fiona told me," Kate interjected. "Haven't you figured it out already? She's been blessed with a gift."

Talib's eyes moved to Fiona. Her head was low, but when she felt his eyes on her, she lifted her head. Their eyes met, but Talib was slow to understand.

"It is like a gift to understand things that are hard for others," Kate added.

"Do you mean like a gabamnoteh?"

"Maybe." Kate was hesitant to answer.

"Is that the same as being possessed?"

She laughed. "No, it's something you're born with. For people to be possessed by spirits or something like that, they must allow it. This is different. We all have our own gifts." Talib was comfortable with Kate's explanation.

"His name was Yaron, right?" Kate asked.

"Yes," he confirmed.

"He was a giant. The Irishman I spoke of figured out the name."

"Yaron," Talib whispered. "Yes, that was his name."

"He was a very special man, kind and protective."

"You talk about him as if he were real."

"Oh, but he was very real," Kate said. "The old Greek people had their religions, and they told stories to their children that we now believe were innocent ways of telling them what really happened a long time ago. It was as if they wanted us to remember something very important—perhaps something that would change the world or maybe protect it."

Talib continued his meal as Kate narrated more about her ancestor, Joseph Konstantinos. She had a talent for telling stories. Talib could clearly see the images she painted in his mind. He imagined, just as Kate described, Joseph sitting in the garden at this very same mansion as the sun set behind the tall courtyard walls. There were seven men seated with him; they were founders of their brotherhood, so named The Enlightened Titans.

*****

At that time, a year had passed since the discovery of the scrolls and the theft. Joseph vowed to track down the culprits and even went so far as to incorporate the search for the missing artifacts as part of the brotherhood's organizational agreement.

He invited Edward the Irishman to his home, and at their garden meeting, Edward disclosed his discoveries. He explained to the seven other men that the first scroll told about the creation of the universe. From what he could understand, the description compared to what was recorded in the book of Genesis. The details in the scroll were more specific, especially since it included a description of what he called the World of Demons. Edward believed that the scrolls described different races of hellions, some of which were compelled to destroy mankind by means of violence and procreation deviances.

"From what I have deciphered so far," Edward informed. "The scroll bearing the seed of life symbol speaks about a massive division of worlds. These worlds are in conflict. It seems that there is a barrier placed between them. It is not clear to me, but the worlds overlap in some ways, and in other ways they are totally disjointed. There are barriers between them, but it is unclear."

"When you mention barriers, are you referring to legitimate places?" one member asked.

"No," Edward explained. "These are not like the New World across the ocean. These are nonphysical boundaries. Take, for example, a sorceress or a warlock; these people have learned how to penetrate the spiritual world. During the Crusades, various books that were believed to be written by King Solomon were discovered. In these books are written many procedures. Some we understand; some we do not. For those that are misunderstood, there are angels who, if properly summoned, will come to our aid and help us. If I understand it all correctly, the scroll speaks of a time before these barriers were created and the spirits were allowed free access to our world—this world of mortal men. Today, there are limitations, but these limitations are ours. If properly trained, we could penetrate these fortifications."

"And what do you think will happen if breached?" Joseph asked.

"I don't know. A unity with the spiritual world can do many good things for mankind. Within the spirit world, there are answers to the problems we have in the physical world."

"Then we must breach the barrier," Joseph declared. The adrenaline began to boil in his body as he contemplated the possibilities of common knowledge between men and spirits.

Edward protested. "I have to caution you, Joseph. These things must be delicately carried out. Some things must not be known to men. Even worse, if we breach the barrier, who is to say we can prevent something from the other realm from entering into ours?"

"Is that possible?" asked one of the other gentlemen.

"If I stick with this, I can learn more. Perhaps one of these scrolls outlines a procedure. Gentlemen, I must caution you again that this is a very delicate matter. Only well-trained men should have access to this knowledge. The mere fact that you possess these scrolls may attract some ungodly spirit to you and possibly to your homes."

"Edward," Joseph spoke warmly and almost patronizingly, "and all of you honorable men in this room, hear me out. Nearly one hundred years ago, the world witnessed the fall of Constantinople, an empire that lasted more than a thousand years. The Crusades, which our prestigious Edward Kelly just mentioned, failed to suppress a Muslim force that continues to pound on our door. In the West, the Lutherans have weakened the Catholic Church and all but destroyed its power. Every day men kill men over the debate of God's authority. There is no end to these wars. I can promise you that much. Now I ask you, what spirits are behind this? Is it God? Is God in conflict with himself, compelling mankind to kill each other? I dare say it is not so, and I am sure you agree. But what if it was meant for us to come across these scrolls, and what if it is meant for us to find this barrier? What if something exists in a netherworld that is the antidote to war? Should we not open the door? And if we do, what else lies behind it? If all things that are secret to men are known to spirits, and if we have the ability to interact or even ally ourselves with them, what more can we learn? What sicknesses can we cure? What famine can we not foresee and contend? Now with that, I do acknowledge that I may be wrong. You may say, what if none of this is possible? Then I ask you, how different would the world be if I am wrong? If I am wrong, war, sickness, and tyranny continues, but if I am right, imagine how beautiful the world would be."

Joseph's speech was compelling, and he saw in their eyes a

commitment to support him. Joseph was fully in agreement with Edward Kelly. The brotherhood should preserve the secrecy of the scrolls and the lessons they contained. He devised and presented an oath to the men that each member would take. He called it the Order of Olives. They each memorized the oath and vowed to induct their children as members. It was a promise to "end global strife, to ensure global peace through the consolidation of men under the same cause, to unite the worlds under the banner of justice, to restore efficacy to the laws of the universe, to see the unseen, to know the unknown, and to compel the forces of evil by channeling through one intentional universal benefit beyond the reach of normal men and into all realms adjacent to or submerged with ours and to be ever loyal to the one supreme truth."

Joseph was a proud man when he witnessed the induction of his first son into the brotherhood. He stood beside him as took the vow. "I do swear as a brother of the enlightened to be a titan and a tyrant against decadence, separation, and injustice and those who seek to prevent the advancement of the worlds."

Joseph took the words of the vow to heart in much the same way as the others. Each of the original members saw to it that their sons joined the order. As their need for resources grew, so did invitations to outsiders who shared their resources—and made the vow. When Joseph, weary and aged, witnessed his grandson's induction into the order, he contended himself to resign from leadership. Some members had already passed away, and Joseph believed that his time was near its end. When he thought of his accomplishments with the brotherhood, he regretted that there were not many. He was pleased at the organization's growth but disappointed with the effectiveness. The war between the Lutherans and Catholics had escalated into what appeared to be a world war with the involvement of the Russians and the Ottoman Empire who opposed the Habsburg States and the Catholic League. The Bohemians switched sides in the war, and the French had suddenly sided against the Catholics, despite their claim of being a Catholic state. It appeared to Joseph that his efforts to win peace were futile, and it was obvious to him that to have a peaceful society something needed to be done about the religious conflicts. He theorized that the fighting was less about religion and more about personal differences between France and Habsburg, but there were already 4 million casualties and mass devastation in every European region. Disease, hunger, and homelessness permeated the lives of 4 million others.

Despite the pull from other members, Joseph never fully accepted the idea of supporting one side over the other during the war, but he agreed that something had to be done. The fighting started locally but spread rapidly. The Catholic army suppressed the Bohemians, and the Dutch were in retreat after a failed attempt to rescue their Lutheran brothers from the Pope's onslaught. There was talk about the Swedes building an army to liberate the Bohemians and chasing the Catholics back Rome. At the time, Joseph thought that diplomacy would prevail in the end, but when Erik Andersson approached the brotherhood to inform them that he had just received correspondence from the Swedish King Gustav, Joseph realized that his organization would finally be forced into recognizing the totality of their vows.

Joseph was well aware that Erik had close connections to the monarchy in Sweden through his mother, Brigitta, who, at one time, was the official nanny to the royal family. He nearly predicted Erik's request as he addressed the brotherhood.

"Good gentlemen." Erik spoke very cordially. "Nearly thirty days have passed since the Swedish crown sent correspondence asking for financial support. It appears that King Gustav and his military minds have created a prototype for an advanced weapon to add to its arsenal." He passed the letter to the member on his left. As he spoke, the letter made its way around the table. It had drawings—a blueprint of movable artillery. Until then, armies had stationary cannons, so when they fired, it was easy for the competing army to locate them based on where the shot came from. At that time, it seemed an impossible task to produce cannons with mobility—they were heavy and would sink into the mud, and the wheels that supported them did not prevent the cannons from rolling backward upon discharge. The Swedes, however, seemed to have solved these problems with what they believed was advanced weaponry that could very likely defeat the Catholic mercenaries and ensure religious freedom for the Lutherans.

"He is asking for investors for this project," Erik continued.

"To what end?" asked Rudolph.

"To end the fighting before it becomes global; to force the Pope into making a reasonable treaty." His voice grew louder.

"You see the effects of treaties?" Joseph asked. He wanted to lay a foundation for his protest. "We spent months on the Peace of Augsburg, and it did not work."

"The Peace of Augsburg was incomplete. It did little more than give reasons for more fighting. Bohemia showed us what happens when a ruler chooses a religion different from his people. We need a serious treaty that guarantees total religious freedom. The Danish are already in retreat. When they are pinned down in the snow, the Holy Roman Empire will tighten her grip on them, and more fighting will ensue. Make no mistake—the Swedes will attack, and if they don't get our support, they will get it from someone else, perhaps the Russians."

"I don't understand how our support ends the fighting," noted Bartholomew Zwingli. He was an investor from a prestigious family in Switzerland.

"Are you asking for our collective support?" Joseph asked.

"Yes," Erik answered. "Yes, I am. A decisive Protestant victory will humble the Catholics, and they will negotiate a real solution— one that is peaceful. I believe that if the king gets support from someone else—let's say the Russians—we will have no leverage in setting the terms of peace. If, however, the king is victorious, we set the terms of peace as a condition to our support."

"We can ensure a balance of power," Frederick commented.

"We will also gain financial indebtedness from a sovereign state." William pointed out an advantage that most in the room appreciated. "If the Swedish king is financially indebted to us, we can take a position in his economy and gain leverage in his nation's economic policy."

"Until he decides to hunt us down and kill us so that he would not have to pay his debt," Rudolph suggested.

No one wanted to consider such a possibility. Most of the men at the table were members of prestigious families; some of them were noblemen all the same. Only two of them gained wealth through a history of family endeavors. Rudolph was one who could honestly say that his grandfather was a humble blacksmith. Joseph's family benefited from the rewards of loyalty to the Ottomans more than a century earlier. His grandfather spoke warmly of them and described the Ottomans as fair and tolerant people. Joseph felt guilty that the Ottomans were overlooked during the Peace at Augsburg, and he did not want to duplicate his mistake as he considered Erik's proposal. "What about the Calvinists?" he asked.

The room became suddenly quiet. It was obvious that no one cared about the followers of John Calvin.

"If we do this, we'll need to set terms in the peace agreement that will allow Calvinist followers the freedom to practice."

The room remained silent. None of them had any affinity for that particular Protestant group or their struggles. The practice of their religion was outlawed by both Catholics and Lutherans. No one in the room, with the remote possible exception of Dudley, who replaced Edward Kelly, had ever mentioned any disposition to Calvinist followers.

"It seems to me," said Dudley, breaking the silence, "that if we allow for the suppression of Calvinism, war will break out again. We may all have Catholic or Lutheran dispositions, but considering what we know, it may behoove us to have no specific loyalty to any particular religious dogma. Did we not each swear 'to see the unseen and know the unknown and to compel the forces of evil by channel through one universal benefit'? It appears to me that neither Catholicism nor Lutheranism is universally beneficial. Either we abolish all religion, or we accept them all."

Joseph felt that Dudley was a perfect replacement for Edward. He was young and energetic. He had an unwavering focus on interpreting the scrolls. Hearing him, Joseph nodded his head. "I agree," he said in support.

"Well then, as a condition, it must be established that every man has a right to privacy of worship," Bartholomew suggested. "If we succeed, history will claim this as mankind's last religious war."

They each agreed to invest in war. Frederick and Michael assured that they would use favors from fellow Frenchmen so that the financial support appeared to come from the French treasury rather than the brotherhood. In this way, the brotherhood would protect its surreptitiousness.

Within months, expenditures were made, weapons were built, and all the while Catholic mercenaries chased the Danish army to their own lands and took over whatever territories were left in the wake. Further, and just as Erik predicted, the Pope tightened his grip on the Lutherans. His tyranny over them and the Catholics was short-lived, however, as the Swedish king took reign with his advanced weaponry. But peace did not ensue, for the king was killed in battle. Alas, the French betrayed their church and went to war against the Pope. Many years passed, and no peace was procured.

During that time, six of the eight original members of the Brotherhood passed away; only Joseph and William remained. The membership had grown to eighty-seven men, and in his last years of his life, Joseph realized that he barely knew anything relevant about more than half his brothers. He understood that after witnessing the induction of his grandson that it was necessary to yield the governing body to his son. He was saddened at the thought that true global peace would not occur during his lifetime, but hope lived in the sight of growing membership. There were more men dedicated to obtaining the dream than he ever imagined. His grandson, Hector, was born eighteen years after the brotherhood was established; now at age twenty-four, he too took the oath. Joseph was content with knowing that the Konstantinos family would remain part of the governing body for many years to come.

There were eighty-seven members at the New Year celebration, and Joseph recognized very few of them. On that day, he concluded that protecting his family's legacy was more important than pushing a peace proposal between the Catholics and the Lutherans.

That night he spoke to his son Matthew and grandson Hector. "Your dad was just fifteen years old when we made this brotherhood," he said with a gentle touch of his soft, wrinkled hands on Hector's shoulder. "He would stand outside my door trying to listen to our meetings. Your grandmother would chase him away. He used to say, 'Papa, I want to help you,' and I would tell him, 'Someday.'" Joseph then turned to Matthew. "It is time to help the world now. It is your time to help the brotherhood, the family, and the universe." He moved slowly across the room and sat in his chair. Beside him were a small table and cup of wine. He took a sip. "I drink more wine now than before." He smiled, returning the cup to the stand. "Sometimes I think we made a big mistake, financing this war. It has grown out of control. Millions of people are dead; the German states are all bankrupt and so are the Italians. This has gone on for nearly thirty years, and I don't see any end. First, we gave money to the Swedes and now the French. We've turned Catholics against Catholics, and still there is no end in sight." He sipped from the cup again. "If it was all a mistake, I apologize to you."

"Papa," Matthew said. He could see the regret on his father's face. "No apologies. Remember?"

"I didn't want to go and leave you the burden that was mine."

"Go?" Hector sounded confused. "Where are you going?"

"Oh, Hector, you are far from naive. You are far more intelligent and educated than I am, and you are not blind. You see the gray hair and wrinkles. I can't stand on my feet for long. I will soon be a memory. You will hang my portrait on the wall beside my father's and tell my story to your children. I ask you both to remain steadfast. Keep our family on the governing board. Matthew, you will be my successor. You must ensure that our side wins the war, and if that doesn't happen, then our terms must be part of the peace agreement. Hector, I am putting you in charge of the most important thing—the relics. Right now, Dudley is overseeing the work. We've learned a lot, but this war has sidetracked our progress. Make it your mission to keep the relics in this family's possession. Make it your mission to learn the vocabulary and teach your children to read the scrolls. Take possession of Edward Kelly's notes, as well as those of John, Thomas, and Dudley. That is our most important work. Put everything in a family library accessed only by our family. There is someone mentioned in the scrolls: Yaron. Our ancestors called him Orpheus. When you find the connection, I believe you will find a source of power here on earth waiting for us to tap into; we must resurrect and own it. When that happens, we will put an end to global strife."

Within six months, Joseph was laid to rest. Matthew and Hector were successful in accomplishing the tasks placed upon them. Upon Dudley's death, Hector was delegated to be his successor on the governing body. Soon afterward, the war ended; a treaty drafted by the brotherhood was signed, and both sides agreed that the Spanish would leave the Netherlands, the Swiss were granted solvency, and the begrudging Catholic diplomats had to accept that, among many other things, all men were granted freedom of private worship. The father and son made a special toast to Dudley who had spent nine years in his grave. It was his dream to end religious wars forever.

*****

"So, who was Orpheus?" Talib asked.

"Legend has it that he was born of a union between a human and a spirit. He was what we now call a Nephilim. He had a very special gift. It was music. He played a lyre, and everyone loved to hear him sing. He was powerful with his talent, so much so that when his wife was bitten by a poisonous snake, he used his music to free her from the jaws of death. As the story goes, he traveled to the underworld—the land of the dead where spirits go when their bodies die. There, he played his music to the keepers of hell, and he so charmed them that they released his wife to him."

THE GIFT

Three days passed before Talib was privileged with a tour of the mansion and the areas where he was invited to roam freely. Three sides of the building were considered private, and a fourth was considered exclusive. It was separated from the main building by a long hallway and had a separate garden prepared with an Asian flair. The section that Talib was permitted to roam included his bedroom, personal bathing room, and a flight of stairs leading to the dining area where he first met the sisters. A door inside the dining area opened to a garden where he could feast and familiarize himself with the arrangement of blossoms that kept the conservatory well scented. The garden was in the early stages of springtime bloom; still, Talib found fascination in the care and attention the workers gave to its cultivation.

On the opposite side was the door where he followed Kate and Fiona. Down the stairs was the room where they stored the sensitive artifacts. Up the stairs was a long hallway. Hardwood floors with heavy varnish stretched thirty paces to an end where a door led to the library. This door was an exit that was kept locked and seldom opened. The select few who entered came from a different entry point. Between the stairs and the library were four other doors to various rooms. The room closest to the library was floored with mats colored with a grayish hue. When Talib first spied it, there were three people inside engaged in a yoga session. One was a middle-aged man, graying at the edges of his hair. He was the instructor. His students were both females who were older than Kate by perhaps ten years. They were flexible and strong. Talib was impressed at their ability to hold their positions for as long as they did, showing no evidence of shaking muscles or gritting teeth. Although they made it look easy, Talib was not convinced as such.

A second room contained one extremely large white rug that nearly covered the floor from corner to corner. The center was printed with a red circle large enough in diameter for perhaps one or two people Talib's size to lie in the center and not touch the edges. Surrounding the circle were twelve small candle holders, no larger than the size of a man's hand. They were precisely placed at thirty degrees apart like numbers on a clock. At the three, six, nine, and twelve o'clock positions were painted triangles that contained larger candle holders for larger candles. To the north of the twelve o'clock position was a long trough filled with water, attached to a small fountain that was lit with gentle red and blue lights. Seven koi half the size of a man's arm swam inside. The trough extended the length of the wall from the east to the west. Against the south wall were two small, restaurant-style ovens used as food warmers. They were made with glass coverings. These, however, were not used for food; they actually warmed rocks, gems, and crystals. Twelve such rocks, gems, and crystals were set in multiple small containers and placed inside the warmers. When Kate gave Talib the tour of this area, she explained that each item had a specific energy.

"The bloodstone affects your courage. The emerald supports positive energy." She pointed to each gem as she spoke. "The garnet is for self-esteem. The lapis lazuli is my favorite; it stimulates wisdom. Malachite provides protection from danger; moonstone promotes unselfishness. Here is my sister's favorite—the tigereye for clear thoughts. Oh, and this one is moldavite; it increases the energy of the others, but more importantly, it increases your ability to communicate with your higher self—your soul." She turned to him. "Have you ever listened to your soul?"

"No." Soul listening was new to Talib.

"You should try it. Sometimes our souls try to tell us things through our dreams. If we listen, the frightening dreams may stop."

Talib was more than interested in stopping the nightmares. "How do you listen to your soul?"

"I'm happy you asked." Kate smiled. "I will teach you."

There were other crystals in the warmers, but Kate spoke nothing of them. On the east wall stood an altar with pedestals on either side that were as tall as Talib's shoulders. On each were porcelain objects used to burn fragrant oils. Talib could smell the rosy scent wafting through the air. Kate continued to explain the significance of the four elements.

When Talib asked of the purpose of the room, she answered, "This room is used by those who want to better both themselves and the world."

A third room had an earth-toned carpeted floor. Scattered in no particular order were a variety of rugs that Talib identified with prayer. Four people were there. One was a very old man, bald with a white beard. He was dressed in a hooded robe, the hood draped behind his neck. He sat with folded legs and balanced a green crystal between the eyebrows. The three others practiced differently. One pulled beads one at a time around a thread as he recited words. Talib related this to meditating Sufi worshipers he often saw. He was curious to know if the man indeed practiced Sufism, and if so, on which attributes of Allah did he meditate? The other two faced each other, seated with folded legs, their hands placed on their knees, and palms faced upward. Together they made soft hums. They pressed their chests upward and closed their eyes. Around the room were thirteen potted house trees. From two large windows, the sun entered the room, mixing with the colors on the walls, reflecting and bouncing around the room. There were also mirrors that deflected the sunlight, making it reach every tree.

"This room is where people come to listen to their souls," Kate explained.

The fourth room was closest to the stairs. It was here where Talib often found Fiona sitting on a stool in front of an easel. She spent much of her free time painting in this arts-and-crafts room. Painting was obviously her talent and hobby. Talib thought it was her way of escaping or separating herself from whatever pressure he imagined was placed on her. He soon learned that he was wrong. Fiona's burden was never spared, and Talib could not begin to understand. Even in her waking hours, she was often haunted by thoughts that were not hers and feelings she should not endure. The depictions in her mind were portrayed on her canvas.

Talib was standing in the doorway observing her once and wanted to ask about the images she conjured. Fiona's back was to him, and she was dressed in green. She often wore green clothing on Friday. Even though he made no sound, she knew that he was there.

"This is a place where I go," she spoke to him as if he was beside her.

"I apologize, I wasn't trying—"

"I know," she interrupted him. "It's okay. You may join me."

Talib walked cautiously into the room and looked at her unfinished artwork. "What is it?"

"A prison."

"It looks like a maze."

"It is a prison and a maze. If you enter, you may not return."

"Where is it?" Talib questioned.

"The astral plane," Fiona explained.

"Where is that?"

"I won't say. Kate will tell you." She turned to face him after a long, silent pause. "I have to learn to not fear you."

"Why do I frighten you?"

"Because of what you can do," she sighed. "But mostly because of what you want to do."

"What do you think I want to do?"

"Burn the world."

Talib did not respond. It was true. He hated the world, and he wanted vengeance against everyone who failed to distinguish between the innocent and the guilty.

"How did you get this way?" he asked in his attempt to redirect her. "Is there a lot of witchcraft in this place?"

"There are no witches here," she answered. Her eyes studied him, scanning over his black hair, copper skin, and gray eyes. She surveyed his thick black eyebrows and small nose. Lastly, she took notice of what appeared to be the perfect proportional measures of his lips, chin, and jawbone ratios. "My gift is inherited. It was passed down from my mother. She died soon after I was born. I never met her—at least not here." Her voice trailed off.

Talib was curious to know what she meant. From the sound of it, she had met her dead mother somewhere else. He concluded that she referred to her dreams. He was saddened by his own occasional dreams of his father, just the same as it appeared with Fiona. She did not tell stories as well as Kate, but she was effective enough.

Fiona spoke of ancestors: Two daughters born to one of the sculpted faces in the lobby outside the artifact room. Their father's name was Paul, Joseph Konstantinos' great-grandson, born ten years after his death. As some would say, Paul had the misfortune of having four daughters—none of them would inherit his position on the governing body of the three-hundred-member Enlightened Titan brotherhood. But Paul loved his daughters dearly. They were twins: Agatha and Anastasia. When the time came for his twin daughters to marry, he arranged a union between a not-so-distant cousin and Anastasia, the selected bride.

Anastasia often suspected that Agatha was Paul's favorite. They spent many private moments in discussion. Paul revealed the scrolls to Agatha and taught her the words that were deciphered. He spoke to her often about science and told her of the experiments the brotherhood sponsored. It was as if he wished that she had been born a boy. Although such suspicions did not make Anastasia jealous or vindictive, on occasion she was purposefully reckless in her attempts to garner attention from her father. She suspected that the sudden marital arrangement was a strategic ploy to make someone else responsible for taming her. She resented that idea and rebelled just two days before her wedding while attending the traditional prewedding dinner with her family in Constantinople.

That day, by means of her father's status, Anastasia was surrounded by women from the wealthiest families in Europe, East Asia, and the Middle East. With the influence of the Enlightened Titans and their agreed-upon decision not to finance Ashraf Holaki's political move against Turkish authority, the brotherhood had conducted business on three continents; they financed scientific experiments, astrological research, anthropological digs, hostile government coup d'états, and suppressions. These exploits made Paul very popular, and as such, Anastasia's wedding was equally popular.

Without hesitation, Anastasia agreed to abide by her father's wishes to marry Lafayette, her cousin, although she was never attracted to him. He had traditional Greek features, including the nose that Anastasia could not get past. Despite her efforts to look away, she could not help shifting her eyes back to his nose. She held her reluctant secret close to her heart, and no one would have ever known until, by some obscure chance, Anastasia happened to come across a gray-eyed server who seemed to recognize that she wished to marry someone else.

Just one day before her wedding, Anastasia sat in the dining hall in harmony with her sisters, mom, and other women—older ones whose eyes pierced behind their pleasantries and smiles. They had their fill of the delightful Mediterranean cuisine when the server placed a sorbet on the table in front of Anastasia. She barely glimpsed at him, although she couldn't help noticing the wondrously scented oil he wore under his collar. He spoke something to her under his breath, using her native language in such an uncouth way and with such a heavy Persian accent that she almost missed what he said.

"Congratulations on your marriage, but it is a shame you wish to marry someone else." He spoke softly, but just loud enough for Agatha to hear.

Agatha did not make out the totality of what he said, but Anastasia understood him thoroughly, despite his heavy accent. She was instantly astonished, not simply due to his insolence but also to his awareness. Just before dinner she uttered the same exact sentiment to her sister in private; now a servant stood at her side echoing her words. She was appalled. Had he eavesdropped on their private conversation? Furthermore, why say such a thing while standing in the circle of so many important people?

"How dare you!" She stood from the table, the suddenness of her movement causing her drink to spill.

As one might imagine, this prestigious group of people in such a historically volatile city—despite its beauty—would have a company of body guards dispatched appropriately. The server could take no more than three steps in retreat when he was apprehended. Anastasia was joined by her sister, Agatha, who stood beside her. Their height and appearance remained identical even in their older years.

Agatha was nearly ready to demand an apology when Anastasia spoke. "You insolent creature; you have the audacity to insult me on the day before my wedding?"

"I could show you what it feels like to be with a real man." His laugh was cut short by a hand around his throat, choking him to prevent him from saying more as he was dragged away.

The remainder of the evening came with complimentary desserts, wines, and apologies from the hotel manager who even promised to refund a portion of Paul's money, as well as dismiss the servant from employment. He called the servant a "scum gypsy—an Assyrian who was better off as a con artist in the streets." According to the manager, men of such stature were given fair chances at employment, despite the likelihood that their peasantry and unmanageable nature were often revealed. He explained that the server's parents were deceased and that he spent his youth pretending to read minds—a foolish trick that his people were known to pull on others—but his skill was so good that he survived by use of it. He had worked at the hotel for six months, and until that day, he'd given the managers no issue. But as it goes with his people, according to the manager, the gypsy nature came out, and it was impossible to know what would trigger such outbursts.

What the manager did not know, and what Anastasia admitted later to her sister, was that the server's words were nearly identical to her thoughts at the time. The two girls were alone inside Agatha's chambers when she mentioned as much when they were suddenly drawn to the window of the third-floor room by loud yelling. They had heard so many apologies and excuses from the manager earlier that they recognized his voice. Although neither of them understood the Turkish diatribe, they raced to the window to look down upon the figures of both the manager and the Assyrian server. The manager threw out articles of clothing, foot gear, and a box that sprang open when it hit the street. The contents were scattered in every direction, and the server was left to gather his personal belongings. They were watching him search the dark for his items when he came to an abrupt stop and looked upward. He spied the window where they stood in observance. Agatha screamed and then laughed as they moved away.

"Papa told me once," Agatha whispered. "Do you remember Uncle Isaac talking about atoms—those little things that make up the world?"

"Yes. They were atoms." Anastasia remembered. "Why are you whispering?"

Agatha begged her sister to speak softly. Her expression changed from childlike jovial to serious contemplation. "Papa said that those atoms had smaller parts, and that some of those parts were connected in such a way that they would always work together. If one turned right, the other left—they were always opposite."

"So?" Anastasia had little patience. "What's your point?"

"He said that atoms gave off energy that people could use through concentration."

"So?"

"What if that man's brain worked the same way? What if he knows how to concentrate just the right way to use that energy to read someone's mind?"

"The manager said it. Those Assyrian people are great tricksters." Anastasia hesitated, and doubt spread over her face. "But I know what my thoughts were, and I know what he said." Then something came over her. "I have to see if it's true. Let's switch clothes."

Agatha protested, but Anastasia said that time would not allow for discussions or explanation. She asked Agatha to play along and hide in the closet when she returned with the server.

"You can't bring him here."

"It will be all right," Anastasia promised as she left the room. She was always one to take risks. Now she was willing to risk her safety and her pristine reputation by bringing into their hotel room a peasant who could turn violent against them.

Agatha cautiously returned to the window and peered out with one eye while half her face was blocked by the wall aside the window. She saw that by the time Anastasia had eluded all possible eyes assigned to protect her, the server had completed his search for his personal items and had walked away. He was not so far gone when Anastasia called out to him.

"I was told that you read minds," she said when he stopped and turned in her direction.

"It is only rumors," he replied, not approaching. He spoke to her from a distance.

"Are you saying that the rumors are lies?"

"It would all depend on what you call a mind," he said, struggling to find the proper Greek words when he spoke.

"If it is true, I want to use your talents. I will pay for your time if you come with me."

The promise of money was motivation enough for him. He came with her. Using her cunningness, Anastasia slipped past her father, his friends, the hired bodyguards, and the ever-watchful eyes of her former nanny. When they reached the hotel room, Agatha was hidden in the closet just as ordered.

"Now, first, you owe me an apology," Anastasia said.

There was a long pause until Anastasia shifted her weight impatiently. Then, he spoke. "I do apologize," he said cautiously. "I had no way of knowing that what I said would offend you."

Anastasia feigned surprise. "You had no way of knowing? So I guess it *is* a rumor, and you *are not* a mind reader."

There was a long pause, and as awkward as it was, the server said nothing. Anastasia looked at him and noticed how handsome he was. He seemed younger than she, barely twenty years old. He wore his hair long and combed backward; it was black and accented his eyes well. Something about those gray eyes was enchanting. They seemed to have a blackish hue at times. The shifting eye colors made her stare deeper, but he did not turn away or look down the way a servant typically should. He was tall and had broad shoulders. She imagined he had spent much of his life lifting heavy things.

When Anastasia stopped looking over the servant, she remembered that her sister was hiding. She was also certain that Agatha knew by then that the servant could not read minds. Then Anastasia pulled back her shoulders and lifted her chin to assume the posture of a wealthy lady when she prepares to give an order to a servant.

She spoke to him firmly and looked past him as if he was not there. "I am sure you have a family to get to; so, you may now leave."

The server did not move. "I have no family," he said. "And you promised to pay me."

"I promised to pay you for your talents. You obviously have none."

"I apologize."

"You are filled with apologies." She pointed to the door. "You may leave now before I scream."

The server smiled and shifted his weight looking directly into her firm and seemingly immovable eyes. "You will not scream," he said.

"I will too scream."

"I don't believe it. You are interested in me. I am like an experiment or a toy to you. Did I not say all the things that I should say? I did apologize."

"You should leave," she said, her voice less demanding.

He was right, of course. Something that Anastasia could not explain was interesting and magnetic about him. He was unlike any man she had ever met or spoken to. He was vulgar and wild. His eyes were like a savage, bearing no concern for rules or formalities. This man was a nonconformist, and Anastasia felt compelled to be as such. The rules and expectations of her culture were shackles to her. She wanted to be free of them, if just for one night. Yes, bringing him to her room was all part of her adventure and, as he put it, experiment, but it was not enough. She had only begun to feel the rush of excitement when she maneuvered through the hallways and corridors to see him and escort him to her sister's chambers. She didn't know what else there was to feel, but she wanted something more. The server in front of her was suddenly a symbol of everything adventurous that she wanted, and somehow, he seemed to know what she felt.

"If I leave, you would be so unsatisfied."

"You are an arrogant man."

"Am I?" He took one step closer to her. "Is that what you were thinking when you were looking at my shoulders?" He shook his head. "No. You didn't think that."

Anastasia found herself melting. Her eyes invited him to take one step closer. She did not retreat when he did.

"That is not what you thought when you looked into my eyes, right? Are they black or gray? Is that what you thought?"

Her mouth dropped, and she gasped for air. She was thunderstruck.

"You thought you would test me, right? You wondered about my touch, about my hand on your shoulder." He gently reached out and touched her shoulder. She felt a surge of energy in his touch that vibrated, and she shivered in ecstasy. He moved closer to her and whispered into her ear. "Yes, madam, I am the adventure that you hoped to find."

His words frightened her, and she was suddenly conscious of her private fancy. She had wished to be, one day, taken away in passion by some man. She dreamt of it, but the man had no face. Anastasia was bred for traditional courtships and marital arrangements. She was trained to appreciate the rules of her culture and class, but those rules did not award her with the rush of energy and passion that she wanted to experience. She once saw her uncle, her mom's brother, cheating on his wife with a servant. She knew it was wrong to watch, but she could not turn away. They made love like fury—an out-of-control wagon way. They panted like dogs gasping for air. The thrust of their hips, and the sounds of their colliding bodies struck something deep inside her that made her want to feel the same. She thought of the experience as an adventure, and suddenly this server spoke using the same words, as if he could predict what she had witnessed.

The server touched her in places and in ways that made her slow to resist. She had never been touched like that before. She reached out to move his hand, but he moved it first—to another part of her body—her breast, then to the small of her back, and then he pulled her close. Before she could push away, he kissed her lips. Before she could protest his kiss, she had reciprocated. Then it all became a blur. She was lost in the moment, consumed with passion, and enthralled in the sin of it all. He gave her exactly what she hoped to have. Anastasia lay beneath the server, feeling the exact same way that servant girl felt as she made love to Anastasia's uncle.

After suffering through the revolting sounds of kissing, sighs that became sudden, short breaths, and extended exhales that became violent collisions of naked bodies, Agatha burst from the closet and accused her sister of whoring, but Anastasia promptly refuted the accusation.

"A whore is paid for what she does. I just paid him. What does that make me?"

Agatha had no answer. It was true that when the server left, Anastasia gave him two gold coins. But the server left Anastasia with something more than an adventure; she was left implanted with his offspring to develop inside her womb. At the time, neither girl was aware. Anastasia was married the next day just as planned, and within a month, Agatha was married as well; the secret of the bastard child was left between them and the earthly spirits.

She called him Charles, although the man who would be the presumed father officially named him Ajax. In the beginning, Anastasia's husband, Lafayette, was offended that more people took to the name Charles, but after conceding to accept it, he changed the child's name to Charles Ajax Stanis. It was not long before it was discovered that Charles manifested a special gift. He was merely four years old when, using his easel and canvas with a paint set, he painted an image of a rainbow, flowers, a smiling sun, and butterflies. He presented this painting, which was made as best a four-year-old could muster, to his aunt Agatha. At the time, she lay in bed mourning the loss of her unborn child. The news of her miscarriage had spread to only her immediate family, and

Anastasia had not yet been privileged to this information when Charles asked his mother if he could take his painting to his aunt. "Your aunt is not well today," Anastasia said to him. "You just saw her yesterday, and she needs her rest."

"This will make her feel better," Charles answered. "Maybe she will not be sad about her baby dying in her belly."

Anastasia hesitated and looked at her child. She felt her heart tremble. It had been five years since her premarital adventure with the hotel worker in Constantinople, and Charles reminded her of him whenever she looked into his gray eyes. Agatha had only once mentioned her fears of a miscarriage to her sister, and Charles had not been present at the time. Anastasia was frightened that the Assyrian blood was thick inside of her son. The Assyrian left her almost certain that he could read her mind. She recalled the moment when he climbed out the bed. Perspiration dripped over him like a waterfall. He said nothing to her at first, but when he had dressed and received his two gold coins, he said, "Now that you've had your adventure, you may live your life as a wealthy wife. Also, I know your sister is hiding in the closet." He walked to the door, and before exiting, he spoke again. "I hope she enjoyed the show. I expected her to join us. The Greeks are famous for their orgies. But perhaps that is only rumor."

She never saw him again except for the moments when she looked into her son's gray eyes. At that moment, she feared her son in much the same way that she had feared the Assyrian. Hiding her fear behind a smile, she squatted and held his hands. Despite her resistance, she looked into his eyes. "Did your aunt say this to you?"

"No," he answered.

"Well why do think she had a baby in her belly?"

"I felt like I had something in mine, and then I thought it was dying."

"What do you mean?" Anastasia was dumbfounded.

"You told me I should feel sorry for people, so that's what I do. She was sad, so I felt sad with her."

Anastasia forced a smile, attempting to hide her fears. If Charles possessed the ability to pick up on a person's thoughts and feelings, he could one day learn that Lafayette was not his biological father, and the truth of her affair would leak out to the embarrassment of the family. She stroked his hair and concluded that perhaps she should not think of the Assyrian server from Constantinople. If she had no more thoughts of him, then Charles would never know, even if he possessed some uncanny ability to read minds. Anastasia focused her thoughts on conversation they were having. He spoke so well and with such maturity that she felt proud of him.

"You spend too much time around adults," she said. "You're beginning to sound like a man."

The following day, Agatha revealed to her sister that she had miscarried. It was the second time she had attempted to bear a child. It was the second time she had failed. Anastasia spent the entire day with her sister as she had often done since the wedding. She tried to ease Agatha's mind. Anastasia had always been a loyal and loving sister—never envious of what seemed to be Paul's favor toward Agatha. But on that day, just before leaving for home, Anastasia realized that she needed something from her sister. There was no one else she could speak to regarding Charles and his natural father.

Anastasia seldom involved herself with the rituals that Agatha learned from their dad. She was never taught to read the words on the scroll or to summon spirits, but she knew that Agatha had practiced the art. She inquired about these things, and Agatha told her that when the Enlightened Titans were young, they were warned by Edward Kelly that it may have been an unwise choice to keep the secret relics inside the confines of their home.

"There is a fundamental rule of the universe," Edward said. "One reaps what he sows. We are engaged in sowing seeds of an unnatural curiosity, and this curiosity will no doubt attract things to us that we do not yet understand."

Although Joseph did not understand most of what Edward said to him, Agatha understood much more about how various universal energies find ways of consolidating their strength to create specific vibrations that cannot be explained by eighteenth-century science. After hearing what Agatha had to say, Anastasia suspected that within Charles—as with his father—was a concentration of energy that gave him access to the vibrations of other people in such a way that he could physically and perhaps mentally connect to and partly comprehend what they felt or thought. She did not believe that Charles could read a person's mind or thoughts, but she hypothesized that he would appear to read another person's mind—when, in fact, he was using cues to guess what a person thought or felt through a process of elimination.

With this hypothesis, Anastasia wanted Charles to learn the lessons that Agatha learned from their father. Anastasia believed that if he—with such ability—understood the world in the way that Paul did, her son would become the son Paul never had. She hoped Charles would be able to tap into a vast sea of information and accomplish all that her father and his father before him wished to accomplish: global peace.

Agatha agreed and promised to teach Charles everything she knew. "But there is no better teacher than Papa," she admitted. "He's going back to England in a few days. Why don't you permit Charles to go with him?"

With that, Anastasia surrendered her son to the teachings of the arts and the business that Paul endeavored. She explained that he should pay close attention to his grandfather, who had recently been placed on an oversight committee for the brotherhood's construction project in England. Charles was extremely excited to join his grandfather, but more thrilled to spend more time with Agatha who became his instructor for many things. He lived in the family mansion with his aunt and was the student of two private instructors; one was for science and arithmetic, the other for language and literature. He learned to speak and read in Latin and other languages, including English, Aramaic, Hebrew, and Mandarin.

Agatha taught him the arts in the same way that Paul taught them to her. The first lesson was of the planets and solar system. He learned that each planet emitted a distinct energy that imposed on nature. He learned that the energy was stronger on some days and weaker on others.

"The moon's energy is strongest on Mondays," he regurgitated during his first quiz.

"And Tuesday?" Agatha asked.

"Mars."

"Wednesday?"

"Mercury."

She was pleased. "And which day is the best to make business decisions?"

"Thursday."

"Why?"

"It is the energy of expanding, growth, and business success."

"What is the proper name for it?"

"*Tzedek.*"

She smiled with approval and hugged him tightly. Above all else, Charles aspired to please his aunt.

Two days before his eighth birthday, Charles accompanied his grandfather to England for the celebration of their completed project. Until then, Charles had not been allowed on the building site, but this time, Paul was happy to show the finished product to his grandson—his future successor.

Three years of the building's construction, and finally, it was serviceable for use. The Enlightened Titans had created a system based on previous ones, of course, but this prototype that was used in London had far-reaching possibilities that could one day fit into the brotherhood's vow and mission statement. Charles tried to understand these things as best as he could, but it was not until he stood inside the building that he realized his grandfather's importance to the world. When he reached the destination after his long trip with his grandson, Paul escorted Charles directly to the great hall. There, a statue was erected of a man Paul identified as William the Third. Engraved in the structure were words written in Latin. Charles, seeing the words, was prompted to read them.

"For restoring efficacy to the laws, authority to the courts of justice, dignity to Parliament, to all his subjects and their religions and liberties, and conforming these to posterity, by the succession of the Illustrious House of Hanover to the best of Prince William the Third, founder of the Bank, this corporation, from a sense of gratitude, has erected this statue and dedicated it to the memory in the year of our Lord 1734 and the first year of this building."

Charles felt accomplished when he saw Paul's approving smile and felt the gentle tap on his shoulder. Then Paul beckoned Charles to follow him outside the building to another engraving in the foundation. There, he pointed to his name and asked Charles if he knew what it meant to have his grandfather's name engraved in the cornerstone of a building.

Charles answered, "No."

"It means that this is your inheritance. You were born into this legacy. Do you remember the first line on the statue?" He did not give Charles time to answer. "For restoring the efficacy of the laws ... I don't want you to forget that."

They walked to a place where they could eat. There, as they waited for supper, Paul spoke of his father and of the brotherhood. It was important to Paul that his grandson—his only grandson—understood the brotherhood and the power and responsibility of it, as well as his inherent place within it.

Paul explained that his father was Joseph, named in honor of Joseph, the founding father of the brotherhood. Joseph, Paul's father, was four generations removed from the inception of the Enlightened Titans. He lived a short life that robbed him of witnessing Paul's induction into the brotherhood and his initiation into the governing body. In his short tenure, Joseph made a major impact.

"When you join the brotherhood, you will have to make a presentation explaining how you hope to make the world a better place. When your great-grandfather made his, he told the committee that we cannot create global peace because we are too reactive. That means we wait for things to happen first, and then we try to fix the problem. You see, Charles, it is the governments of the world that cause so many of our problems. The brotherhood tried to help, but kings and princes and politicians are very arrogant men. They are selfish and do not take good advice. Because of that, we could do very little to help them in making the world a better place. My father believed that he had a solution. He said that every man in the brotherhood should give up his loyalties to his ethnic group, to his country, and to his religion. We should be loyal to the world and the universe—to the realm of men. We will never be able to stop war; at best, we can maintain peace in small chunks of time. Peace without war is impossible. Therefore, we should control war. We should determine where it happens and when it happens. We should control the balance of power between one king and the next, between one country and the next. If we give up our loyalties to the countries of our birth, we can do this without prejudice.

"He proposed that we control the balance of power through economy. We were already on the path to doing this, but we needed to control the entire world economy. If we could control the king's money and all the monies of the world, no one entity could make war against the next without the brotherhood's approval.

"Now I want you to imagine this: a bank that owns more gold than the king's treasury. Imagine an entire population without gold or even access to it, but one that continues to buy and sell goods using paper as a substitute for that gold. The paper itself has almost no value and is nothing more than a promissory note. The bank produces these notes and loans them to the government, and in turn, the government extends them to the people. The citizens will work and receive these notes as payment for their labor. The kings collect notes from the citizens in the form of taxes and repay us in kind. In this way, the king is convinced that he does not have to repay us the gold he borrows, but will repay us by returning the notes we finance, after which time he will need more. Then we will exchange the paper notes for his gold. It will be up to us to decide how much paper currency is worth the return of his gold. Eventually, we have all the gold, and the nations will run on an alternate payment system, all controlled by the one bank that has the ability to completely control the flow of the notes and the value of the work that men do for it.

"The most difficult thing in this, we found, was to identify a starting point, but your great-grandfather, my dad, had a solution for that. This is why we are here in London. This is where his plan took place. There was a war going on here; they called it the Glorious Revolution. Some of our members were big supporters of King James, for they knew he was a good man. He was Catholic but believed that everyone had a right to choose his own faith. He even let his daughter marry a Lutheran—that was a big deal back then, although not much has changed today. The true test of our brotherhood came during those days, but somehow the members stuck together, just like a brotherhood should. Your great-grandfather was a genius. Things played out exactly the way he plotted. The English exhausted their wealth fighting against themselves, and they came to the brotherhood to gain more. When we offered the idea of this central bank to William, he allowed us the freedom to establish it here if we helped him win the war. That was tricky, but not impossible. Admittedly, we betrayed King James in the process by manipulating him into attacking England again. When he did, he was killed, and the brotherhood succeeded in making your great-grandfather's dream come true. The real lesson in this story is a law of the universe that you must never forget it. Whatever you believe is possible becomes possible if you do all the right things to make it so.

"Many people in the future, if they ever knew about our part in the war, will think that we did an evil thing against King James, but soon you will learn that deeds both evil and good are all the same. They are no different from your hand. There are two sides to it, but it is the same hand."

"How did we win the war?" Charles asked. He was fascinated with his grandfather's story.

Paul obliged. "We had help from the French. The brotherhood has done much of its work in disguise as French operations. William went to Ireland to fight King James, the French Navy utterly destroyed the English Navy, and the new King of England had no money for his country.

"Our bank started in a building owned by the grocers. Now, we have our own building." He smiled at the accomplishment. "It's too bad your great-grandfather is not here to see it. This new system is good. We're helping a lot of people who never had gold or silver. Now they don't need either to buy food. The world is a better place because of your great-grandfather. Now isn't that something to make you proud?"

Charles looked at his grandfather drift away in thought and realized that there were more lessons to Paul's story. He asked about them, and Paul said, "It is better to be a king maker than to be a king."

*****

When Charles was fourteen years old, Agatha introduced to him the sacred alphabet. She first presented each letter, then taught the sounds that she believed each letter made, and later graduated to full words. These were words that Edward, James, and Dudley had deciphered and translated from the scrolls that Agatha taught him. Charles was excited to learn his new skill. He gravitated to the lessons like a moth to a flame. The lessons seemed to strike something inside of him. Agatha was two days into her teachings when, on the third planetary Wednesday, Charles saw the scrolls for the first time. When he looked on them, and his eyes moved over the letters, he became light-headed and his legs became rubber; everything went black and he fainted. When he was conscious, he remembered that he dreamt that he had wings to fly and that he became friends with an incredible giant.

A week later, he tried to read the words from the scroll again. This time, things were different. He took to decoding the words on his own and continued without hesitation. He read with such fluency that he unraveled the mysteries of certain sounds that the brotherhood had deciphered in error. When he finished, she asked if he understood the meaning.

Charles paused. "I don't know," he answered. "I think I understand. I'm not sure I do, but I have pictures in my mind. I should read it again."

"Yes," Agatha said. "Yes, you should, but next time, go slowly and tell me what you see."

When he reread the words, he envisioned life-forms that were not men but had legs and arms all the same. They were giants that appeared to be made of light. "They are marching some other creatures to a prison deep into an ice mountain. The prisoners are like men with wings. They are sad."

"Is that all?"

"No," he answered, grappling for words to explain what was painted on the canvas of his mind. "I think it is explaining how the shackles were made. They are cold and iron, and they take away the power of the prisoners. They are tortured so much that the mountain bleeds from their wounds."

He hesitated, and Agatha asked if there was more.

"No," he answered.

She told him that they had done enough for the day and cautioned him against telling anyone about what he read or thought the words said. She promised to bring paper and a pen next time, so he could take one word at a time and explain the images that came to his mind. He agreed, and together, Charles and his aunt Agatha became exclusive researchers of the scrolls, decoding their contents and making considerable progress until misfortune was imminent. Agatha became incredibly sick to the point where the doctors felt there was nothing left for them to do.

Charles, at sixteen years old, had not imagined life without his aunt until then. The notion distressed him tremendously, and he spent hours in severe lamentations. Anastasia tried her best to soothe him with flavored teas and his favorite desserts.

When Paul attempted to comfort the youth, he said, "There are things in life that we can neither avoid nor prevent. Life is a mere shade cast against the ground; just as the sun moves, so goes life, until at some point the shadows and the night all merge together. I know you dearly love your aunt, and I love her as well, very much. It seems unfair for a child's light to fade before the parents' lights. If I could take away the last five years of my life and add them to hers, I would. But no one fire can cause another to burn if there is no fuel to burn." It seemed that he spoke more to himself than to Charles. His voice trailed off as his speech became barely audible. "We are all atoms and molecules—condensed energy. Energy needs fuel, and her fuel is very low."

"So, what is the fuel for life?" Charles asked.

His grandfather's gibberish jarred a sudden awakening. He remembered something he read in the scroll. He had skipped ahead without permission to satisfy his curiosity. There was something in the last portion pertaining to the desires of man—his willpower. He could not state what he read or even begin to explain it. He just knew that the scroll caused him to see or understand that the energy of life, fueled by the desire of man, could cause him to extend his life. Man's energy is immortal; it does not die but merely transforms. Charles started thinking that maybe there was a way he could combine his desire for Agatha to live with her desire to live, and if possible, the sickness that sapped her life's energy would cease, and she could revive. She could beat death. The ancient scrolls mentioned such a person who did just that.

Charles stole away to the upstairs chambers to privately read the scroll. Standing right before him as if very real stood a giant so tall that Charles felt like an eight-year-old boy standing beside a man. It was the same giant that he had seen before; it was Yaron. Seated around him were many spectators in what appeared to be a theater. The stage was lowered, and the spectators' seats were raised so that the people looked down upon it. A man in a hooded robe approached a much younger man with a dagger. For a moment, Charles could feel the young man's energy. He was not afraid. He felt a rush of adrenaline from the unmistakable notion that despite the approaching dagger, there was nothing that would take away this man's life. His eyes were focused on something—a symbol that Charles could not see. He must have been aware of the threat of death, but he seemed to disregard this and kept his focus on the image. Charles believed the image to be the fuel of this man's desire to live, so when the hooded attacker thrust the blade, lodging it into the young lad's chest, his life was yet spared. He first fell flat on the ground, given the impact; however, he arose just moments later—alive and unscathed.

Charles understood that the would-be victim's focus on the image spared the man's life. He also figured that he could adopt letters from the scroll to devise an image on which to focus to revive Aunt Agatha. If Agatha was willing to accept it, Charles was convinced that he could transfer his own energy into her being. He would step outside his body and merge with hers, hopefully increasing her willpower to survive. The key for success was not his wish or focus on survival but on his aunt's *will* to stay alive.

With that, Charles selected letters from the scroll and

positioned them to create an obscure image. As he labored, he imagined that Agatha's will to live increased. For all her tenacity, Charles's mission was to magnify her resolve; her inner strength would be visually depicted in the image he composed. He produced a portrait of the construct and meditated on it for three days; during that time, it seemed that Agatha was increasingly weak.

For two days straight, Charles visited his bedridden aunt. She coughed blood numerous times over a twenty-four-hour period, and her loved ones had come to the realization that they would leave her bedside, and Agatha would cough no more. She was believed to be lying in her deathbed. What concerned Charles more than anything was that Agatha had come to accept the same.

"I can feel you, Aunt," he said. "It makes me sad to know you have given up. Why are you so willing to die when living is so much better?"

"Fate is something I cannot control," she whispered to her nephew and then turned her head to look into his eyes.

"But it is a gift with which you are blessed. Your fate is yours. It belongs to you, not I, not your papa, and not even God."

His eyes seemed to come alive and reach out to her as he spoke. "If you believe you can get out this bed, then without a doubt, you will do so. I can help, but your every thought must be fixed on returning to the lady you were born to be—the one who taught me about the stars and planets. You have more to teach me. Promise that you will."

Charles sensed Agatha's surge of pride in him. She reached out and took his hand. He could feel her heart rate increase, sensing that she wanted to survive as she made her promise. Charles was happy. He stood, thinking about how his work was unfinished. He knew he had to bring to life the painted image of her desire, just as the young man from the story in the scrolls did. Turning away from his aunt, he looked upon the two nurses who provided care for Agatha—an elder one and her younger assistant. Charles looked into the elder lady's face; she was divorced with no children of her own, so she claimed, but Charles knew differently. He knew that she longed to be with a man to relive the passion she felt when she was younger. Her thoughts of being taken and penetrated were strong. Charles even felt her discomfort with him. His eyes told her exactly what he wanted to do, making her uneasy.

He wanted her to feel that precariousness, so he stepped close, never changing his expression or shifting his eyes. He saw her as a piece of meat to be consumed. She moved her hand to the collar of her dress as if to hide the cleavage.

Still standing close, he demanded, "Come with me."

She followed him out the door into a dimly lit hallway.

Charles issued a declaration. "You will have sex with me."

Apparently shocked, the nurse gasped for air. Her hand instinctively moved again to cover her cleavage, but there was none revealed. "I will do no such thing," she said. "You are but a boy."

"Never mind what I am. You have an itch that needs to be scratched. I have a need for a female body. You will do as I ask, or I will see to it that my grandfather sends you packing, along with your assistant who is your daughter, while you both pretend otherwise."

He knew his words struck like a sledgehammer. Charles was aware that the servants alleged he possessed an uncanny ability to read thoughts; they rumored about it for years. He also knew that despite the servants' inability to keep secrets, the nurse had somehow managed to keep her daughter's identity concealed. Charles perceived her loss for words and her fears that Paul would terminate her employment. He knew that she needed the money but also sensed her unwillingness to take his virginity.

Reaching out, the nurse gently took his hand and led him down the hallway, around a corridor, and into a closet where the servants kept supplies. There was no light in the closet, but she found two candles to light. The nurse turned to Charles and saw his frustration. He followed her to the closet, but he was not expecting to engage in sex there. She placed a hand on his member, and he understood that her intentions were to show him other ways that a woman could please a man.

"Please allow me to do this," she begged. "It will feel the same." She tugged at his pants until they fell past his knees and then fondled him. "You see?" she asked. "This is good; it's just the same."

Being a virgin, Charles had no way of knowing that the grip of her hand felt different from the grip of her vagina. It was nonetheless pleasurable to him, and he was quickly aroused. He understood that he didn't need her body; what he sought was an orgasm and the emotional high that only an orgasmic climax could render. Such energy, if projected properly into his contrived image, would benefit the spell he created.

He stopped the nurse just long enough to reach into his pocket for the folded paper. He unfolded it and stared at the image he had created three days prior. She carried on to his enjoyment until he realized that he had to exercise mind over matter to keep from losing focus on the image. His concentration on the image was necessary in order to pour into it that which he felt from her touch. The speed of her strokes increased, and Charles felt his skin quiver at his toes and fingertips. After a short moment, his lips tingled, and vibrations stiffened his back. He was at a sudden loss of breath, but he refused to take his eyes off the image. Charles fought that ecstatic feeling until he reached a climax like never before. He expelled a loud and vocal sigh—almost a scream. Warm seminal fluids erupted from his shaft like a volcanic reaction. His body jerked involuntarily as the semen poured over the nurse's hand. With her free hand, she lightly stroked his back feigning like she genuinely cared for him or enjoyed the experience.

"Are you okay?" she asked.

Charles did not speak. Instead, he took the paper and held it to the fire of one of the candles. The flames caught quickly, and the paper burned rapidly. He felt the searing heat on his hand and dropped the paper to the floor. It fell and ignited a wooden box that was on the floor. The nurse called for Christ and reached for a towel. She doused the flames, but the suffocating smoke filled the closet. They both sprang for the door, Charles, pulling at his pants as the smoke escaped the closet.

Charles started to chuckle. He regarded the smoke as a symbol of his energy, permeating the space inside the closet, escaping into the hallways, and reaching Agatha, thereby completing the transfer of his sexual energy that he believed would transform into her very own will to live.

It took three days before the nurse noticed that Agatha had not coughed blood. Five days following Charles's experiment, Agatha asked the nurse to lift her to a sitting position. He witnessed the return of her appetite. Seven days later, the doctor confirmed that Agatha's sickness had started to regress. She lived for ten years more before dying in her sleep. She was the first of Paul's four daughters to depart from life. Although she had no children of her own, she spent her lifetime working diligently to educate her nephew on interpreting the contents of the scroll. Paul's wish that his children bury him was fulfilled. Agatha attended his burial ceremony, and three years later, she was laid to rest near him.

Both Charles and Agatha were enlightened by the first scroll's explanation of the barriers that Edward Kelly once spoke of. They were equally interested in one specific impediment to a realm of the universe known as *The Book of Life*. This was not a book in the literal sense; instead, it was a place. It was suggested that one particular spirit—not an angel, but one nearly as old as any angel—had a desire to instruct men to enable them with the ability to find this place through projection of his soul. Unfortunately, the scroll they had in their possession came short of supplying information. Charles assumed that more data was contained in the missing scroll, which was stolen and had been missing for more than one and a half centuries. Charles vowed that he would diligently search far and wide to recover his family's property. He suspected that the thieves destroyed the scroll and that perhaps they thought too highly of it to demand ransom. He imagined that the crooks would learn to read the script and use it in much the same way as he had. The scrolls, among many other things, proved to be a roadmap to realms of consciousness where men and spirits could correspond and perhaps form alliances. If this was true, Charles theorized that at some point, the path of the thieves would conjoin with his path, and when that happened, those who possessed the second scroll would pay for their interference.

TALIB'S BOOK OF HATE

From what Talib learned about Fiona's family history, he assumed that the gift empowered her to do many things—some that were frightening and others that were beneficial. The fact that she had the ability to save someone's life, like Charles, made Talib envious. He would have liked to own such a capacity to save his father's life.

Fiona arose from her stool and escorted him around the arts and crafts room. Four other easels held previously completed projects. One was a detailed image of an elderly man in a folding chair. His head was covered in a white ghutra. It was held in place by a black egal. A tan bisht covered his shoulders and most of his clothing, down to his ankles. His eyes gave the impression of a wise man, and his expression held a look of concern. His mouth was open as though he were engaged in conversation. A gaping hole made it apparent that he had lost a front tooth. To the left and right of him were seven young men who were around Talib's age. They sat cross-legged on rugs, arced around the wise man. Behind them stood one person in a white thobe.

Talib felt tears forming in his eyes as he observed the painting.

"I apologize," she spoke softly.

"No. You don't have to."

"It's just that I cannot get past you if you do not get over it."

"When did you paint this?"

"The day you arrived."

"I remember this, Sheik Mustapha," he whispered. "But I don't see me."

"It is from your point of view."

"Is this what your gift allows you to do?"

"Painting is a gift of its own. Sometimes, when I am working on an illustration, my pains disappear. My grandfather's dad did the same. He also wrote a lot."

"Does it work?"

"Sometimes." She continued to watch him. As he studied the painting, she studied him. "Would you like for me to show you more?"

"What more?"

Fiona touched him in such a way that prompted Talib to face her. He noticed the look of fear in her eyes and hoped she wasn't fearful of him. Slowly, she dropped to her knees and then transitioned into a sitting position with folded legs. Then she stretched out her hand, silently asking him to mimic her behavior. When he did, she took his hand in hers, but Talib pulled away.

"What are you doing?"

"If you will allow me, I will see the source of your hatred."

Talib felt his heart tremble. He was suddenly frightened of her.

"I will only see what you allow."

Talib felt conflicted. He wanted to trust her, but he held fast to his religious teachings that admonished him to avoid sorcerers, wizards, and palm readers.

"I am none of those," she explained. "We shouldn't fear each other."

He watched as she again extended her hand, and this time, he slowly reached for hers. When their hands met, he gazed into her gray eyes.

"Breathe slowly," she advised. "Close your eyes and allow me to share your memories."

Talib advanced back to five days shy from his sixteenth birthday. One would imagine the anticipation he felt about the date, but he was more excited about it being the first day of school. He had waited many weeks for his chance to sit under the tutorage of Instructor Hassan Abu Bakar. Hassan had been away for nearly five years, locked in an Israeli prison where he was charged with inciting violence against Israeli militia—the army unit that patrolled his neighborhood.

It just so happened that four tanks and eighty foot-soldiers from this unit passed through a neighborhood heading to their patrolling assignment in Gaza, when an eight-year-old child struck one of the tanks with a rock. None of the soldiers actually saw the child throw the rock, but at least six of them knew from which direction it came. Fingers pointed, but the boy had already escaped.

The commander demanded that the people in the community turn over the culprit, but no one complied. The military units were ordered to dispatch and take assigned positions in the area. Some soldiers stood at corners. Others took post in the center of the street. Four other soldiers were ordered to go door to door and into resident homes to cattle out all members at gunpoint into the street to face the commander.

When they arrived at Talib's door, he walked out ahead of his father, whose hand was placed gently on Talib's shoulder. They were ordered to sit when they reached the street.

It took nearly an hour before every home was emptied and every present neighbor sat on the edge of the road. Sobbing women and mumbling men were all around him. There was talk about attacking the soldiers, and Talib's father whispered to his brother to pay no attention to the foolish talk. Talib saw no sense in fighting; they were outgunned and outnumbered. He sat patiently; it wasn't the first time that the Israeli military had ordered everyone from their homes to conduct searches.

The commander first promised that no harm would come to the person who identified the culprit, and the same promise was extended to the culprit if he confessed. He called the act of throwing a rock an attack against them and their country. According to him, hiding was a cowardly act that would not go unpunished if no one stepped forth. He then promised that he would cause them all to suffer if the culprit was not pointed out. Still, no one said a word.

The commander would get no answer from the citizens. Giving his order, he called for one of the tanks to advance toward a home. The intent to demolish was apparent.

"Does anyone wish to confess now?" he asked as the tank continued approaching. "If you do not speak up, every home in this neighborhood will receive the same treatment."

The tank rolled forth until it collided with a house. The structure, built more to endure heat from the sun than the push of a tank, quickly gave in to the force of the three-ton block of steel.

A loud cry escaped from the lady who owned the home.

Hassan stood. He was a rather tall young man with a perfectly trimmed beard. His skin was golden brown, and the youthful glint in his eyes hid his resentment for the Israeli army. Every rifle near him pointed in his direction, but he showed no signs of fear.

Although Talib admired Hassan for his actions, he feared that the man would never return. When word to the contrary spread, there was celebration among the neighborhood people. Soon after, Talib had heard a rumor that Hassan would be an instructor at the school. Talib was ecstatic about the opportunity to study under him. He anticipated Hassan's lessons, but more importantly, he couldn't wait to inform Hassan that he was the child who'd thrown the rock.

Hassan had an influential way of teaching, and Talib found the well-versed instructor to have the most interesting stories. "How did you learn so much in prison?" Talib once asked.

"There is nothing else to do in captivity except learn. Reading is not allowed so much, so I spent time in discussions with older men. There are hundreds of highly educated men in the Israeli prisons."

The two of them sat in the courtyard at the school. Before heading home, Talib and his friends Abdullah and Sami usually met under the one tree in the courtyard that provided ample shade. On this day, Hassan joined them and answered questions regarding his imprisonment. He explained how he once believed that it was possible for Christians, Jews, and Muslims to coexist but that he no longer subscribed to such impossibilities.

"There was this English man who had been in that prison for twenty-six years. The first time I spoke to him, he had intruded on a conversation I was having with a Pakistani who had joined HAMAS. I told him that Mecca was conquered by pilgrims who carried no swords or weapons. It was a peaceful invasion. Then the English man joined and told me I was naive. He said, 'There will never be peace between the religions. There are people who are content with making sure of that.' Then, I said, 'By the mere concept of religion, it is impossible to follow any of them without striving for a peaceful community.'"

As Hassan related the story, Talib envisioned the dusty prison floor. He pictured two mattresses on opposite sides of a small cell. He could see the bars separating Hassan and his cell mate from the Englishman, who leaned his back against the bars and spoke—his voice dry and old. He could imagine the blue eyes and the gray hair that Hassan described. "I remember when I was as stupid as you are now." He smiled, his aged eyes turned upward. "Boy, was I stupid." He looked at Hassan. "Religion is a facade, son. It is a distraction! It is a tool used by the wealthy to control the masses almost like a mass hypnotic trance. Have you considered the possibility that some religious nuts believe that peace can only be achieved if and when every follower of any other religion is dead?"

"Then they would be in violation of their own faith," Hassan replied.

"What if the religion called for them to fight and kill and even commit genocide? Just like your jihad."

Hassan said, "No religion is as such, my friend. It is written in Islam that you should fight against oppression, fight against slavery, fight against those who prevent you from prayer, and in that, you fight them until they stop fighting you. That is jihad. But the deeper meaning, the true meaning of jihad, is to fight the weakness within you. The weakness that prevents you from—"

"Yeah, yeah, yeah! I can take what you said and make it mean anything I want! That is the beauty of religion. Have you ever heard of the Christian Rights?"

"Christian rights?" Hassan repeated. "Their rights are not different from others, no?"

"No. I don't mean their rights. I'm talking about organizations. They're called Christian Rights. Their rights supersede others' – so they believe. They also believe that every nation should be governed by the Ten Commandments. Their way of establishing it is by kidnapping children and making them fight in their armies. They rape women and force them into marriages. Take a visit to middle Africa and ask anybody there about the Lord Resistance Army. If you think that's bad, try India and ask the children of dead Hindu worshippers about the brutality of the National Liberation Front of Tripura. Check out the Catholic Reaction Force or the Orange Volunteers. These Christians make your little Muslim antics look like child's play. Then, of course, there is the Aryan Nation and the Christian Identity Movement. By the time you identify those people, it is too late. Some of them believe that one day Jesus Christ will return to this earth just as he said he would, but get this—he cannot return until the earth is ready. It is the people's job to make the earth ready. Any idea of the most important task they must accomplish?"

Hassan answered, "No."

"They have to rebuild the temple of Solomon." He turned to look Hassan in the eyes. "But they cannot rebuild it until every Muslim in Jerusalem is dead. Do you know why?"

Hassan did not answer.

"Because of Al-Aqsa Mosque. Solomon was a wise man, the wisest ever. The world will never know anyone like him again. He was the one who created the House of God. He used men, demons, and angels to do it, but Nebuchadnezzar came along and demolished the temple. The rubble remained on that spot until, on a February day, a Muslim caliph, Omar, entered Jerusalem on a white camel. He and his men wore tattered clothing. They were a tacky but disciplined group. The chief magistrate of Jerusalem, Sophronius, was with him. When they rode to the site of Solomon's Temple, Omar climbed from his camel, looking appalled at the waste and rubble on the mount. Sophronius declared, 'Behold the abomination of desolation, spoken of by Daniel the prophet.' It became Omar's mission to build his Muslim mosque on the mount, and there it is until this day."

"But how does that justify genocide?" Hassan asked.

"'So the people shouted when the priests blew with the trumpets: and it came to pass, when the people heard the sound of the trumpet, and the people shouted with a great shout, that the wall fell down flat, so that the people went up into the city, every man straight before him, and they took the city. And they utterly destroyed all that was in the city, both man and woman, young and old, and ox and sheep, and ass, with the edge of the sword.'" He smiled as if he was pleased with his quote. "That, my friend, comes from the Holy Bible and the Torah. Is that not genocide? Would you like to hear more?"

Hassan answered, "No."

The British man continued to quote regardless of Hassan's lack of want. "Then the Lord said to Joshua, 'Do not be afraid; do not be discouraged. Take the whole army with you, and go up and attack Ai. For I have delivered into your hands the king of Ai, his people, his city, and his land. You shall do to Ai and its king as you did to Jericho and its king, except that you may carry off their plunder and livestock for yourselves. Set an ambush behind the city.'" He laughed when he saw that Hassan had become flustered. "If you didn't know, the Israelis killed everyone from Jericho. Shall I go on?"

As Talib listened to Hassan's prison adventures, he understood more than what Hassan made obvious. Talib understood that prison was not simply a place of brick and iron bars; it was a place of despair where dreams became haunting ghosts. Talib understood that Hassan had transformed while in prison. He could not attest to what Hassan had become, but his new pedagogy was interesting and enlightening.

"We cannot have peace until the peace breakers are eliminated."

Many people saw Israeli settlements as a military occupation. Over the years, the British gentleman made many accusations against the Israeli people from his prison cell. If all his recitations and points of view were correct, there were no more Israelis. They were all destroyed or taken away by an Assyrian army and had become a genetic mix of many different ethnicities. What right did they have to the land in Palestine? What right did they have to inflict misery on the people who had lived there for more than a thousand years before these "new Jews" arrived?

Hassan explained these sentiments in simple ways that Talib and his friends understood. Hassan was not far removed from the boys' ages, and because he was highly intelligent and enlightened, Talib accepted his words and beliefs as if they were the words of the Divine. He did not like the harassment he faced whenever he entered Jerusalem for prayer. He expressed how it was inherently wrong for Israeli soldiers to deny his people entrance for prayer.

Talib sensed that Hassan wanted to change things, but he had lost hope for peaceful solutions. Talib's father cautioned him to avoid anyone who could not accept peaceful solutions. Although Talib feared that Hassan had become one of those people, he knew there was more to this man than his political views. He gave spiritual lessons that were not in the Quran. Talib loved to hear stories about Solomon and djinn. Hassan knew dozens of such stories, and Talib ensured that he heard them all.

"As you know," he once said. "King Sulemon lived in Jerusalem and built the most glorious house of worship for Allah's sake. But did you know that what made the temple unlike any ever made before it or after it was that it was made by men, djinn, and angels?" When Talib first heard this, he was surprised. "Djinn?"

"Yes, it's true. At first, there were only men; one was a boy who Sulemon loved greatly. He paid him double and provided him with extra food. Despite this, he noticed the boy growing weaker each day. The king was perplexed about this, and one day, he called the boy to ask why his size was decreasing. The boy said 'Please believe my story, oh, King. Each day, after leaving work, I lay down to rest and am visited by a djinni. He is an evil sort who wants to deter construction of the temple. He casts a spell and bites my thumb. The spell causes me to sleep; when I wake, half my earnings are missing. My soul is oppressed so my body grows thinner every day.'

"When Sulemon heard this, he was deeply moved and went into the temple to pray. His prayers lasted for the remainder of the day and deep into the night. He was weary and sad. Then Allah sent a messenger—the angel Michael—who offered Sulemon a ring. Michael told him, 'Take this gift that we offer you. It is the highest Sabaoth. With it, you will hold captive all the shaitans and djinn that you desire. None in the earth, male or female, will be able to resist you. Those who wish to destroy your work will be compelled by your desire for them to help build all of Jerusalem.'

"He gave Sulemon the ring, and the king was content. The next day, Sulemon called for the boy and instructed him to use the ring to strike the djinni in his chest when it came and then bring him to the king. Sulemon implored the boy to report regardless of what the king was doing or what time it was. The boy obeyed. When the time approached for the djinni's usual visit, he came like a burning fire and began casting his spell. The boy, equipped with a defense, did not hesitate to throw the ring. 'By the name of Allah, you are the prisoner of King Sulemon.'

"The boy ran straight to the king while the djinni followed, screaming loudly. It begged to be released, but the kid would not.

It offered riches of gold and silver to no avail. When Sulemon heard the noise, he rose from his sleep and met the youth. There, in the vestibule of his throne room, was the djinni, much like a man; his feet were covered in smoke and his legs seemed to grow from the dark smoke. Despite its intimidating looks, it was afraid and trembled before the king."

"'Who are you?' asked the king.

"'I am Ornias.'

"Sulemon stared at its face. It was like a fiery transparency. It did not appear solid at all. 'And from what energy of the universe are you derived?'

"The djinni was surprised, and astonishment was evident in his voice. 'How do you know such things? You are but a man.'

"'What energy are you?' Sulemon demanded.

"'I am begotten of the one whose symbol is the water pourer and of those who are consumed with desire for the noble virgins upon the earth.' The djinni turned to the boy. 'Like him. He wishes for one of the king's daughters.'

"The boy ashamedly lowered his head. The truth was spoken, and it was clear to the king that the djinni was called forth by the lad's desires.

"'Lustful soul like him I strangle. But in cases where there is no disposition to sleep, I may take on one of three other forms. A man becomes enamored of women, and I metamorphose into a beautiful woman, then I take hold of the man in his sleep. When I am satisfied, I grow wings and ascend to heavenly dominions. If I am angry and wish to strike fear, I morph into a lion.

"'And which of the Lord's angels compels you?' asked the king.

"'Uriel. I fear only Uriel—so you, dear King, will have no authority over me!'

"Sulemon was not intimidated by the spirit's sudden fit of rage. He knew more than the djinni realized. 'This may be true, but I now control your fate. Perhaps I shall condemn you to eternal imprisonment much like Semjaza, Araklba, Ezeqeel, and the others!'

"The djinni's fire cooled, for it wished to eschew such eternal captivity. As it chilled, its body solidified into human flesh that had been burned by fire. Then Sulemon gave the djinni his sentence. 'You are my prisoner. Just as you attempted to destroy my work, you will now be my stonecutter for the construction of the same temple you sought to betray.'"

Talib, upon hearing this story, became infatuated with the idea of the supernatural. He was curious to know more about spirits and wondered if they interacted with modern men as they did in ancient times. For his entire life, he had heard stories of Allah, angels, and djinn, but it wasn't until he heard Hassan's stories that he came to appreciate the spirit world.

Hassan made the entities seem tangible—as if they lived like men. As he described them, each spirit possessed a personality and a will that did not necessarily include the destruction of mankind. Talib was left with the impression that the spirits were like humans in that they chose who they would affect; the difference was that they did so on their own accord as opposed to succumbing the devil's orders and commands. In this, Talib wanted to know more: he wanted to know the truth.

Every adolescent who latched onto Hassan did so for some personal reason—but mostly because of his charismatic mannerisms of walking, talking, or laughing. There were many simple reasons why others respected him as well. His manner of dress was not traditional. He wore bold colors that made him stand out, but he contrasted that boldness with a humble nature. Talib and his friends often imitated Hassan's movements and word choice. While having dinner with the family, Talib often sat with his legs curled behind him in much the same way as Hassan did.

When Talib visited Hassan's home, he was surprised by the vast difference between him and the older, white-bearded scholars. He did not oppose television or music like the elders. Hassan possessed a television, a video recorder, and a stereo system. There were blue jeans in his closet and a pair of Michael Jordan shoes. His walls were decorated with framed Islamic artwork. It was obvious that he had an affinity for green plants for they were in every corner of every room. The oil he burned smelled of sandalwood. He was, if nothing else, organized. Everything in his room seemed to be lined and squared perfectly.

What Talib and three other visiting students loved more than anything was the collection of firearms displayed on mounted racks fastened to a wall in Hassan's back room. In all, there were five weapons: three automatic weapons and two handguns. Naturally the question arose as to why a teacher would have so many weapons—or a need to have them.

"There is a promise I made to myself that I intend to keep," Hassan answered. "I will not spend another day in an Israeli prison."

This answer was acceptable to the youths, and it was obvious that Hassan had taken a different approach to coexisting with Israeli soldiers.

"I learned many things in those five years." He continued. "I was there for a reason, a bigger reason that what I first thought."

"What's the reason?" asked Abdullah. He stood next to Talib, who the shortest of them. Abdullah's hair was long and black.

"It is time to free our people. Everyone here needs to know the truth. We need an army. We have a right to an army, a recognized country, and a right to govern ourselves."

He motioned for them to follow, and they complied. Hassan stood taller than most Palestinian men. He had narrow shoulders and a slender frame. Next in height was Amir who was also considered tall for his age. His dad was even taller, so it was understandable how Amir grew faster than his peers. Talib, however, was unusually short. Whereas Abdullah had experienced one growth spurt and hoped for a second, Talib continued to hope for his first one.

Hassan took them to a neighborhood of row houses where they found a man older than Talib's grandparents, if they were alive. He sat comfortably in a wheelchair under a shaded tree. In his lap was a half-filled bowl of dates. He was generous and offered dates to his visitors and invited them to take a seat on the grass.

Hassan sat also, and introduced the man as Sheik Mustapha. "I brought these four young fellows to hear you speak. They have questions and you are the best to answer them."

"Ah yes," the sheik said. "There is much to be confused about. I think, with every generation, the confusion increases." His brown eyes looked over them.

Talib knew of the sheik's reputation, but he had never seen him. The legendary man was surrounded by armed guards. "How well do you know your history?" he asked.

Abdullah confidently raised a thumb. Amir and Talib both mumbled "Okay." Sami said nothing at all.

The sheik smiled. Even with missing teeth, he had a pleasantly warm smile that made them feel comfortable. "It's a strange thing history is. It is not absolute. It is personal, and although a single event may include a hundred men, it will have different meanings for each of them."

Talib was in awe at the sheik. He had never been privileged to sit at the feet of a man who was so reputed. Talib saw him as a man who could order a thousand men to war with one simple command. He was powerful and respected, yet he was as simple as any man. Talib admired the simplicity of the sheik and clung to every word as that humble man told his story. As he spoke, Talib understood why the disdain for the Jewish festered among his people.

The sheik spoke of a time when he was Talib's age. He grew up in a simple community near a plot of land that was dense with foliage and inhabited by so many insects that the young Mustapha hunted and captured them in a glass jar. He visited that field twice each day—once to capture the insects and later on to release them—by his mother's command. He would do this for three to four days each week until one day, to his disappointment, he found a fence erected around the field. Now, although he climbed the fence to continue his exploits, eventually, he was no longer able to catch the insects. The field, to his dismay, was destroyed by fire and charred black for as far as he could see. Bulldozers and large dirt piles were mixed with the uprooted shrubs and trees.

It was then that he realized that the field had become a construction site for a Jewish community. After a short while, the insects were forgotten. Instead, young Mustapha watched the workers drive bulldozers and dig ditches. He noticed construction workers too. They had pale skin that turned red in the heat and spoke a language that he had not heard before. His teachers explained that after losing the war, the Ottomans had to pay the British with the surrender of his homeland.

The sheik laughed at the audacity of the European demands on the Turks. "Can you believe that? We were the price. Our land and our lives were all handed over to the British for their disposal."

Although he was smiling when he spoke those words, the look in his eyes betrayed the apparent joy in his voice. Emptiness cascaded his face as he described how the community around him changed. First, homes went up and replaced the field of insects and foliage. Next, Jewish families moved into those homes. Following that was an influx of Christians now interested in visiting Jerusalem. Some of them also took up residency, and the sheik explained how Christian people frightened him. They brought with them reputations from years past when they sent Muslims to the guillotines for refusing baptism.

"We were told not to allow them to baptize us. The sheiks told us to die as Muslims and the reward in the hereafter would be far greater for those who become martyrs."

He reflected on the rumors and realities of friends and relatives who lost their homes for the construction of new ones and the eventual exclusion from the marketplaces. He remembered the days when life became violent. There was the gang of Jewish terrorists, Irgun, that turned against the British.

"They were the cruelest and most violent men you ever met," he said. "They killed our people by the thousands; they killed my parents, pillaged the neighborhood where I grew as a child, and took my wife and child from where we lived in Deir Yassin. They chased the British out of the country first and then turned against us with tanks and automatic weapons. We had nothing to defend ourselves. The Egyptians were our only friends; we relied on them to defend us, but they were outnumbered. The Americans, British, and French all joined against them, and when the Egyptians were defeated, we had nothing. I was left with no parents, no wife, and no child. All I had at that point was my religion.

"It was clear to me that the Jews and the British had one goal. It remains their goal even now: the total subjugation or extinction of the entire Arab race in Palestine. I decided to learn as much as I could about my enemy. One of the first things I found out about was an agreement between the governments of Britain, France, and Russia."

Hassan nodded in anticipation of what Sheik Mustapha was about to say. "It was the Sykes-Picot agreement." He muttered just loud enough to be heard.

"The pact was made in secret. They decided to break up the Ottoman Empire and divide the parts between them. We had no representation. The Jews had friends in Britain, but there was no one to listen to our concerns. The same is true today. We try to barter with the world through the Palestinian Liberation Organization, and meanwhile, the Israeli people attack everyone— Arab and British alike. Even after they betrayed the British, the queen continued to support them.

It is because of all this that I teach to our brothers and sisters about our responsibility to end our suffering." He made eye contact with Talib.

Talib understood the sheik better than he had ever imagined.

He understood for the first time why it was so commonly believed that the blood of his countrymen was on the hands of the Americans, British, and French. He understood that Americans supplied the Israeli government with tanks, fighter jets, and assault weapons to use against Palestinians. He understood the hatred and disdain for the Americans and the cry for revenge each time the Israeli militia killed one of his neighbors. For the first time, Talib understood the pain of his countrymen, and it was clear that the sheik's message was correct: the future of the Palestinian people could not rest alone in the attempts to negotiate with their enemies. And as Talib contemplated how he could do his part, the sheik said something he would forever remember.

"No American agreements are honorable. They keep no vows. America is a land of contradictions and lies. They only seek to brainwash you. What do they say ... land of free? So why own slaves? Enslaved people built America. They claim everyone can become wealthy and educated, but it is all deception. They murder, discriminate, and subject their own people to poverty. They are Christians, yet they burn churches. They imprison innocent men and women, and they permit homosexuality and any vice you can imagine. America is the modern Sodom and Gomorrah.

"There is no wonder why they support Israel. Allah will not free them from punishment. Their society will fall by their decadence. The time will come when men take on other men for wives—and the children will kill their parents. The evil that the Americans make will fold in on them. They need no other nation to destroy them. They are already destroyed, and they do not yet know it.

"For us, there is just one sensible solution. Each of us owes a responsibility to all of us, and to those who sacrificed their lives, and to those who have not yet been born. We owe it to bring peace to our lands and our people in any way possible. Not everyone will understand or agree, but sometimes the end result matters more than the methods. It will be then that Allah decides—for He is the best planner."

Talib had never heard history told in such a way. He could hear the pain in the sheik's voice when he spoke of his murdered wife and child. Even in all of that, the sheik seemed to harbor no regret or animosity against those he recognized as his enemies. He suggested that the war be fought in two realms of reality. Talib did not completely understand what the sheik meant, but he did realize that he spoke against hatred and for the inevitable war, a jihad both inside and outside of every man. No one would escape it.

On the return home, Hassan attempted to explain to them that there were three wars to fight. "There is one to protect our right to live the way we choose. Then there is another inside each of us to remain disciplined and free from hatred. Then there is the war against the spirit world that wishes to destroy all mankind— not just Jews or Arabs."

Talib, for the first time, disagreed with his teacher. The sheik referred to something else. It was something more elusive than and not as obvious as a simple war between men. Talib kept his thoughts to himself. His friends, however, were interested in joining the organization.

"Are we allowed to join the liberation organization?" Amir asked.

"Yes. You can join, but first, you must learn many things. You should never join anything until you know exactly what or who you are joining."

Talib was comfortable with Hassan's sentiment. He felt he was being recruited and was certain that his father would not have approved of any membership with any political organization. In fact, Talib was sure that, if his father ever heard about his visit to the sheik and the recitation of Palestinian history, all future visits would be prohibited. The incessant talk about war, history, murder, and violence was a bit gloomy. Talib wanted more stories about Solomon and his djinni.

It was time for them to leave, however. Hassan knew that most parents preferred that their sons to be home for Magrib. Nonetheless, he agreed to one short story before sending them on their way. "I will tell you about two of Sulemon's most dangerous djinni. Do you remember the djinni Ornias?"

They answered together, "Yes."

"Well, Sulemon ordered this djinni to retrieve the strongest of them. Ornias protested and begged the king to release him, but with the threat of summoning the archangel Urial, Ornias agreed to obey. He left and went to find Beelzebub. When he found the huge djinni, he said to him, 'The king of Israel, Sulemon, summons you.'

"Beelzebub laughed. 'Who is this Sulemon?'

"'He calls for you, and I must obey orders to bring you.' He threw the ring, and Beelzebub transformed into a blazing fireball. All around them, the place was filled with grass and shrubbery, but the heat from Beelzebub's infernal rage turned everything that was green to hues of brown and the vegetation perished. There was nothing Beelzebub could do to resist the power that was placed on the ring."

Talib had a question. "Tell me about this ring—how did it work? Aren't spirits invisible?"

"No, they are not, but sometimes we cannot see them. There is a difference. There was a Sufi master who wrote about his experience in the realm of angels and djinn. He was shown a metal that was partly composed of elements from our reality, but it also contained substances from the spirit world. When all the substances are combined into an alloy, spiritual energy is affected to enable men to capture spirits. For this reason, the temple was not erected with iron tools. Once in contact with this material, the djinni becomes visible. Its energy is arrested, and its body cool into a physical form. When this happens, they can then feel pain, receive punishment, and even procreate with women or men with solid, physical forms."

Talib nodded. He admitted that the thought of spirits materializing into fleshy creatures was spooky and made his skin quiver.

Hassan continued with the story. "When Beelzebub stood before Sulemon, the king asked his name." 'I am Iblis, also known by men as Beelzebub the exarch.'"

"'And what function do you serve in this universe?' asked the king."

"'I am he who teaches the djinn their apparitions.'"

"'Well,' said the king. 'I have much work for you. Bring me all of the unclean spirits. They will help me build the house of God.'

"Why would I do that?' Beelzebub laughed at the king. "'Silly mortal, what need does the Creator have for a house? The universe is the place where it rests its feet.'

"'I have been given authority over them and you as well. If I am made to hunt them down myself, I will torture them with iron. They will not have men to torment for I will bind and imprison them in much the same way as the Watchers. They will dwell in cells of iron and brass with a curse of containment, much the same as on Tartarus.'

"Beelzebub was not at all interested in being responsible for the Watchers' fate. 'Very well,' he said. 'I will bring them to you, and you will swear by your God to make no such containment.'

"Sulemon agreed. He chose his words very carefully so that he could, if needed, create something else that would serve as containment for the unclean djinn. Then the king sent the Djinni to retrieve a female sprit if there were any. Beelzebub agreed, and then he left. His speed was lightning fast; within a moment, he returned with his charge. 'And who are you?' the king asked.

"'I am called Oroskelis,' she answered.

"'Tell me all about yourself.'

"'I am a spirit inside of a body. I am she who will strangle men with a noose. I stalk precipice points to taunt men until they leap to their deaths. I dwell in caves, ravines, and places of folly. Many times, I consort with men who bear dark skin as if I am a woman of like hue. I cause them to privately and sometimes openly worship my star without knowing that they harm themselves in doing so. These are they who whet my appetite for more of what I do.'

"So, Sulemon commanded her to spin the hemp to make the ropes. There she sat night and day, spinning the hemp. Then Sulemon made a seat for Beelzebub to sit beside the king. He then asked the djinni from where his power derived and to explain why he was the strongest.

"Beelzebub told him, 'Because I am the lone watcher, left to roam the earth. I escaped the wrath of the angels when they came down upon my brothers.'

"'You were the only Watcher who got away?'

"'There are others. They serve the angels faithfully. When I left them, none came along. Only those who were not Watchers followed. Then my brethren fought against us, but it was not long before they left their heavenly abode for the bounties of men, so the angels came for them. My sons and all others who followed me escaped the wrath.'

"Sulemon was interested in the sons of the djinni. 'Tell me about these sons.'

"'One was born to a mortal. He is the greatest of the Nephilim. He vowed to free my brothers from their prison. If he fails, we have conspired for him to succeed in a different life at a different time. When the seventy generations have passed, those who will come forward will come to him and teach him the words. He will break the curse, and the gates of Tartarus will open. Then men will see the power of my race.'

"'Nothing born of a woman will live so long. You deceive me?' Sulemon started to grow angry.

"'I cannot deceive you so long as this seal is on me. It is written in the book of Asmodeus.' Beelzebub said. 'If needed, my son will hide for seventy generations—and he will still fulfill his promise.'

"'And what of the other son?'

"'He haunts the Red Sea. On any suitable occasion, he comes up to me and reveals what he has done. I give him my blessing.'

"Sulemon was anxious to see and imprison Beelzebub's sea-dwelling son, so he commanded that he present his son to the king. Beelzebub refused.

"'I will not bring him to you, but there will come by the wind another djinni, Ephippas. He will oblige to serve you. Then, at your request, he may bring my son to you.'

"'What is his name, your son?' the king asked. 'And why is he in the depths of the sea?'

"'You cannot learn it from me, but one day, he will come to you and openly answer your questions.'

"Beelzebub was wise about not revealing his son's name to the king. In the spirit world, your name is a doorway into your mind. It is said that if someone asks your name while you are dreaming, never say it because it allows the djinn access to your mind."

"What will happen to you?" asked Sami.

"You will go insane," Abdullah answered.

"My dad said that most people who are mentally ill are really mentally infected," Talib added.

Hassan, mindful of the time, did not add to their side conversation. He continued with his story. "Beelzebub went on to tell the king of his mischief. 'I destroy kings.' And he gave to Sulemon a dreadful glare, filled with hatred. 'I ally myself with tyrants, and I cause them to worship my family of djinn. We feed those men power to rule, deceptions, lies, greed, frustration, fear, and injustice until they are full. I also do this to the chosen servants of the Creator and faithful men. I cause them to love my djinn, and we lure them to break their vows with heresies and lawlessness. Then these men obey me, and I give to them the will of destruction. I inspire them with envy, and they desire murder and wars and sodomy and every imaginable thing. They turn on their loyal servants, and their most trusted men are killed or condemned by their own hands. And these are the ones who will destroy the world.' Then he smiled and said something that should have angered the king. 'You should be grateful to me … for if I had not done the same to your father, you would not be here.'"

The four students were terrified. "This is what Beelzebub does to us?" Sami mumbled.

"Not to us," Talib answered. "He goes after kings and priests and people like that." He turned to Hassan. "What did he mean by that? Is Iblis responsible for Sulemon's birth?"

"Yes," Hassan answered, watching his student's eyes enlarge. "As you know, Iblis and Beelzebub are the same. Now, Islam does not support this belief, but Christians say that one day King Dawud was visited by Iblis and Asmodeus. These two djinn made it so that the king would see Bathsheba bathing, and they made Dawud lust over her. So Dawud, according to the Christians and some Jews, had sex with her, made her pregnant, and then tried to cover up this sin by sending her husband to war. He was killed, and then Dawud married her."

"I don't believe that story," Abdullah said.

Hassan laughed gently. "I never told you about Asmodeus, have I?"

"No."

"He was another djinni that worked the temple. He was perhaps the strongest of them, and Sulemon had to take extra precautions to control him. When Asmodeus was brought before the king, he was bound in chains. Sulemon had to place two seals on him—one in front and one on his back. When Sulemon asked his name, the djinni gave him a glare that was twice as frightening as Beelzebub's. With the evil stare, he yelled. 'And who are you?'

"'As you are already punished, it can be worse. Answer me. Who are you?' The king yelled back.

"Then the djinni answered. 'How can I answer you when you

are nothing but a man—a son of a man? I am the firstborn of this earth. I hail from fire, son of an original djinni, forged by the Creator's words. No words of my heavenly born race addressed to the earth-born can be overweened. My star is bright in heaven, and men call it the Wain, the Dragon Child, the Great Bear. I am close to my star, so ask me not many questions because your kingdom will in a short time be disrupted. Your glory is for just a season. Short will be your tyranny over us, and then we shall again have free range over mankind. They will revere us as if we were gods! We will devour their families. We will rise up a race of men who cannot be destroyed, and they will enslave the world; every man, every creature, every herb will submit to their collar. Long after you are in the ground, we will multiply your tyranny over us twelvefold and give it to one race of men to unleash on the world.'

"Sulemon ordered his men to bind Asmodeus tighter with an iron collar around his neck. The iron was very painful to him. Sulemon had him flogged and promised to continue with the floggings until the stubborn djinni answered the questions.

"Finally, the djinni said, 'I am called Asmodeus by men. My business is to plot against the newly wedded and prevent them from knowing one another. I serve them with many calamities. I waste away the beauty of virgin women and estrange their hearts. I transport men into fits of madness and desire when they have wives of their own. I cause them to leave their wives and go off by night and day to others who belong to other men. And I allow each of them to know of the unfaithful deeds until they become infuriated and fall into murderous deeds.'

"Then the king asked the djinni of which angel he was most afraid. The djinni said, 'Raphael.'

"'And what on earth causes you to flee?' the king asked.

"'The liver and gall of a fish I cannot bear when it is smoked over ashes of the tamarisk.'

"Then the king asked for the name of the fish, and Asmodeus said it was the glanos, found in the Assyrian rivers. He then asked the king to keep him away from water, but Sulemon did not listen. He ordered the djinni to make clay for the temple, put him to work, and bounded him with iron. While Asmodeus worked, Sulemon ordered his men to burn the liver and gall from the fish around the perimeter to prevent the djinni from escaping. Although Asmodeus was the strongest of the djinni, he had the ability to see the future of many things—except his own."

Time expired, and Hassan released his students, satisfied with what they learned that day. He bid peace to all of them and their families. "If you return tomorrow, I'll teach you how to fire a rifle."

Needless to say, the four boys were excited at the thought of firing a rifle. They also had much to say about the sheik's story. Each of them had comparisons from other stories they had heard from others. There was not one life that the cold hand of murder and war had not affected. They all had grandparents who, in sadness and pain, refused to reflect on their childhoods due to the horrific realities they had faced. While three of the four boys restricted their conversations to the tragedies of war, Talib's focus was on the stories of Solomon and the djinn. He had an incessant curiosity to know if the djinn were real or if the stories that Hassan told them were no different from the *Arabian Nights* stories his mom use to recite when he was a toddler. Talib wanted to know the truth, and he needed to discover a way to meet or see a djinni.

In Palestine, it was extremely difficult to learn about spirits and communications with them since such knowledge was protected due to its illegal nature. It was forbidden by his Islamic faith, but he still wanted to know. He admitted to having a curiosity about the spirit world and if he could solicit the assistance of angels or djinn.

Talib was aware that not all djinn were evil or wanted to destroy men. Some of them were good—like the ones that helped Muslim warriors in battle or those that helped men find their way when they were lost in the desert. When the legendary Mansa Musa fought for his kingdom, there was a djinni at his side to assist. Talib fantasized about the possibility of having a friend that was not easily seen by others. The possibility that such a friend could give him secret information or answers to school tests thrilled him. He thought such advantages would make his life exciting and possibly empower him to end the decades-long conflict in his homeland. His abilities could be limitless. With such thoughts, he wanted more information and knew that only Hassan would give him the answers.

When he had the chance, Talib picked his mentor's brain with probing questions. "So how did you come to know the stories?" he asked.

They left Hassan's home and walked through the streets and around corners for nearly an hour until they came to an old marketplace that was now a field of rocks and rubble from mortar shells and tanks. Twelve stores and merchants once gathered there each day to do business. There was once a slaughterhouse to buy meat, a clothing store, and an old man who sold prayer rugs made of the softest goat skin. All the boys were too young to remember the marketplace, but Hassan told them about his visits there as a child and how his aunt purchased a pet bird that he taught to speak.

"There was a man I met in prison. He told me that if I studied the life and actions of Sulemon, I would one day be privileged to answers that could help resolve many of our issues. I did exactly as he suggested."

"Did it work?" Talib asked.

"Well, I'm not finished. He was released about a year before me. I visited him once. He is the smartest man I've ever met. He teaches now at the University of Cairo."

"I don't understand what old stories can teach us about today," Abdullah said. "In those days, no one had tanks or rocket launchers to kill a hundred people at once."

"There were tyrannical and evil men in those days. There was—and will always be—greed and oppression. What the stories can teach you is the sources of these things. Men are used sometimes as tools without knowing. If you have a hammer that breaks, you easily replace it. This what the spirits do with us; once we die, they are off to manipulate another. When we are knowledgeable of them, we can avoid their traps."

"Tell us another," Talib asked.

"Yeah," Amir said. "But no more about djinn. Those stores give me nightmares."

Hassan laughed and said, "I don't believe I've told you about the queen of Sheba."

"No," Talib answered.

"It all starts with a bird. Sulemon, with all of his blessings, was able to communicate with animals just the same as with men and spirits. So, he summoned many of these birds since they could tell him about faraway people and places. One of these birds was a hoopoe.

"The king was initially frustrated with this particular one until it said, 'For three months, I've traveled the world trying to find a place or a kingdom that has not heard of your fame. After all those days, I found a city in the south called Kitor; it is a city with more wealth than any I have seen. Dust is more valuable than gold and silver is like mud in the streets. The trees are so strong they must suck water from the Garden of Eden. The men know nothing of war, and they wear garlands on their heads. Their monarch is a woman. They call her the queen of Sheba.'

"With that news, the king forgave the bird and called for his scribes to write a letter to the queen. When they were finished and the king approved, it was given to the hoopoe bird who flew off to deliver it.

"It took weeks for the bird to reach the city, and when it arrived, it was morning. The queen had awakened and was en route to pray to the sun as was her custom, but she was interrupted by the bird. When she noticed the letter tied around its foot, she took it in her hand and read it. Finishing it, she went right away to summon her advisers. She asked them if they had any news of Sulemon. None of her men knew anything of him, but they promised to investigate. After two days, they met with the queen again. The eldest of them said, 'He is a king who is rumored to be the wisest of any man who ever lived. It would be wise to entertain him—but not here. If he and his men were to come, they would like what they see and then conspire to overtake us. It would be best that you visited him.'

"So, the queen took his advice and sent word to the king that, although the trip should take seven years, she would arrive in three. This gave Sulemon plenty of time to build some very lavish chateaus, one of which was a glass building where he set his throne. There was rumor that the queen of Sheba was not entirely a person but part jackal—even part djinni. It was believed that she covered her legs and feet because a djinni has feet like birds. Sulemon thought of a candid way to learn her secret. He came up with a plot to build a pool of water covered with glass directly in front of the throne. When he invited the queen to sit beside him on a throne that he claimed to be her own, she was astonished. 'I thought you would be better comfortable seated at your own throne,' he said.

"When she caught sight of the pool of water, she did not realize that glass covered it. She walked up to the steps, and Sulemon watched carefully to see if she would lift her gown to avoid getting it wet, but one of her guards—sensitive to her secret—covered the pool of water with his garment so that she would walk over it. Sulemon's plan, although very clever, failed. He would figure out another plan to get what he wanted from her later.

"When she reached the top, she inspected her throne, thinking it was just a replica. There were some alterations to it—the images of her polytheistic gods were removed—but other things about it were familiar to her. She could not understand, however, how was it possible for her throne to arrive before she did, especially when she left it at home.

"The interesting thing about how it got there is that a djinni whose name was Dhakwan asked the king if he could retrieve the queen's throne from her hall—for such a deed would prove to her that Allah is the supreme of all gods and there is no comparison. The djinni promised that if he was entrusted to carry out the deed that he would return with the throne before Sulemon could finish his sessions of judging over the people. The king liked that idea but thought that the time away was too long for Dhakwan to be out of sight. Dhakwan was a very powerful djinni. If he was permitted the time to do as he said, he would have caused great mischief in the land and caused many men to do wrongs. The things that a man will do in a year can be done by djinni in an hour.

"Then a nice and friendly djinni that gave worship to Allah promised that it could retrieve the throne with much more speed than Dhakwan. With that promise and the trust of the king, he was granted the task and delivered just as promised.

"You would think that by now she was convinced of his might, but she was not convinced so easily. She said that she had heard of his wisdom and naturally had expected to see such wondrous things. 'If now I inquire of your concerning a matter, will you answer me?'

"The king agreed, and she said, 'Seven there are that issue and nine that enter, two yield the draught and one drinks; do you know of what I speak?'

"Of course,' the king answered. 'Seven are the days of a women's impurity, and nine are the months of pregnancy; two are the breasts that yield the draught, and one is the child who drinks it.'

"You are wise—but maybe not as much as your reputation.'

"The king laughed at the challenge. 'Do you have another question?'

"She nodded, and he told her to ask until she had exhausted them all—and she did. 'A woman said to her son, "Your father is my father, and thy grandfather is my husband. You are my son, and I am your sister.'"

"'How comes it that you know of such things?' he asked. 'You speak of the daughter of Lot who spoke as such to her son.'

"Later, she was escorted to her chambers—inside of a beautifully made building of stone and glass that the king built especially for her. When the king came to visit, she placed before him seven male and female children of the same age. None of them had reached puberty. They were similar in height and bore similar haircuts. 'Distinguish between them the males from the females,' she said.

"The king was not worried at all for this challenge was simple to him. He asked that each of the twelve children were given bowls of water. He had them wash their hands and promised to feed them nuts and roasted ears of corn. When this was done, he observed that some rolled up their sleeves before washing their hands where as others did not. 'Those are the males,' he pointed to those with wet sleeves.

"'Indeed, you are wise,' she said, but she continued to challenge him. 'There is an enclosure with ten doors; when one is open, nine are closed; when nine are open, one is closed.'

"The king answered her. 'The enclosure is the womb, and the ten doors are the ten orifices of man—his eyes, ears, nostrils, mouth, the apertures for discharge of urine and excreta, and the navel. When the child is an embryo, only the navel is opened, and the others are closed.'

"She asked him many questions for every day of her visit. At night, she contemplated more ways to create a question that he could not answer. The last question was this: 'Tell me this. It is a door and a seat, a shield and a sword, and it keeps you stationary and simultaneously takes you away. What is it?'

"The king was not at all lost by her question. 'You speak of a chair, one that is mystical and opens doors to parallel worlds. While sitting in it, the magician is protected from the djinni—and he may order the djinni to do mischief in the land. He who sits in it remains, but his soul transcends the energy of the chair. It is your prized possession, your throne.'

"'Yes,' she answered. 'And you have destroyed its ability by defacing it.'

"'I did better for you than you know. Yet I do fear that your counselors will restore its sigils.'

"'We have no army—none to defend us—save the spirits we seek.'

"'Do not worry, my queen,' Sulemon said. 'I will give you something better.'

"He offered her the Arc of the Covenant."

Hassan ended the story when they reached the field where he would teach them to use a rifle. "Now that I've told you that story, each of you must determine what it teaches."

That was the first time he suggested that his story was not for entertainment but for teaching a lesson. Talib, perhaps more than the others, was very interested in understanding the point of the story. He thought there was perhaps hidden information that would enable him to communicate with some member of the spirit world. He tried to figure out the meaning while engaged in shooting paper targets and tin cans. Hassan was a good teacher. He did not allow his students to use the automatic functions on his rifles, explaining that it was far more advantageous to learn to aim efficiently before using the automatic function.

They carried with them only two weapons. While two of the boys fired away, the others spoke, hoping to find the answer to the story's meaning.

Sami said, "If you consider that the queen did not invite Sulemon to her country because she was advised that her people would be in danger because she had no army. She had many riches—but little means of protection. Sulemon was very powerful and destroyed her throne. Wouldn't it make perfect sense for her to ally with him? With Sulemon as her friend, no one would attack her people?"

"That's good thinking," Hassan said. "When people speak of the queen of Sheba, they fail to consider her intellect. She was indeed brilliant. Her intellect is evident in the riddles and tests she presented to the king. It makes perfect logical sense that if she asked him riddles, she knew the answers as well. I am certain that, of all the women he ever knew, none were more brilliant than she."

Abdullah said, "So the point is ... make friends with powerful people?"

"I think that is a good way of saying it."

"But what happens if your friends turn against you?"

"That is something very likely to happen. In those days, monarchs ensured that would not happen by sealing their agreements and treaties with marriage. Sulemon had three hundred wives. Many of those marriages were parts of treaties and alliances."

"Why didn't he marry the queen of Sheba?" Talib asked as he surrendered the rifle to Sami. They all found out on that day that Talib had no talent for aiming a rifle.

"Oh, but he did," Hassan said. "Not only did he wed her— he put the future of the Jewish people in her belly." He saw the astonishment in their eyes. "Well, you know that Sulemon had the djinni Asmodeus as his prisoner. Asmodeus was very powerful especially since he could foresee future events. One day, Sulemon ordered the djinni to speak of the future.

"Asmodeus said 'The futures are many; new ones are created, and others are eliminated before they come. I will tell you of one that I hope will come to pass. In it, you choose just one from your many sons to rule over Israel. Iblis will visit him, and your son will heed the words of the master djinni. This offspring will become a tyrant over his people as you are over us. Then the people will hate him. Ten of your tribes will go away and the sons Judah will battle his brothers. We will rip your nation into twelve parts and cause your people to kill themselves. They will make objects to worship. Your temple will mean nothing to them. We will cause the children of Judah to wrestle naked in synagogues. When they have busied themselves, warring against each other and worshiping, my brothers, Kartikeya, will raise men from Assyria ... and Chamunda the Chaldeans ... Abaddon the Medes ... and Papingingara will raise them in Babylon. You will be in the grave, and your people will turn from their worship, their culture, and their God. They will become dispersed and absorbed, and the land will become a wasteland of dust and vultures. Rest assured, oh King, your daughters will bring shame to their fathers for they will voluntarily have their wombs seeded by Gog and Magog. Their skin will be as white as snow, and they will reconstruct your religion to please their desires. They will replace the words of Musa with the mystics of the Babylonians. I assure you, oh King, there are fifty different futures, and only one exists with your people destined to the greatness that you wish. You are a vain king, your hopes are vain, and all is vanity with men. You will build, and your sons will destroy. That is your future. It is for sure that you will be the last to die as king of the twelve tribes.'

"Sulemon became deeply saddened by the djinni's words. He thought of a way to preserve the Israeli tribes. When the queen came to Jerusalem, he married her and gave her his child so that when the future Asmodeus spoke of arrived, the Jewish people—through his seed—would survive."

Talib was amazed. "Did it work? Where are they now?"

"It worked," Hassan answered. "But they remain oppressed. Even the people who claim to be Jews now reject them and discriminate against them. I heard once that the Jews who came from Europe do not even recognize the descendants of Sulemon as their Jewish brothers."

Amir said, "So, the point of the story is that we must find ourselves a strong ally. The Israelis have the Americans and British ... we need to do the same."

Sami said, "Well, perhaps the Palestinian Liberation Organization will do that … find a powerful friend."

"Yes, but there is only one problem with that." Hassan injected. "Islam prohibits Muslims from seeking help from *al kafiroon*. We should rely on Allah and what He has already provided."

There shooting lesson ended, and Hassan walked home with the boys. It was then that Talib understood Hassan's frustration with the Palestinian Liberation Organization. "It is failing us," he said. "Our president wants our enemies to recognize our right to exist. I am beginning to believe that you don't ask your enemies to respect your rights; you force them to. How can they respect you if they want you dead?"

Once again, he kept his thoughts to himself. Talib, however, learned later that Hassan had serious thoughts of joining the Harakat al-Mugawamah al-Islamiyyah Party, an organization that was created in the past five years to accelerate the fight for Palestinian freedoms and rights. Many of the younger men were already leaving the Palestinian Liberation Organization due to their lack of progress and diminished confidence in the president's success potential.

Talib learned about Hassan's thoughts after a frightening conflict at a checkpoint when he went to pray. It was the first Friday of Ramadan, and Talib's father announced during morning breakfast that he would take a group of people into Jerusalem for the Jumah prayer. "We'll have to leave early to get past the checkpoint. I'll wake you—don't sleep too hard after Fadgr."

Talib remembered the checkpoint at Ramallah. He didn't like going there. There was war all around him, and he knew nothing of the peaceful days that older people spoke. In Talib's short life, there was only playtime, school, Quranic study, and sleep. He had not yet come face to face with the reputed hatred that the Israeli people—their soldiers particularly—had for the Palestinian natives.

He made the trip for the first time a year ago, and he

remembered the congestion of cars and long lines of people. At that time, it was forbidden for Palestinians to drive their cars into the city. Talib's father, Amid, informed them that they would walk to the first checkpoint and then take a taxi to the second checkpoint. From there, they would walk since it was considered a special act to walk to the mosque for prayer.

After an early breakfast, Talib, Amid, and Nadir—Talib's brother—started out for their long trek. They were joined by Hassan and others who, sharing the same idea and belief, took to the journey with happy feelings. It was like an adventure—a community adventure. The dozens of men walking together brought comfort and a sense of unity to them all. Each man was encouraged to walk the distance by the sight of another man joining the morning crowd as they strode toward the checkpoint.

The checkpoint site had an ominous appeal that had a drastic impact on the crowd; it put a damper on the upbeat feelings that the men carried with them. The area looked like a militarized zone. There were guards posted in the road with automatic weapons. There were more in the guard tower. There were two car lanes; one consisted of taxis transporting elderly men, and a second was for those who had not heard about personal vehicles being prohibited. The car zone was blocked with barbed wire to separate it from the pedestrian waiting area, which was quickly becoming crowded.

There were soldiers at the staging area. An officer requested that each visitor have proper identification and a permit in hand to expedite the process. He stood on top of a military jeep with a bullhorn. There were bricked booths with two men inside of each. Behind them, a gate lifted anytime someone was permitted to pass. In front of the gate, four armed soldiers stood nearly motionless with their weapons held in front of their chests with both hands.

Talib and his father waited patiently. Nadir, Talib's brother, after a full forty minutes inside the waiting area, was less tolerant.

He was not alone; other boys of similar age also complained. "I don't understand," said one. "They already checked our identification and our permits ... why the second time?"

"They must read the permit and check for authenticity," Amid explained to Nadir as if it was he who had asked the question. "Be patient. We're almost there." His voice was calm—the epitome of composure.

The murmuring grew louder with the continued influx of people. The possibility was very real that some people would not get past the first checkpoint in time to make it to the next checkpoint. One worshipper was told he was not allowed to pass and became irate. He claimed that his permit was valid since he applied for it many days ago. His identification was indeed valid, but the soldier had no explanation to give him. Neither did he aspire to provide one. A second soldier asked the disgruntled man to step aside, but he refused in protest, looking for a reasonable explanation.

"This is our homeland," someone yelled from behind. "Not yours."

"Go back to England!" someone else yelled.

The soldier was joined by a second who assumed that the situation would require a more forceful approach, and he reached out to grab the irate Arab by the arm.

"Take your filthy hands off me," the man yelled, pulling away.

"You can't deny his right to pray!" Yelled a deeper voice.

Other man yelled, and a loud scream of anger followed. Talib never saw who made the first move of violence, but there was sudden pushing and pulling in the crowd. He saw a mass of bodies move suddenly backward. Someone fell, and someone else seemed to climb across the top of the crowd. The next thing Talib knew, a mass of bodies was on the ground. Tear gas and rubber bullets were released into the crowd. Talib ran for safety at the behest of his father, but Nadir was missing. For a moment, Talib thought he recognized his brother in the mass of people. It appeared that Nadir had stomped an Israeli soldier.

Many men retreated before the fighting had started, but many more remained, fighting despite the tear gas. Amid was lost in the crowd for nearly two minutes before Talib saw him pulling at Nadir. Nadir—his face bleeding on the left side—wanted to go back. Rage had made him immune to the pain from the rubber bullets and the tear gas. More gas cans were thrown into the crowd, and more soldiers in gas masks coalesced, demanding that the crowd disperse. Nadir eventually submitted and followed the crowd of men who turned to go home.

Nadir made no prayers that day; neither did he join the fasting as he was too angry to participate. His mother tended to the cut on his face. By midday, Hassan visited their home. With him were two others; Valance was tall with jet-black hair, and Kaapo was overweight with a perfectly trimmed beard. They had heard about Nadir's injury and had come to see about him.

Talib's mother, Vada, thanked the men for their concern and invited them to stay. Amid was reading the Quran but set it aside to host the guests. He invited them to sit with him on the floor. While they sat, Valance informed Amid about one person who was killed in the fighting. From what he knew, ten men were arrested—and five others were hospitalized.

Nadir entered the room, agreeing with Valance that something had to be done about the checkpoints and the violation of their civil rights. Valance justified the fighting because of their brother being denied access to prayer. "It is prescribed for us to fight in such cases," he said.

Amid disagreed. "He could have prayed whether he went into Jerusalem or not. In the days that the Prophet—peace and blessings be upon him—spoke these words, there were not as many mosques as we have today."

"I respect your point of view," Hassan said. "But the fundamental right to pray is what is addressed here. A man has the right to pray in whatever mosque he wishes, and the government has no right to prevent that. We can ignore the real problem as much as we'd like, but it will not go away. We are oppressed slaves within our own land, and there is no one to help us against our oppressors. Unless we become more active as a community, we will not have our basic freedoms."

"The Palestinian Liberation Organization is doing nothing for us," Kaapo added.

"That is because they want the Americans to fight and negotiate for us."

"That will never happen. They are the ones who give guns and tanks to Israel," Valance added.

Amid said, "The Palestinian Liberation Organization is our only official voice in the world. We must give them time. Yasser Arafat is a smart man—"

"My apologies," Nadir said. "Yasser Arafat is too weak. He has no more strength in his words. He does not stand firm with our demands."

"I agree," Hassan said. "No one has strength without a serious military force to uphold his words."

"We have a military," Amid said.

"We have a police force. We have a few undisciplined and untrained men with guns and mortars. That is not an army. We need a stronger hand."

"A powerful friend," Valance said. "Someone who the Americans fear."

"The Quran states that a Muslim should not seek help from the nonbelievers," Amid said.

"And yet there were Muslims sent to Abyssinia under the protection of a Christian king," Hassan said.

"Asking a foreign king to permit Muslims to live in the safety of his country is far different from asking foreigners to supply us with tanks and guns."

Hassan said, "Amid, you have a point. I agree. Still, I

strongly consider the option of leaving the Palestinian Liberation Organization in favor of Harakat al-Muqawanah al-Islamiyyah."

Amid passed no judgment against Hassan. "I understand why you young men are anxious for the freedoms we deserve. I also know that Harakat al-Muqawanah al-Islamiyyah has a strong appeal to young and educated men like you three. I only implore you to remember that this is our holy month, and it was by peaceful means that Mecca was conquered. If peace is our one option, we must take that one. If not, we are as evil as the Americans, the British, and Jews alike."

Talib, who only played the role of listener, was torn between the two positions. Seeing the blood flow from his brother's face gave him no additional love for an Israeli soldier. Hassan's five years in an Israeli prison for a crime he did not commit had always been a matter of contention in Talib's sense of reasoning. However, he wasn't sure he could stomach the act of shooting an Israeli— despite his obvious disdain. He only hoped for some type of peace. He wanted his life to remain as it was: school, play, Quran studies.

He saw his father later that night sitting outside with a cup of tea. He was looking up at the thin crescent moon in the star-sprinkled sky. Amid had always held an affinity for staring into the night sky at the stars and moon as it waxed and waned. He admitted to Talib that he had a hard time sleeping and assumed that his mind was troubled by everything that had transpired that day. Talib also had difficulty sleeping and was happy when his father invited him to sit and drink tea. Talib talked about his strange dream—it was a reoccurring one that always seemed to end the same way.

Amid was humored. He could remember having similar dreams when he was Talib's age. They stopped just before Talib's birth. Amid assumed it was a common thing for boys in his family to have such dreams, as he remembered his father once speaking of a reoccurring dream.

"My father dreamed that he was a wizard on an island. He

was there to help free black slaves from white masters. That did not seem so bad to me, but he said that he was not a good man. He was evil because he used witchcraft to help them. He was always in conflict with himself. I think that is what the dreams meant.

"I remember there was a girl in my dreams. It was the same girl every time. I can't remember much, but she had these gray eyes. She was like a guide or something. She always took me to a door, and on the other side, I would see strange things. Once, I went through a door and was suddenly in a land of giants with fiery red hair."

"Were they nice giants or mean ones?" Talib asked without disclosing that he too had dreams of red-haired giants.

"Some were nice, but some were very mean. The nice ones died, and the girl with gray eyes turned to me and said, 'Don't forget.' Every time I saw her, she'd say, 'Don't forget.'" Amid burst into a loud laugh. "I've forgotten all those dreams except for the giants. But I'll never forget those eyes. I think that was because my eyes were so much different from my sisters'. I was the only one, aside from my father with these eyes. He said he got them from his mother."

Talib smiled. He inherited his father's eyes, and the realization that there had been at least one person in each generation with the same color eyes comforted him. He wanted to tell his father that he saw a girl in his dreams, however, she had green eyes. He also dreamed about giants, and the green-eyed girl appeared in other dreams as well. He remembered her being at a wild party where men drenched their heads and faces with blood. In that dream, she simply stood and watched. Her thin lips turned up into a smile. She had dark skin painted over perfect facial bone structure. She was beautiful. Talib remained silent about his dreams to his father. He simply sat and listened.

"There is one dream that I doubt I'd never forget. I had it soon after your brother was born. I admit that I was a little frightened about being a father, and I always thought this dream was somewhat symbolic. I dreamed that I was on a very important mission. I traveled with men on a boat. These very prestigious men were out to find a very rare item. It was a piece of a man's soul. Somehow, we learned that a man was going to die. He was a huge man—so fat that he was unable to walk and couldn't even sit himself up. I pray to Allah that no one would ever get that fat."

Talib laughed, and his father joined him. Then his eyes rolled upward, turning thoughts over in his mind to remember more details of the dream.

"So, we found the man and gathered around his bed when he died. His soul came out of his body through his mouth. It was like a little ball of light. I had a tiny vial made of glass and iron, no bigger than my thumb. I had the task of catching the ball of light with the vial. When I did, the vial was suddenly snatched out of my hand. I don't know for sure what happened after that, but there was some figure … something or someone larger than life. I think it was the angel of death because as soon as I saw him, I was frightened out of my sleep. It was a frightening creature, like it was made of green light.

"I believe this was a message from Allah. Each man is responsible for his own soul. We cannot steal a man's deeds or pay tribute for the deeds of our loved ones. This is true for a father. His job is only to provide his sons with proper direction. To leave behind a righteous child is one of only three impressions a man can leave behind after he departs from this world.

"It is my wish that you and your brother grow up in a world of peace," he said warmly to his son. "But peace is not meant for this world. It is, however, meant for individuals. Be at peace with yourself and the choices you make; understand that those who fight for peace are filled with anger and hatred, and they can never be at peace. You've heard of the murder of Uthman, the great caliph?"

Talib nodded. "Yes."

"Well, there was a lot of conflict surrounding his murder. Ali did very little to investigate or punish the responsible traitors, so people became naturally suspicious that Ali was part of the conspiracy. He had been passed over as the next khalifa, and now that Uthman was murdered, Ali had his chance. One person, Aisha—who was by far one of the most righteous—became furiously angry with Ali to the point where even she believed he had become a traitor of Islam. His actions seemed more suspicious when he dismissed some of the men who Uthman had placed in prestigious positions. His actions angered her until she declared herself Uthman's avenger and proceeded to conspire against Ali. Bani Umayyah, who was part of Uthman's tribe, was also suspicious of him and invited Aisha to join him. Yala, the governor of Yemen, was fired so he left the country with the treasury and gave it to Aisha to finance a war against Ali. Many men, hearing of Aisha's cause, joined in. They were men like Talha and Zubayr who were once Ali's supporters.

"After building their army, they chose to attack Basra. On their way, they came to a town in the valley of Hawab. There, as Aisha rode, she was suddenly surrounded by dogs. Their barking reminded her of a prophecy of the Holy Prophet's, peace and blessings be upon him. He once told his wives that one of them would participate in an ill-advised war of religion, and she would have the dogs of Hawab bark at her. It was then that she realized the error of her ways and refused to proceed.

"All might have been resolved at that point and peace would have been restored had it not been for Talha's dishonesty. He gathered witnesses to convince Aisha that they were not in Hawab and that she should continue without worry. You must understand that she was very important to the fighting. Talha and Zubayre both understood that, without Aisha, there would be no war. The people would follow her before them.

"They continued marching to Basra and made their attack, successfully capturing the governor. There was massive fighting, and many Muslims died at the hands of other Muslims. The well-being of Islam has not been the same since then.

"Islam, the greatest gift given to mankind, was soiled by the anger and the hatred of men. Do you see? Muslim men resorted to deception, dishonesty, and violation of the sanctity of the mosque because of hate and anger. Son, I hope you hear me clearly. There can be no peace if the peacekeepers are hateful and filled with anger."

That was the first time that Talib saw his father in such light. In most memories of Amid, Talib saw a devout man who was committed to follow a specific path dedicated to worship and the provisions of his family. He was an extremely intelligent man who had a photographic memory. He had committed the entire Quran to memory when he was sixteen years old but had no aspirations of being an Imam. Talib was happy that his father was no Imam because he would have little or no time for friends. Those who he knew were children of an Imam seldom had time away from their studies.

He felt more connected to his father after that night and did not protest the next family adventure to prayer at the Ibrahimi Mosque in Habron. The mosque was located within a collective of subterranean chambers that were once purchased by the Arab ancestor, Ibrahim, as a burial plot. The mosque inspired conversations of Ibrahim and his firstborn son, Ishmael. Amid, was a firstborn, and the warmth of the story where Ibrahim placed Ishmael on the altar for sacrifice gave Amid a humbling feeling. "This was a man who had no children. He always wanted a son, and finally, after many years, Ishmael was born. Then, after all that waiting he was asked to sacrifice that son—the one thing he loved most—and the Prophet, peace be upon him, obeyed. But not only does Ibrahim obey, Ishmael, fully aware of what his father had to do, submitted by making no protest. If not for the bravery and the obedience of both Ibrahim and Ishmael, I believe there would be no Arabs, no Israelis, no Islam, no religion for mankind at all. It was through the willingness of sacrifices that the world was given hope."

There were hugs and kisses between the men as they entered the cave. It was indeed a historic sight bearing stories from Ibrahim to Sulah-ad-Din to the present day. Talib believed that he could feel the warm embrace of the spirit world as he entered the cave. There was the call to prayer, the formation of lines—men stood shoulder to shoulder, feet to feet—bare, clean, and connected. The scent of fragrant oils floated in the air above; the soft plush carpet massaged the soles standing upon it. The sanctity of the heavenly sanctuary was calming, and Talib exhaled in perfect relaxation as the Imam recited Al Fatiha.

"'By the name of Allah, the most Gracious: most Merciful. All praise is due to Allah, the Lord of the universe.'"

Talib stood among the crowd of men, his arms folded. He recited the words of the scripture in his mind as the Imam chanted them aloud. Outside of the mosque, however, was another man, one Baruch Goldstein—a physician by trade who had once immersed in learning to provide medical attention to men—to save their lives and heal their sicknesses.

"'The most gracious, most merciful, Master of the Day of Judgment.'"

Reciting those words in unison with the Imam, Talib thought about committing himself against judging other men. He would not judge the Jewish people but learn to pity them for their fears and aggression.

Baruch, on the other hand, had already made his judgments. He had become a member of the Kach movement and was convinced of Israeli preeminence.

The Imam recited, "'You alone do we worship. You alone do we ask for help.'"

Talib remembered his father's statement that Muslims should not seek help from nonbelievers. The problems in Palestine could be resolved more quickly without outside influences. The

Americans, British, French, and everyone else should simply stay away. While he thought these things, Baruch's helper was already inside the mosque. John was dressed in traditional Islamic clothing and waited in the area near the fountains where men washed their heads, hands, and feet before entering the prayer sanctuary.

"'Guide us in the right path.'"

Talib believed that his father's understanding of peace was the best. It worked for the Muslims of old; they conquered Mecca as pilgrims, not soldiers. Baruch, on the other hand, lived by the creed that no nation forged without bloodshed. He was an Orthodox Jewish citizen who was familiar with the way his people slaughtered the children of Canaan, the Philistines, the Jebusites, and the multitude of other infidels. The nation of Israel was created for Jews and should be preserved for only the same, he believed.

"'The path of those who You have blessed—not of those who have deserved your wrath nor of those who have gone astray.'"

John, although dressed as a Muslim, had not come prepared to pray. It would have been very difficult to do so with the Israeli military-issue Galil assault rifle, which was concealed in his loose clothing. He once heard that, per the words of the Imam's recitation, that Jewish people deserved the wrath of God—and Christians were those who had gone astray. Talib, however, understood that many people deserved the wrath of God—not just the Jewish. At times, perhaps even he deserved it. He was grateful that Allah was a merciful Creator and stayed his wrath. There were people like his brother who were led astray, but with the love and wisdom of his father, Talib was certain that Nadir would be okay. Hassan as well, Talib hoped.

While Talib hoped the best for Hassan, Baruch entered the mosque with a full notion that anyone who knelt and placed their heads to the floor inside the mosque deserved the wrath of God. Make no mistake, he believed he was the messenger and the iron fist of the Creator when he pulled the weapon from its concealment and opened fire on the praying Muslim men.

A sudden grip of fear caused everyone to become suddenly motionless. Then there was a sudden free-for-all for survival, pushing, pulling, panicked attempts to escape the gunman, but as they evaded Baruch, they ran into John's opened fire.

Talib stood motionless in the midst of the commotion. It all seemed to move past him slowly, as if in his dreams, and he found himself waiting for the green-eyed girl to appear and bid him to remember. John commenced to firing his weapon while Baruch reloaded. He had entered deep inside the mosque, strategically positioned to seal off every escape route. Talib's vision was momentarily obstructed by a body flying in front of him. At that point, his eyes shifted, and it seemed as though he made direct eye contact with Baruch, who had the automatic assault rifle pointed in Talib's direction. Talib saw sparks of gunfire. He would later contemplate why the bullets missed him, but at that moment, he could only see Hassan's flying body, parallel to the floor, diving at Baruch. Their bodies collided. Baruch fell, his hand still on the trigger.

Two others fell before there were no more sounds of attacking bullets and sharp whistled sounds as they pierced the air. Instead, there were massive screams and thuds sounding off from a dozen fists pounding Baruch's body until he was dead and utterly disfigured. When Talib looked around, he saw dead and wounded bodies circled all around him. He was afraid for his brother and for his father. He searched for both of them, not long as he immediately found his father crawling over bodies toward him.

Amid was wounded. He had taken three rounds: one in his chest, another in his thigh, and a third in his hip. Talib stood transfixed, having not seen his father attacking the second gunman, sacrificing himself long enough for the other men to apprehend him. Amid could barely breathe but whispered, "Find your brother."

"No," Talib said, not wanting to leave his father. He rushed foward and embraced him.

Amid said, "Make sure your brother and mother are safe."

"No." Talib rolled his father on his back, his head resting in the bend of Talib's arm. "You come with me. You come with me."

Amid could not go with his son. He had become the firstborn sacrifice that saved many men from the hateful deadly bites of the remaining ten bullets in the shooter's rifle. When Nadir saw Talib sitting in tears, his father's head resting in his lap with blood pouring onto the carpet, he knew Amid was dead. He ran to his brother and stood over him. Talib, feeling Nasir's presence, turned and looked upward to see his brother standing there with bloody knuckles.

"Is he dead?" Nasir asked.

"No." Talib answered what he wanted and not what he knew. "I don't know," he corrected himself.

Valance joined them. "Check his pulse."

"I don't know how."

Valance squatted and put his fingers to Amid's neck. He felt no pulse, and for a moment, he stood motionless, head hung, and then he started to cry. Amid was a good man of moral consciousness. He was naive to think that there was ever a possibility of Arabs and Jews living side by side.

Talib's body was motionless, but his blood boiled with rage. He could feel the hatred swelling in his chest and pounding in his head. Something had to be done about this attack. He wanted someone else to feel his pain. He imagined there was some Jewish boy in Tel Aviv who was, at that moment, sitting at a table, eating with his father, and enjoying a life made for him on the backs of Palestinian blood. That boy should not get to live so freely and peacefully. That boy, whoever and wherever he was, should know what it feels like to lose a father. There was no one free of guilt. The entire world was to blame.

When the men united at Amid's home, Valance echoed aloud

what Talib felt. There were six in all, each committed to joining HAMAS and bringing the fight to their enemies. "It is better that we kill them all before they kill us," he said.

Hassan agreed. "The shooting that happened today was evidence that the PLO has failed us."

Nasir hesitated, being the one exception to making a commitment to HAMAS. Each of them sat silently, awaiting his decision.

Vada, surprisingly enough, showed no emotion. She sat at the table and, like Nasir, was in deep thought. Talib's eyes shifted from brother to his mother and then to Hassan. His hurt caused tears to swell in his eyes, but Vada said, "You are not allowed to cry. They do not get the satisfaction of your tears. It is they who must cry." Her eyes shifted to Nasir as if to encourage him to join the others.

"I'm in," Nasir said. "But that means you are in danger." His eyes shifted from his mother to Talib. "Both of you are."

"It is true," Hassan added. "The Israelis will look for you. You'll have to leave. Is there anywhere you can go?"

Veda did not answer right away. "There are things your father wanted you to have," she said to Nasir as she walked closer to him, pushing a chair aside. The heavy chair, now moved, revealed a square swath cut in the carpet. Veda had Nasir remove the cutout; underneath was a thin board that concealed a hole in the floor. Inside the hole was a chest that Nasir pulled out. When he opened it, he saw that it hid his father's most prized possessions. Inside was Egyptian currency, a book with Arab folklore, and three pieces of jewelry. Nasir stared at it for a while. Talib stood over him and understood that the box contained Nasir's inheritance. It reflected all Amid's work to be passed down to his eldest son. It now belonged to Nasir, but he closed the box as if he did not wish to accept it.

Hassan handed his extra money to Talib. "You must leave. At some point, it will be discovered that it was your father who was murdered in the mosque and that your brother has taken to

HAMAS. When the Israeli Secret Service realizes this, they will
come looking for you."

Talib said, "I will stay and fight too."

Hassan reached for Talib's shoulder. "Someday, but not now.
You are too young, and you are a terrible shot. I will tell you how
you can help HAMAS."

Talib was alert and anxious to lend his assistance.

"It will not be easy, but you have to get to Egypt. Use this
money and find a way to get to the University of Cairo. Find a
professor named Abdul-Salam Bin Laden. Explain to him that
I sent you." He paused to look into Talib's solemn eyes. "You are
very smart, and he can mentor you. You are one of the brightest
boys I've taught. The next time I see you, I expect you to know
everything he knows. Do you understand?"

Talib nodded in obedience.

As he fought back tears, Nasir reached into the chest and took
out a square charm. It was made of brass and had thirteen small
stones in it. It dangled from a silver chain that he placed around
his brother's neck. "Maybe this will bring you good luck," he said.

THE PACT

When Fiona released his hands, her face was wet with tears. Her breath was short, and she gasped for air. Her heart pounded against her chest. She stood, and without a word, she raced for the exit. Talib watched her silently. He heard Fiona running through the hallway and down the stairs. He heard the door open and imagined that she had run into the garden. He had no concept of the pain she felt; he only knew of his pain and hatred.

He hated Israelis—not just one, he hated them all. He wished for vengeance, but as he rose to his feet and looked upon the painting of Sheik Mustapha, he understood that there were many more people and nations responsible for his father's death. He hated the Palestinian Liberation Organization for its weakness. He hated the British for leaving Palestine to the Jews. The United Nations—the world representative—had turned a blind eye to the genocide that his friends, who were depicted in the painting, would inevitably endure. He grew angry at his father for insisting they attend the mosque in the cave to pray to a God who, like the United Nations, turned a blind eye on a defenseless people.

He wiped away the tear that squeezed from the corner of his eye and slid through the crease of his nose as he heard footsteps climbing the stairs. He was a proud lad and sought to avoid appearing weak and teary-eyed. As he moved away, a stack of paintings in the corner caught his attention. He stood over the collection, peering upon the first and assuming Fiona had made them all.

The painting he studied depicted a terrifying event. Many

creatures appeared desperate and frightened as they tried to escape a rising tide of water. On a hill, centered within the canvas, a centaur was standing on his hind legs. Above him, a winged unicorn's feet were turned toward the angry sky as it plundered the water below at the devastating command of a lightning bolt. On either side of the hill, various creatures were climbing to the safety of high ground. To the left, a man was standing beside a woman; both were dressed in rags, their brown flesh wet from the cascading water. Their hands dug into the mud on the mountain. On the right, four other creatures were shaped like men and women from the waist up and goats from the waist down. Their tails trailed behind them. One of the creatures was curled into a ball, tumbling down the side of the hill past the others. She was just inches from the water. At the front of the hill was a giant. The painting revealed only its back, which was wide and incredibly muscular. From its head grew two bones that appeared like shoulder blades. The giant was also climbing the hill to escape from the water.

Talib heard the approaching footsteps grow louder. Without turning to see, he felt that Kate had found him. She stood at his side and looked upon the painting. For a short while, neither said a word.

Kate said, "It's remarkable, isn't it?"

"It's spooky," Talib answered. "Is this something Fiona dreamt or imagined?"

"It's something she envisioned after reading the scrolls."

"What is it?"

"It's the great flood."

"Do you mean with Nu? Where is the ark?"

"The most educated historians and world archaeologists dispute the great flood. Did you know that?"

"No," Talib answered.

"But all over the world whether it is Utnapishtim in Babylon, Cessair in Ireland, Gun-Yu in China, Noah or Nu, all over the world, people talk about the great flood." She turned and walked away, inviting him to join her.

They left the room and entered the hallway, heading in the opposite direction of the stairs from which they came.

She said, "If we understand the writings correctly, at some point, there was a terrible flood. At that time, there were different species of life that died. A single man who was gifted with foresight was able to save his family and save the human race."

Talib listened to Kate until he spied the open door to a room where he had seen rocks and a large circle on the floor. Inside, two people in hooded robes sat inside the circle with their backs to each other. Talib could not tell if they were male or female. He stopped for a better view, but he was suddenly obstructed by a third person in the room who approached the doorway, looked lifelessly at Talib, and then closed the door.

"What are they doing?" he asked.

Kate stood four paces away from him. Her voice became distant as if she wanted her answer to be vague, but honest yet aloof. "They are looking for something."

"Something like what?"

"Are you certain you'd like to know?"

He paused. "Yes," he answered, curiosity taking the best of him.

"They are searching for others—those who are not near. They are searching for weapons and allies to help us."

"Help you do what?"

"Bring peace to this world."

Talib was confused. He had entered the room before, and to his recollection, there were no places for hiding weapons, people, or anything else. "What do you mean by people, weapons, and allies? There's nothing there but rocks and fish."

"There is a lot more in that room than you think." She smiled. "Come." She reached inside her pants pocket for a key to the library—through the door that was seldom opened.

Talib was curious and followed anxiously behind her. Upon entering, he saw that the library was larger than he had imagined. It had a high ceiling with high windows. Four rows of bookshelves extended some twenty paces into the center of the room. Talib saw a second door that accessed another part of the mansion. Near that door, there were three large oaken tables and twelve chairs. Three large crystal chandeliers were hanging from the high ceiling. The sunlight danced through the glass, throwing red and blue sparks, and Talib admired their beauty. The floor was carpeted in a royal red fabric that muted the sounds of their steps as they made their way to one of the tables.

The main entrance to the library was to the west side. It was a set of double doors painted white. To the left and right of the entrance were portraits of family ancestors framed in gold.

Kate continued past the tables and walked until she stood under the portrait of a clean-shaven man with salt-and-pepper hair and long sideburns. He donned a black tie with white stripes and a white shirt under his black suit coat. Talib surveyed the gentleman's narrow nose, slightly parted lips, and highly noticeable gray eyes. His facial features suggested a lineage that was not completely European. Unlike the portraits to the left, this man was distinctly different.

"This is Charles," Kate announced. "He lived six generations ago."

"Is he the one who saved his aunt's life?" Talib asked softly, almost in a whisper of admiration.

"Yes, he did," Kate said proudly. "He also did much more." She offered him a seat.

Talib noticed that each table had a carving on its face. He sat at one that bore the image of an owl. A butterfly was engraved in the table to his right and on another was the wheel that a ship's captain would use to guide a ship.

Kate said, "Charles was perhaps the most important of us. He was just like Noah—if you wish to call him by that name—but he was the one who made it possible for men to acquire everything the Brotherhood hoped for ... for the sake of humanity."

Until then, Charles had been the youngest to have ever joined the Brotherhood of the Enlightened Titans. He became a member just a year before Paul's death. His credibility among the members of the Brotherhood grew rapidly after winning the approval to take his grandfather's place on the board of directors. His position was solidified after making a statement that set policy for the Brotherhood's direction. The policy became known to them as the Order of Perfectibility. The genesis of this order occurred in two parts. The first was the issue of the English colonies that were governed by men thirsty for their share of power. These men had insulted their king with many forms of rebellion, including the creation of their very own currency. Before then, the Brotherhood showed little concern for the colonies or the laws the British Crown imposed upon them. However, when it was understood that the colonies rejected the king's currency, the Brotherhood was rife with havoc and disdain. They took the colonists' actions as a complete insult and unquestionable undermining, so the Brotherhood agreed to support an English invasion to apprehend those colonists who betrayed their king and fellow Englishmen. It was vital to the Brotherhood that the economic system met as little resistance as possible. If they could eliminate any competitive currency, a vast majority of the members would stop at nothing to rid themselves of competition. It was at that time that the concept of a single world currency raised its head within the organization. They debated in France over the fate of the colonies.

That day, Gregory Lancaster, chosen to represent a growing group of members who were interested in the hostilities between King George III and the colonies, addressed the board of governors. "There is an enormous threat that will expose this brotherhood. That threat is symbolized by the life of one William Pitt who very recently made the comment, and I quote, 'There is something behind the throne greater than the king himself.'"

Eugene Mavrocordatos, Charles's second cousin who had recently been placed at the governing table, interrupted Mr. Lancaster. "Sir William Pitt is an old man who should be more appreciative of our help and favors to him. He is a man of the people, and history has taught us that the masses are seldom a threat as long as they can be pacified. We have done a very good job of pacifying them. Did he mention the Brotherhood?"

Gregory Lancaster admitted that Pitt had never mentioned the Brotherhood by name or the names of those whom he knew to be members. Gregory Lancaster also admitted that he agreed with the success of the Brotherhood's pacification of the masses as well as its distractions – namely the overwhelming success of the African slave trade.

Although Charles made high efforts to keep his talent secret from the Brotherhood, he did not spare to use them. He understood that Gregory Lancaster did not expect support from Eugene Mavrocrdatos who had recently conceded to the Brotherhood's decision to not interfere with his uncle's imprisonment in Russia. It was not in their best interests to take covert actions for the sake of revenge or personal vendettas. Charles knew that Gregory Lancaster hoped, just as those he represented, to rally enough of the governing body's support to consider the power balance and the threat of exposure if the English colonies continued their insolent ways.

Charles was also aware of the more tenacious voices within the Brotherhood—now three hundred members strong. Affiliates like Jean Jacques Rousseau and Denis Diderot were in a constant debate over the future of global government. They were at the forefront of fancying the notion that aristocrats should be removed from authority and the working class, mostly merchants, should have a voice in government. Charles understood that Gregory Lancaster and his supporters did not favor such radical change. They held onto the belief that power balance—offset by the will of the working class, partly educated people—would create dangerous civil volatilities and little or no control. In many ways, Charles agreed.

As always, when proposals came from the circles of common members, the governors expressed their viewpoints, debated if necessary, and then voted. If it was determined that the proposal was in the best interest of the Brotherhood, the governors assigned committees of men to carry out the orders of the proposal. Usually, the orders were given names like the Order of Spreading Snow, a proffer that determined that revenue from the fraternity's investments was to be collected and saved until the end of the solar year. When that time expired, the funds were distributed to members of the organization based on a system of seniority.

When it was Charles's turn to offer input, he greeted Brother Lancaster with a basic understanding of his fraternal brother's disposition. He grappled with Lancaster's rage toward the British colonies' betrayal. Lancaster's flaw, according to Charles, was that he and his small group supporters failed to realize that the Enlightened Titans heeded no concern as to whether or not the people of the colonies were insolent because the Brotherhood had no loyalties to any principalities or monarchies. Charles understood that such loyalties were difficult to ignore, but he believed that his new reform would make it easier for all to do so.

"You are a man of vision and passion," Charles continued. "I, for one, appreciate it. My position is simple. We should not concern ourselves with those men in America. Their threats mean nothing to us. We were here long before any British colony, and we will be here long afterward. In fact, the opposite is truer. They represent an eternity of wealth and power. If they rebel, let them rebel against King George. If they succeed, they will become a nation of innocents and naïveté, easily influenced. What traditions do they have? What character of government? They will become easy pickings for us to involve ourselves and construct the framework of a new nation with our principles and our direct control.

"Within fifty years, our policies will be their laws. The symbols of our dogma will be encoded in every patriotic image they make. Their currency means nothing. We can change it with simple exchange rates. They will need imports and exports to survive—so we will control the exchange rates. They'll need finances for their slave trade and expansion. What will happen if we choose to call all our loans on any state that supports the African trade? We can break the Americans' backs by simply ending the slave trade. What will they do without free labor?"

He reached to his left and touched the arm of the gentleman sitting beside him. "I've spoken to Brother Smith about this matter. He has a plan that, if successful, allows us to consolidate the global economy; there is no way the Americans will escape it. It may take some time, but in the end, our influence is the dominant one. Allow the Americans to revolt if they like. If they succeed, we recruit some of them—those who fit the criteria. Allow them to build their nation on the backs of their slaves, and when they are so dependent upon their free labor, we devise a way to take it away from them. We cut the threads that bind them together and watch them kill each other and destroy their own economy. Then we sew their nation together with our needle and thread." He paused and read the emotions inside of Gregory Lancaster. Charles saw that his speech appealed to Lancaster's internal sense of authority and power, and there was more wooing to be done to appeal to more emotions. Since he held the floor, Charles thought it was the perfect time to move on to his next point.

"Gentlemen, this brings me to my second point. I know this is a bit out of order, but what I must present to you is important—so before we vote on the proposal before us, please allow me to make an addendum to it." He paused to wait for a counterargument, but there was none. "I would like to introduce you to a man who I personally nominate as a candidate into our brotherhood to fill the position of senior councilman to the committee board."

Charles enthusiastically rose from his chair and walked to the closed door.

Every eye focused on the door in utter curiosity. The men were intrigued by his actions, and there were no objections. This room where the ten men sat at a long table, facing the entrance, was spacious. Not more than eight paces from the center of the long table was a smaller one with an empty seat that Gregory Lancaster chose not to occupy. Behind that same chair were twenty-five additional paces to the door. Charles opened the door and motioned for someone to enter. They watched as a man of less than thirty years entered the room. His attire suggested he was a member of the upper class. His gait and posture confirmed as much. He had an aggressive nose and a dimpled chin. His eyes were focused like a man who was not easily intimidated. He exuded a confidence that assumed the Brotherhood needed his membership more than he needed to be a member.

Charles invited the man to take a seat behind the smaller table and asked Gregory Lancaster to join the governors' table. Since there were no chairs, he stood. The eleven men faced the nominee as Charles continued his speech.

"My dear brothers, I would like to introduce to you the esteemed Adam Weis. I came to know Mr. Weis less than five months ago, while visiting our brothers in Bavaria—things are going very well there, I might add. Since then, I have kept close correspondence with Mr. Weis, and I've learned that he has a special interest in something you all know I hold dear—the spiritual realities. Mr. Weis shares my interest in metaphysics of worlds both tangible and intangible. I will not say much about this fascinating man; I will let him speak for himself."

Charles, with another motion of his hand, invited Adam to speak to the men before him.

"Thank you, Charles, for your kind words." He stood and moved away from the table. "Good gentlemen, I would like to tell you a little about myself. I was born to a Jewish family in Ingolstadt.

My father died when I was young, and my godfather, for all intents and purposes, became my guardian. He served as a professor at the University of Ingolstadt. I was enrolled at a Jesuit school at the age of seven. Later on, I followed the path of my father and godfather, which led me to study law at Ingolstadt, but something much greater captured my attention. At first, I suppressed my feelings because, as a Jesuit, I was not supposed to allow myself to have a controlled interested in the world of the unseen. I could not escape the burning curiosity, and I converted to Protestantism. When I graduated, I was made a tutor, a catechist, and then a professor of law. I joined other brotherhoods in hopes that some members would share my interest and assist me in my studies of these realities.

"To my disappointment, many men fear my work because of their religious dispositions. The popes of the past and old indoctrination have caused men to assume that an attempt to learn such mysteries is satanic in nature. I marvel at that because they all believed in prayer, but what is the nature of prayer if not to communicate with the spirits of saints or of God himself? Is not the heavenly Father a spirit?

"As logic holds, it cannot be wrong to communicate with beings not of this world if it is permissible to communicate with the saints or with God through prayer. Is it not written in the very same Bible used by these men that Mary the mother of Christ spoke to angels? What about Joseph, Noah, Abraham, Lot, even Adam, the first man to ever walk the planet? Did they not speak with the unseen? Were their acts sinful?

"After speaking with Charles, I was made aware that your brotherhood stands guard to some very sacred knowledge that may possibly assist me in my research and mission. I have many things to share with you in this regard. Think about this example: it is possible and highly likely that a bond between men and spirits can seal the fate of your brotherhood until the end of time. As the spirits are immortal, your covenant should be the same. With such a covenant, the mission of your brotherhood could last for an eternity. As such, the Brotherhood of the Enlightened Titans could become the most powerful organization that the world has known or will ever know."

Upon finishing his speech, Adam Weis was voted in unanimously by the governors. Charles continued forming his policy for the Brotherhood with Adam's advice. Adam explained that, for the sake of the Brotherhood's eternal success, there was a definite need for certain, specific members to commit and form a pact with immortal spirits. He explained that traditional religious teachings of spirits were extremely inaccurate in that spirits were not to be regarded as one-dimensional. He advised that these beings are very similar in nature to men. They are driven by desire and their desire, above all else, is to change the misunderstandings of their world. When that happened, according to Adam, mankind would benefit from the unseen.

As Adam explained, there had to be a commitment reflected by use of specific words and actions. These words and actions, once joined with an elevated height of emotion, would connect those selected men with the spirit of choice to seal their pact. The most effective way to achieve the results was to participate in a ritual that involved an extravagant, promiscuous bacchanalia. Charles, along with five other men, agreed to commit.

Charles relied on the constellations and planets to select a day for the ritual when the sun was positioned in Taurus and conjunct with Mars. "This will reveal the true purpose and motivation of our brotherhood in amassing tremendous financial wealth, power, and our enjoyment of both," he advised as he chose to have the ceremony on the night of May 1. "The perfect day."

The ritual was held outdoors in a wooded area where the energy of the planets would fall on them directly. The location was adorned with scented candles, grounded to form a perfect circle around a bonfire. The parties were dressed in hooded robes and burned torches. They prayed and chanted in an ancient Semitic language. While engaged in this, they sat with folded legs and meditated over the obscure symbols carved on clay tablets and placed on the ground in front of them. The symbols were said to represent prosperity, autonomy, political power, wisdom and knowledge, and war.

Eight naked women—their faces covered in dark masks with fixed ram's horns that curved downward on each side of their faces—approached from behind. Silently, they busied themselves undressing the men and fondling their genitals. The fondling turned to oral pleasures, and the oral became vaginal. The men moved between the women, and the women found ways to rotate from man to man until each was relieved and seminal fluid covered the clay tablets.

Still heavily panting and tingling with relief, each man tossed a clay tablet into the crackling bonfire. The flames roared louder, and the heat intensified as if the tablets were fuel to the fire. The members burned their clothes, shoes, and everything else they had brought with them. There they stood in the forest, seven men and eight women, basking in the heat from the blaze.

Charles—for a very brief moment—felt a kinship with the burning fire. He felt a warm and cozy sensation, like the reuniting one might have after years of separation from a dear friend. Something pulled Charles toward the fire, suddenly speaking to him and asking him to merge with it. "I see you," it whispered. It was so faint he assumed it was his subconscious. He was content with believing he had found his way, and on that day, he was illuminated.

When the ritual came to a close, the men made their way home dressed in black linen. Adam Weis congratulated them on their commitment. He said they had succeeded in opening a window of opportunity for the goddess Libertas to enter their world. Charles understood that he had made a vow to this goddess that would tie all of humanity to her being. He knew that Libertas was no symbolic goddess, but a true immortal spirit, welcomed through a portal opened by the fire.

Adam presented a gift to the Brotherhood. It was carved from ivory and shaped like an owl. "This symbol represents the illumination and wisdom that you, on this night, inherit."

In the years to come, Charles received many more symbols from Adam. In all, he adored the first more than others. It connected to his Greek ancestors: the Noctua owl of the goddess Athena.

"Such owls have 360-degree vision," Adam explained. "That vision is the representation of knowledge you will receive. We are now the patrons of Athena—not the mythological bedtime story but the true spirit that our ancestors named Athena, the gray-eyed goddess."

Adam implored the Brotherhood to place their symbols on everything they touched so they would achieve the desired success. More than a mere symbol, in fact, it was a talisman. "Place this on your currency and buildings. Place it on whatever you touch, and whatever you touch will be like gold. It will link this physical world to the spiritual one. One day, the spirits will place your symbols in the subconscious of every man. When that happens, each person will willingly accept the terms that the Brotherhood lay upon them. This will give us one giant step to universal peace."

Charles later admonished the Brotherhood to seize the power of monarchs and the church—both Protestant and Catholic. "That power of choice belongs to men. Offer them liberty and Libertas, the spirit will free them from moral shackles and our brotherhood will become immortal."

Charles died twenty-three years later, three months before the turn of the century.

Adam eventually became a member of the governing body and performed many of the same rituals with the others. They witnessed the American Revolution during that same year and the signing of a constitution that was drafted by the Brotherhood and signed by twelve of its members. The French Revolution followed, and more signatures were made by members of the Brotherhood who enacted law and policy for the sake of liberty.

GORGO AND THE RED-HAIRED GIANTS

Talib got very little sleep that night, so his nightmares did not assault him. He was barely able to close his eyes as his mind raced and grieved him. Despite his efforts, he could not quiet his thoughts about all he heard—the ringing sounds of the Imam reciting the Quran as he always did during prayer. Past discussions revisited him including the sound of his own voice when he recited the passages during regularly scheduled Quranic study times. Talib remembered all the teachings that now revisited him, assaulting him as warnings of the dangers of the forbidden practice of sorcery.

After learning about Charles and Adam, Talib grew very uncomfortable with his visit at the Greek host's mansion. Charles, it seemed, was more than a man who possessed a gabmnoteh—and Talib remained uncertain of what a gabmnoteh was—but he was someone who made a pact with a spirit—a djinni. He was also a man who wished to devalue the purpose of religion. Such men, Talib was taught to avoid. He imagined his father's disappointment had he known the trouble Talib had fallen into. He thought about his brother joining HAMAS to seek vehement vengeance against his enemies; his father's disappointment would be the same for his eldest son's deed.

Talib's thoughts fell on previous lessons—Haroot and Maroot—angels who attempted to teach magic to men. "We are a test, so do not disbelieve."' He remembered that the sorceresses would tie knots in ropes and cast their spells on their enemies. There were stories of men and women who died or became ill, hexed by sorcerers. There was a chapter from the Quran to recite if he ever encountered a sorcerer: "I seek refuge in the Lord of the Dawn; from the evil of that which He create; and from the evil of the darkness when it settles; and from the evil of the blower of knots."

As clear as the danger seemed to Talib, he remained remarkably confused and conflicted. The Brotherhood of the Enlightened Titans did not seem evil. In some cases, Talib thought their intentions were admirable. They wanted to bring peace to the world and end violence—the same violence that took his father's life and invariably led him to the Greek island. The Brotherhood succeeded in putting an end to religious wars and managed to institute freedoms of religion and religious practice to people who were subdued by the Catholic Church. What's more, they created currency and standards to benefit the poor and working class. How were these accomplishments evil?

With all of this, however, what did they want with him? How was he to help? Talib stood from his bed and peered through the window into a cloudless, moonless sky crowded with stars. *Why am I here?* As he contemplated, Talib realized that his questions ran deep within until he questioned his mere existence. There was always a simple answer when he was a kid. His mother would always answer, "For the glory of Allah."

That was no longer acceptable for him. The last image he had of his mother was the sight of her face drenched in tears. Her eyes blazed with anger and hatred. He remembered her blessing to her firstborn son. She approved of his commitment to HAMAS. As he thought of his mother, he doubted her answer would be the same. He doubted that she ever knew.

Talib, for one, did not know—and he would not pretend to know the answers. What he knew, or at least concluded, was that he would leave the mansion. He was not willing to sacrifice the eternal life of his soul with the guilt of befriending those who practiced sorcery and made pacts with devils. No matter how much he hated the Israeli murderers, he was not willing to condemn his soul.

He spent the remainder of the night contemplating how he would ask for his hosts' forgiveness and permission to leave. When morning arrived, he joined Kate for breakfast and noticed right away that Fiona was absent. In her place was the uncle, Daniel, who Talib had seen just once since his arrival.

Daniel seemed different. He was more intimidating. His eyes were dark and penetrating. He had a firm jaw and large body with overdeveloped shoulders that seemed poised for attack. He resembled Theodore, and their relationship was obvious from the nose and chin. On that day, however, as they sat for breakfast, Daniel appeared more paternal and nurturing. He wore glasses and held a newspaper over his plate. His eyes looked disappointed when Talib divulged his thoughts and decision to leave. He seemed suddenly disturbed, but not insulted. Talib had no reason to believe that the uncle would not honor Theodore's promise to transport him to Egypt upon request; Talib, nonetheless, thought he should grant Daniel an explanation.

When he spoke about sorcery and his hesitation to befriend those who practiced the arts, Daniel interrupted, "What, pray tell, is sorcery?"

Talib thoughtfully considered his words before speaking. In Daniel's presence, he attempted to exhibit poise and intellect, but Talib's intellectual ability seemed to run for cover upon that question. "It is witchcraft, speaking to the djinn and spirits, reading the stars, and casting spells on people."

Daniel nodded. "And you were taught, all your life, that these things are wrong. Is that right?"

"Yes."

"Why?"

Talib contemplated his answer again. "Because it is not godly; it's from the shaitan."

"It sounds like your belief is rooted in your religious teachings. Is that a safe assumption?"

"Yes. I imagine so."

Daniel sipped his drink. "That's what I suspected." He leaned slightly over the table to look into Talib's eyes. "You are a victim of religion, specifically, organized religion, handed down ideas, and interpretations of spiritual meanings that were seldom understood by the people of the time.

"For a moment, just consider the educational level of the people who lived during the first Muslim era—before they had a Quran to read. Then consider the education of people one hundred years later ... and now centuries later. Do you really think that, with all the complexity found in a religious text, the people of those times understood it all exactly the way it was meant? Can you agree that they did not understand it all?"

Talib said, "Yes." He understood the complexity in the Quran, and considering that his education was more advanced than his parents', Daniel's argument seemed to carry weight.

"It is in the interest of religious institutions to pass outdated interpretations to its members. This has been true forever, regardless of the religion. The Father of Faith, Abraham, spoke to angels. He entertained them in his home. Jesus Christ spoke to demons, or djinn as you would say. He spoke to Satan himself. Is it not true for the Prophet Muhammad? Was he not transported away to Jerusalem? Is there a rule of some sort that says if a man does the same, he creates a sin? I've never heard such a rule. Therefore, if these righteous men spoke to angels, djinn, demons, and transported their conscious energy from their bodies, we are in no way guilty of committing sin for doing the same. Is that a reasonable conclusion?"

Talib felt uncomfortable with Daniel's logic, but he could think of nothing in his studies to contend.

"Both the people here and our friends abroad who study these spiritual sciences are no different. Abraham had no Bible to read or Quran to recite, yet he was a righteous man. No one contends that the Prophet Muhammad was any less righteous before he received the Quran than afterward, yet in those days of his early life, he had no Quran to read. He listened to an angel who spoke to him.

"One of the scrolls we have tells a story about Adam, the first man to live. He had an incredible ability to see and feel spirits—and speak to them just as you and I are doing now. This is part of the pure power of men. If religious institutions told men about Adam's power and full capabilities, men would change their evil and destructive ways. We would have no more need for war, and violence would disappear. We would altogether change as a race of people—one conscious race not bound by the mortal shell but by the laws of the universe.

"When you speak of spells the way you do, it is a disservice to your ability and creation. If not for a spell, magic, or alchemy—or at least the foundation of them—how could Jesus Christ turn water into wine? How could Solomon speak to animals and build a temple without iron tools had he not learned from angels and demons?"

Talib was suddenly in awe. He did not say as much, and his expression grew blank. He was utterly thunderstruck by Daniel's knowledge of the Islamic teachings and the way he juxtaposed them with Christian and Jewish teachings to make one vital point against the modern conception of those principles. He remembered the stories Hassan told. There was much interaction between men and spirits. Talib was perplexed at the possibility that such actions were forms of sorcery.

"Sorcery is just a word," Daniel continued. "What we do is a science. Our family and many others have engaged in it for hundreds of years of study. We try tirelessly to regain the pure power of the first man. We endlessly seek to learn the laws that govern the universe because we want to end the days of sickness, tyranny, and oppression. This knowledge was once at the disposal of every man; now it is privileged to only a few, and those who have it gain it from life forces that are not like us. They are living beings without mortal shells. More importantly, there is something out there in our world waiting for us to realize it—waiting for us to unite so that the gap between our universe and the spiritual one can be bridged. This is why we want your help."

"I believe this is why you are here," Kate added. "I also believe that our mission is connected to your nightmares. We promised to help, and I would like to show you how we can do that." She reached out to take his hand in hers and gently squeezed. "Won't you stay one more night? I promise you will never again dream of the red-haired giant after this day."

The manner in which Kate planned to rid Talib of the sinister giant, Gorgo, was to cause him to dream of it one last time. She asked him to meet her in the room with the large circle and rocks. She called it the Search Room; in it, visitors came to search for answers outside of themselves.

Fiona was there, dressed in a brown hooded robe held closed by a red cloth belt tied into a knot at the navel. She wore loose gray pants, and her feet were bare. Talib dressed the same, but Kate's hooded robe was white. The candleholders mounted on the walls held lighted candles that gave off a fresh lavender scent.

The apprehension that Talib had become accustomed of seeing in Fiona was not there. She seemed more focused than usual as she entered the circle. Her lips moved slightly, but Talib could see that she quietly recited some words. She walked past him, and Kate walked toward him. In her hand was a clay tablet with engraved markings. The markings consisted of lines that formed an abstract image.

Kate placed the tablet in front of Talib's feet and asked him to carefully study every detail. She told him that the tablet was a key to a door that was somewhere in his subconscious. She needed him to concentrate and force the images into his mind so that, when he closed his eyes, he would continue to see them.

Some of the patterned lines moved upward, and some moved to the side. Some lines intercepted others, and some made perfect angles. They were all connected like pen markings that were made without ever lifting a hand from the tablet.

When he thought he had stared at the lines long enough, Talib looked up from the tablet to notice that Fiona had walked to the center of the circle and stood there beside him. Her hood covered her head and part of her face, revealing her gray eyes, nose, and lips. She said nothing, but Talib could hear a thousand voices in his head, whispering in some strange language that he had never heard before. The words seemed familiar and comforting to him. He felt Fiona's touch as she reached out to place two hands on his shoulders while her eyes dropped to his feet. She remained silent as she tried to guide his body to a standing position in the center of a triangle that was marked inside the circle on the floor.

Fiona stood in a second triangle, sat, and folded her legs. Following her motions, Talib did the same. He also noticed that her eyes were closed.

Kate stood outside the circle and held a small shot glass of a clear liquid. Talib asked if he should look into Fiona's eyes like he did previously in the arts and craft room, but Kate said, "No. This is a much more difficult task. Drink this." She held the glass out toward him, but it did not break the plane of the circle.

Talib was completely naive to the meaning of circle and the candles and the triangles inside the circle and the markings on the floor around it. He did notice, from the light cast by the flickering candles, the markings on the wall; one was in the shape of a Greek letter made from the body of an Egyptian cobra. The other he recognized as the shape of the charm that once belonged to his father. He willingly reached for the glass that Kate held and pulled it into the circle. There, he drank the liquid. Fiona seemed to know exactly when he finished because her eyes opened, and she reached out to take the empty glass from his hand. She set it on the floor and shifted her body to lie on her back with her head inside of the triangle. Talib copied her movements and lay flat inside the circle. The flames around him seemed to grow taller. He assumed it was his imagination. His eyes became heavy, and before Talib was aware of what happened next, he was lost in a dream.

It was a familiar dream, but the girl with green eyes was not there. In fact, it did not much seem as if Talib himself was there. It felt more like he was outside of the action, as if he was watching a large screen inside a movie theater. He was once again in the land of the giants. It all seemed clearer now. There were no distortions to this dream—if it was indeed a dream.

Gorgo the giant was very proud of his speed and agility, but what he outright loved about his physical ability was the fact that he could, with a running start, leap the horizontal length of ten men and at least a third of that distance vertically. So, when he emerged from the tree line almost at the climax of his leap, it was no surprise to Raza-Bin. Gorgo was always one for dramatic actions.

Raza-Bin was busy leading the attack on a herd of horned sheep and often accused Gorgo of doing more than what was needed. In the end, he attributed it all to youth. Gorgo was the youngest of the three hunters, and his job was to capture the strays that separated from the group.

Ton-Ton, the largest of them, threw rocks that were twice the size of a man's head. He hurled them with such force that the impact against a sheep's skull was fatal. Despite their synchronized attacks, Gorgo unwittingly landed in the center of the herd. He towered above them, his body covered in animal-skin garments. The thrill of the hunt was invigorating to him, but hunger pains compelled his selfish desires. With the swing of a fist into the rib cage of his prey, he expelled a loud grunt. The impact was so great that it caused the animal to collapse with broken ribs. The sheep kicked and scrambled to regain its footing, but Gorgo would not allow it to escape. Quickly, and with no attempt at any graceful movement, Gorgo fell on the horned sheep, took it by the head, and sank his jagged teeth into the animal's jugular.

He was only an adolescent, but his appetite was growing rapidly. In Gorgo's youth, he possessed a rash carelessness that did not allow him to consider Ton-Ton's disappointment when he interrupted the chase to consume his food right there on the hunting grounds.

"You refuse to think of your mother?" Ton-Ton asked, standing above the adolescent. Ton-Ton had already captured two sheep. He carried one over his shoulder, and the other was tucked under his arm.

Gorgo negated the idea of bringing game to his mother. He contented himself with enjoying his prey while his two comrades retreated to their campsite. Now, pulling the animal's wool from his mouth, he stood and scouted for sheep that had not reherded. They were not so far away that he could not catch up to them with a running start. Knowing this, Gorgo sprang into a sprint.

The herd of horned sheep, seeing and hearing him, collectively took off in an attempt to escape, but Gorgo was just as fast as the fastest sheep, and he had no trouble capturing one that fell behind. The herd scattered into the thick of the forest, and in doing so, they ran into a bottleneck that made it easy for Gorgo. He dropped into a slide on the grass, still moist from the morning dew. As he slid forward, he tripped his prey with his long bare feet. Then, in one smooth motion, as if he performed the move routinely, he rolled over onto the animal, took it by the head, and twisted until its neck snapped.

Gorgo was proud of his strength, and when he stood, he did so with such an air of superiority that Ton-Ton gave a slight smirk and walked away. Gorgo could only enjoy his meal to a small degree. The horned sheep had too much wool that was left to be pulled from his mouth. It usually took two or three days before he felt his mouth was free of strands. Despite the fleece, he was content. Animal blood was smeared across Gorgo's face, and his bare chest was nearly dry by the time he had his fill. He left bones and leftover flesh for the flies. It was time to go home and take the dead animal to his mother.

As he turned to head home, he heard laughter from a small group of Paiutes who casually walked into the field where the grass grew short. He laid low in the taller grass some ninety paces away. He was just barely able to see over the blades but he nonetheless counted six girls and two male escorts. The escorts carried spears while the girls toted animal-skin shoulder bags. They were all dressed much the same, in loose clothing made from animal skins. Stepping into the grassy clearing—totally unaware of the stampede that had just moments ago rushed past their location— the girls came to check the wooden boxes they had set the previous day to trap rabbits.

Gorgo appreciated times when he went undetected. It was amusing to listen in on the conversations of others, especially those not meant for him to hear. Raza-Bin, the wisest of them, said it was simply childish behavior, but Gorgo doubted as much. He thoroughly enjoyed eavesdropping. This was another of those moments that piqued his interest.

The Paiutes were people whom Gorgo had been more than once cautioned against. It was common among Gorgo's race to avoid all people. He had lost his father in a recent battle with this kind. He had no particular resolve for any of their types really— not just the Paiutes. He thought it would have been poetic justice to stand and attack the eight of them all at once, but he chose to simply sit undetected and watch.

This small group of people had a system. They had traps spread out around the field. The girls separated in pairs to inspect each trap. One of them opened the trap; it was a wooden box that she lifted while her partner stood close beside with a small club that she used to crush the head of the small rabbit inside. After the rabbit was knocked unconscious or killed, it was placed in the shoulder bag. Often, as it happened that day, a swift and alert rabbit escaped and raced for the tall grass. As Gorgo observed, to his surprise, one of the fleeing rabbits did not retreat to the tall grass, instead, it darted for the one small area where low grass extended to the tree line.

Gorgo watched as the pair of girls chased the desperate rabbit. It darted in unpredictable left and right movements, evading capture. The men used poor aim in jabbing their spears and missed with every throw. The other six girls gave chase to try to redirect the rodent, but they were unsuccessful. The hare raced for the forest. Gorgo conceded to the notion that it would escape, but it did not.

Just before Gorgo looked away, a hand reached from behind a tree to snatch the rabbit from the ground. Needless to say, Gorgo was taken aback by the sudden change of event. He was not so much surprised by the rabbit being caught but by the fact that it was snatched up by the hands of a giant who stepped from behind the tree.

The giant stood the length of one and a half men, which led Gorgo to realize that he had not yet reached his adulthood. His red hair was stringy and long, similar to Gorgo's, except his was visibly clean and bright. He wore sandals instead of bare feet, and his head was small in comparison to what Gorgo was accustomed to seeing.

What surprised Gorgo was that, until that moment, he believed—due to stories from Ton-Ton and Raza-Bin—that their small community of eleven—Si-Te-Cah—was the only remaining ones of his race. He had been in constant motion, heading west from the day of his birth. People were killing them in the East and their only hope for survival lay in the West. What was equally astonishing to Gorgo was that the giant in his youth was obviously very naive because he held out the rabbit to its pursuers in a gesture of goodwill. He was literally attempting to show friendship, but the girls were frightened by his presence. Five turned and retreated; the sixth stumbled and fell to the ground when she tried to abruptly stop.

Gorgo could not hear what the giant tried to say to the group of humankind. He held the rabbit out in offering to the girl at his feet and waved in an upward motion. It was obvious that everyone feared him, and he, fully understanding this, continued trying to convince them otherwise. The girl who had fallen scurried to her feet while the men retrieved the spears they had foolishly thrown at the rabbit. The naive giant was persistent. He stood fixated in his place, never taking a step closer. The men stood shoulder to shoulder with spears poised for attack. The giant, whose name was Nkupa, slowly and cautiously squatted to place the rabbit, now dead with a broken back, on the ground at his feet.

Gorgo, having trouble seeing over the height of the grass, rose to his feet, assuming there was no danger of being seen by the Paiutes. He had clear and unobstructed view. Nkupa took a step backward to show retreat.

The girl who had fallen stood behind her guards. Her disposition advertised sudden sympathy for the tall figure with red hair. She understood that it meant no harm and moved forward, despite their warnings, alongside the men. One man tried to grab her back, demanding that she remain in a position of safety behind them, but she refused. She continued moving toward the young giant to retrieve the rabbit while the men kept close.

Nkupa took two steps behind the line of trees. He displayed no behaviors of aggression, but as he retreated, he caught a sudden glimpse of Gorgo standing tall over the grass. Their eyes met.

Gorgo knew nothing of Nkupa's clan, and Nkupa's eyes reflected fear—as if he was suddenly found out after hiding for so long. He looked aghast as it was obvious by Gorgo's rugged and wild appearance, which was evident in every part of his being, that the two giants belonged to two separate tribes.

Nkupa stood frozen for a moment, as if expecting Gorgo to do something, but Gorgo made no move at all despite his curiosity about Nkupa. He wanted to know more about him. From where did he come? Where was his family? Why were they separate from the clan? Did they have a different clan?

It was obvious to Gorgo that Nkupa had questions as well, but Nkupa came to his senses and turned to run further into the forest. Gorgo thought about following, but decided it was better to discuss Nkupa with Ton-Ton. In his clan, Ton-Ton was the one intellectual and adviser to the clan leader. Gorgo had very little love for Ton-Ton. He was well respected by others, but Gorgo detested Ton-Ton's never-ending lamentations regarding his immaturity. He was always looking to embarrass or ruin Ton-Ton's pristine image.

"Many years ago, there were thousands of us," Ton-Ton said. "Our ancestors came from the West. They were big men and big women—we do not grow like they did. They had better food, and the sun is changing. We cannot be so strong with the changing sun."

"You told me that we were the only ones. There was no clan other than ours. You told that to everybody."

"It is true. The wars with men nearly killed us all."

"How do you know there aren't others?" Gorgo asked.

"They're all dead. Our race expanded too far east. Those who didn't die from the cold were killed by men. They had help, you know?"

"Yes, you tell us all the time. They have weapons made from another world."

"The spirit world. The spirits want to destroy us, but they cannot do it without the help of men."

"And you say this is good for us?"

"Sometimes the spirits must kill many of us and start over. It is so that we do not consume the earth. One day, we will be large in number again."

That conversation confirmed to Gorgo that Ton-Ton knew less than what was assumed. "I do not believe it is wise to trust

Ton-Ton's judgment," Gorgo said in private to Kordeso, the clan leader. Kordeso was the eldest and was always leaning against trees. His age did not make him any less able to function than Gorgo or any of the others. He was the voice of reason that led the clan southwest and through the mountains to the warmer climate. Kordeso was strong and fast. His leadership was more evident in his ferocity than his intellect.

"Ton-Ton said that we would find warmer weather if we crossed the mountains. He was right about that, so that is good enough for us."

At that moment, Gorgo had nothing more to add. He hoped that he had planted a seed of doubt in Kordeso's mind. He went to sleep that night thinking about Nkupa, determined to find him.

Previous wars between giants and men were devastating to both sides. Many tribes of men scattered abroad to avoid the giants, and Gorgo's clan arrived through the mountains by way of rafts made from tule. He had fought once in battle and developed a thirst for controversy and wanton violence. He thought it would have been a form of poetic justice for Kordeso to turn violent against Ton-Ton. He imagined the sad and pitiful look in Ton-Ton's eyes when it became obvious that Kordeso had lost faith in him. Gorgo yearned to see that. He wanted to make Ton-Ton out to be the fool that he was, and Gorgo believed that Nkupa and the tribe of men would help him.

Gorgo's search led him to the clearing one night. Under the cover of darkness, he often conducted successful espionage on the Paiute village. They were mostly a nomadic people who had settled in the dry, nearly desert area for over a year due to the large supply of animal game. He learned that they had perhaps thirty people—mostly women due to a loss of men from war. For that reason, Gorgo understood that the women were compelled to hunt and trap rabbits for food and fur.

When he entered the Paiutes' village undetected, he was careful to snoop around in silence. There were no guards, and it was obvious that everyone in the small village was asleep. He was too tall to enter their homes, so he stooped and bent over to look inside at the sleeping families. None of the huts had doors; blankets covered the entrances. As he snooped around, Gorgo came across one structure that stored dozens of weapons. This was their stockpile of spears along with some archery equipment. Everything was made of wood and rock, but one weapon was very different. The contraption was mounted on wheels and was a hybrid between a catapult and bow. It had a brass arm and a stone counterweight. Gorgo was confused by the design. He had no idea what he was looking at, but he knew that it was a weapon—and it was deadly.

The next time he saw Nkupa was six days later at the clearing. Remarkably, the friendly giant had successfully won the trust of the Paiute girl who had fallen at his feet. While Gorgo observed from a distance in the shadows of the tree line, Nkupa and the girl struggled to communicate. Nkupa had created a net and demonstrated how to trap rabbits. Until then, Gorgo had not fathomed the idea of men and his race of giants being capable of coexisting in the same area. He had only one thought when it came to humans: kill them. Seeing Nkupa, gentle and cordial with the girl, struck something inside him. He wanted to join, but he knew that he could not. He knew that the girl would fear him, and he suspected that Nkupa would run away. He waited, like a lioness in the bush.

When the Paiute men arrived with their spears Nkupa seemed to grow sad. It was obviously time for the girl to leave him and for him return to his home, wherever that was. Gorgo certainly wanted to know. As the two unusual friends departed, Gorgo followed Nkupa. He intended to be discreet, but he failed. Nkupa was a perfect observer who seemed to be at one with the forest and its noises. When the birds' songs changed from happy tunes to panicked screeches, and they took flight, Gorgo's presence was detected. Obviously aware that he was not alone, Nukupa traipsed the forest in circles until it was obvious to Gorgo that Nkupa was purposely avoiding his home.

Nkupa went to a spot where the foliage lost its density, offering Gorgo few trees to hide among. It was only then that Gorgo knew without doubt that he had been detected; Nkupa turned to face his pursuer. "There are few trees left for you to hide," he said. "You can come out now." There was awkward hesitation, but Gorgo eventually stepped out from behind a tree and emerged from the shadows. He was slightly taller than Nkupa, just barely noticeable, and their age difference was no more than two years apart. Gorgo had an elongated head. His bright, almond-colored eyes were set back deeply into his skull. Nkupa looked at him curiously as if he was the subject of an experiment. Gorgo's eyes were startling. "You are a Flesh Ester," Nukupa announced. "Your eyes are strange, no doubt it comes from eating raw animal flesh."

"Are you alone?" Gorgo asked. "Where is your family?"

"Why are you following me?" Nkupa asked.

"You are interesting," he replied. "Why are you so nice to those people?" He spoke to Nkupa, but his eyes were focused on the background as if he expected something or someone to leap out from some unexpected place and attack him.

"Her name is Istas."

"Is she your pet? Will you do sex to her?"

"No,"

"You should do sex to her. She is woman, yes?"

"Yes."

"Then you should do sex to her. That is what you are supposed to do to woman."

"I want to warn her of danger."

"Danger? What danger?"

"You. You are dangerous—a Flesh Eater. Yes?"

Gorgo continued to look around as if he was looking for something. He walked nearly a circle around Nkupa. He spoke in a low voice as if half-speaking to Nkupa and half-speaking to someone or something else unseen. "Everybody eats flesh, no?"

"I eat it with fire."

"Well, fire or no fire—you still eat flesh." It appeared that Gorgo had seen enough since he found nothing of interest. He had become bored with the friendly giant. "You have a name?"

"Nkupa."

"Nkupa, I'm not dangerous. I'm Gorgo." With that, he turned and walked away. Without looking back, he left to return to his clan.

When he arrived, Gorgo sought to cause more mischief within the clan, specifically a breach in the trust that Kordeso had for Ton-Ton. "Ton-Ton says that all the others are dead. What about them who put fire on their food? Are they dead?"

Kordeso sat back and leaned against his tree. "I do not believe those stories. Only men do that. They have small stomachs, and the fire shrinks their food. We have big stomachs with fire inside to take care of the food for us."

"And you know this because it is what Ton-Ton said. Yes?"

"Yes."

"What if he was wrong? What if there were others like us—who put their food in fire—and they had become friends with men? What if they made a pact and made weapons to destroy us?"

Kordeso laughed. "You think big thoughts. If that was to happen, we would kill them … those who are like us and those who are not. It is our survival we consider first … before anything else."

"One day I will come to you with evidence that what I say is correct. I will take you to a place where a pact has been made between our kind and men. Then you will make a choice."

Kordeso promised that, if such evidence existed, he would entertain the notion to indulge Gorgo's accusations. Gorgo walked away, happy but uncertain. He was witty about being able to take Kordeso's ear. Furthermore, he knew the natives had weapons, but he remained uncertain at how to prove the existence of an alliance.

He waited days before returning to the clearing to observe. His opportunity came in a fit of envy, when he, while hiding in the shadow of the trees, observed that Istas made a gift and presented it to Nkupa. The communication between the two had greatly improved, and Gorgo saw that Nkupa could now use Paiute words in sentences. Seeing their joyous interactions, Gorgo naturally wished to be included. He yearned to have the softness in Istas's eyes turn to him, but Nkupa did not trust him. If Nkupa feared or hated him, Gorgo knew he would have no chance at all at for camaraderie with Istas. He remembered the condescending look in Nkupa's eyes when they spoke. Nkupa was one who put his food on fire. He had straight teeth. He ate duck and trapped his food. Gorgo felt barbaric and small in Nkupa's presence. These thoughts made him furious, and as he watched them, he became committed to driving a wedge between them. When he saw the gift, a brightly colored blanket, Gorgo wanted it for himself.

He watched for many hours until they departed. This time, Gorgo anticipated Nkupa's route and ran ahead so he could intercept him.

Nkupa saw Gorgo approach from the front.

Gorgo said, "So, I see you again."

"Is this by mistake—or were you looking for me?"

"I looked for you."

"Why?"

"I need a friend." Gorgo did not search for anything this time. He fixed his eyes on Nkupa as if Nkupa was the subject of his search. "That is nice. It is pretty. What is it?"

"It is a blanket."

"The woman ... she gave it to you?"

"Yes."

"You will tell her to give one to me?"

"No."

There was a long, awkward silence. Nkupa wanted to move ahead as the sun settled behind the mountains and the shadows of the trees elongated, falling across his face.

Gorgo's countenance had a sinister appeal caused by the shadows, and the glare of his golden eyes made him seem supernatural. He tried to conceal his anger—a task poorly accomplished. He did not like Nkupa's answer or his arrogant tone.

"You should then give it to me, and she will give you another."

"Why?"

"Because you are my friend."

"I am not your friend. You are dangerous." Nkupa attempted to pass Gorgo, but Gorgo would not move. "You are in my way."

"Give me the blanket and I will allow you to pass."

"I will not give you the blanket."

Gorgo, with a sudden flare of anger and rise in body temperature, perspired from the brow, gritted his jagged teeth, and reached for the blanket. Nkupa snatched it away, but Gorgo reached again. This time, he was successful in gripping a corner of the blanket. Nkupa pulled, but Gorgo would not release. For a moment, they tugged back and forth until Gorgo stepped close enough to deliver a forceful fist to Nkupa's chin. It was a shocking blow, causing him to stumble backward, releasing the blanket as he fell. Gorgo smirked in proud accomplishment, turned, and ran away.

While en route to his clan, Gorgo knew he would tout the blanket as evidence of an alliance between Nkupa and the Paiutes.

Raza-Bin, a sort of mentor to Gorgo, once said that the youth had no sense of resolve for temperance. Gorgo was now ready to prove Raza-Bin correct. He wanted to hurt Nkupa as badly as anyone could hurt. Since Nkupa had an obvious affinity for the Paiutes, Gorgo wanted to destroy them as well, starting with Istas. He wanted her to suffer the most, but his first order of business was to present the blanket to Kordeso.

Gorgo proffered his evidence to Kordeso. "There was a boy who was just about my size. He had hair like me, and he spoke to me. His name is Nkupa. He is one who uses fire on his food. He swears that our clan is his enemy. He is not alone, there are others with him, and they have made friends with the men. They make plans now, and they have weapons. I have seen them."

Ton-Ton doubted Gorgo and was suspicious of his intent. "That is impossible."

"Impossible? Are you sure? How can you be sure that we are the last of our kind? Do you have a number of those born and those dead? I think you are incorrect. I have seen this Nkupa, and I have spoken to him. I even fought with him for this." He held the blanket before them. "It is a gift to him from the men. It is a blanket. They are friends, and we are their enemy. One day, we will all be asleep—and our throats will be cut by them. I hope at that moment, just before your throat is slit, you look up into the eyes of one of our kind and know that you were wrong."

Kordeso was torn between the two of them. It was no secret that Gorgo often roamed and explored areas away from the clan. Such conduct was normal for a child. In this, it was also expected for Gorgo to discover new things, some of which were perhaps dangerous to the clan. Kordeso was far from the wisest of them, but he understood that it was his duty to keep them alive.

"Tonight, we will follow Gorgo. He will take us to the place where the men hide, and we will see if it is true that they plan to attack. Others will go forward into the forest and hide carefully. They will look for signs of our kind. If they find a footprint or tools for hunting, they will let me know. If it is true that there is a pact, we will not give them a chance to kill us in our sleep."

Gorgo understood that Kordeso was adamant about the survival of his clan and would take no chances of leaving dangers unchecked. With this in mind, Gorgo spent one night leading, a group of four, Kordeso included. He took them beyond the forest to the clearing that Ton-Ton called the hunting grounds. Beyond the tall grass was a campsite, noticeable by dots of burning fires randomly dispersed. Gorgo was interested in keeping Kordeso suspicious of potential dangers inside the camp. He whispered to him about the warrior men he saw protecting the women when they set traps for rabbits; with each step forward, Kordeso grew more dependent upon Gorgo's narrative.

They reached the Paiute camp site undetected and stepped gently until Gorgo pointed out the spot where he saw the weapons.

Ton-Ton voiced his doubts, but Gorgo insisted that the people inside the camp were dangerous. Ton-Ton persisted. In his voiced opinion, there was no way to know weapons were inside without disturbing the sleeping village, thus causing them to notice the intrusion. The mere presence of intruders would be enough to cause the Paiutes to defend their territory against the perceived danger as such it was not prudent to label them dangerous .

Ton-Ton suggested that the clan leave and wait for the Paiutes to make the first move.

Gorgo knew that Kordeso was not quick to accept such a passive strategy, but he settled in compromise that, if there were no stockpile of weapons stored, he would admit his error and the clan should return to their camp, leaving the Paiutes in peace. His compromise was acceptable—even to Ton-Ton.

The crew entered the campsite just moments before they were noticed by a man who left his hut to find a place to answer the call of nature. He saw the figures of five huge creatures, like mountains, cast by the light from the night sky. The middle-aged Paiute suddenly became frightened and alarmed the entire village with a piercing cry.

Kordeso was startled, and in a sudden moment of subconscious instinct, he assumed an offensive stance. Some of the Paiute men were quick to arm themselves, appearing before Kordeso could consider the possibility of escape over attack—but Gorgo had already lifted a man in the air and tossed his body aside. At that point, Kordeso had no option other than to join the attack.

Panic was spread equally among the giants and the Paiutes. Women scattered and screamed. Brave warriors fled to retrieve their weapons. A hut caught fire. Spears soared to strike their marks. Kordeso called for retreat.

Gorgo used his large hands to twist another victim's neck until it was broken. Spears flew all around them, and some hit their marks. There were so many spears that Gorgo might have been willing to comply, but when he saw the terrified eyes of Istas who abandoned her home out of fear, Gorgo remembered his anger and jealousy. He wanted her to suffer. As such, he chased and captured the young girl. Kicking and screaming, she fought to resist, but she could not prevent her capturer from flinging her over his shoulder and carrying her away in a swift retreat.

Kordeso called for Gorgo, but the young giant did not listen to his leader. Instead, he left, heading in the direction of the lake, through the forest. When he reached the lake, she had not stopped screaming.

the sun had reached its arms over the horizon, and it was soon to lift its face.

Gorgo made up his mind to cross the lake and head for the mountains on the opposite side. Her screams caused Nkupa to awaken from his slumber and walk to the entrance of his cave, which overlooked the water. He lived there with his brother and his mother. Gorgo was unaware that Nkupa was near him. He headed for the mountains, careful to keep Istas from drowning in the cool water. He lifted her high above his head. She continued screaming until all hope of rescue had abandoned her.

When Gorgo reached the mountain, the girl's body was limp. She was so worn and fatigued that her body grew submissive to him. She lay limply over his broad shoulders as he scaled the mountain. All that remained to indicate that she was still alive were her sobs. Finding a cave inside the mountain, Gorgo plopped down to rest and dropped Istas to the rocky floor. He was tired and assumed that he would rape her after he caught his breath. "I will do sex to you the way Nkupa was supposed to do," he said.

She did not understand him. Her head rang from colliding against the floor of the cave when Gorgo dropped her.

The pain of Gorgo's penetration causing her helpless cry to emanate from the cave allowed Nkupa to find Istas. The sun was high above, and the harsh mountain terrain was clearly visible. When Gorgo realized that Nkupa had found him, he was quick to attack the naive giant.

Nkupa was not an experienced fighter. He tried to counter Gorgo's attack with an open-handed charge, attempting to grab Gorgo's neck, but Gorgo was quick and agile. He sidestepped Nkupa and crushed his elbow into the inexperienced giant's nape, sending Nkupa into the wall of the cave. Then, before Nkupa could turn, Gorgo charged him from behind and took Nkupa by the head. He had every intention of snapping the young giant's neck, but Nkupa, reaching backward, held firmly onto Gorgo's arms, preventing him from accessing his full strength. Instead of snapping his victim's neck, Gorgo took a step backward and flung Nkupa to the opposite side of the cave. Before Nkupa could recover, Gorgo knelt beside him, took his red hair in his hands, and smashed Nkupa's face into the rocks. Nkupa put up such a weak fight that Gorgo felt no satisfaction in beating him to a pulp. He left him in the cave with Istas.

Gorgo was stronger and faster than Nkupa. In fact, the same could have been said of his entire clan. However, by the time he reached his clan, he was stricken with a sudden fatigue and weakness. It was as if his body was sapped and drained of energy. He sluggishly entered his village, saying nothing to Ton-Ton or Kordeso. He went to his mother and lay at her feet. His actions were so unusual that no one said a word.

When he finally awoke from a deathlike sleep, Gorgo felt faint hunger pangs that could have been nagging to him if not for the loud noises he heard from the other side of the trees near the clearing where he would usually hunt for horned sheep. His curiosity taking the best of him, Gorgo stood up and walked in the direction of the sound. Ton-Ton noticed him and commented that there was something different about him. "There is a light missing in you."

Gorgo ignored the fool and continued to move toward the sound. It was as if only he heard it, but he was sure that the others simply ignored it. He kept walking until he reached the clearing in time to see the Paiutes take up chase. This time, it wasn't rabbits. This time, it was Nkupa who was pursued.

Gorgo had only caught a glimpse of the young giant taking flight into the forest. Behind him was a mob of men with spears. Gorgo was excited to see how the chase would end. He knew that Nkupa was not a warrior, and he assumed that the Paiutes would easily have their way with him. Gorgo wanted to see. He thought Nkupa deserved whatever fate befell him. As Gorgo hurried through the woods, he imagined that the Paiutes blamed Nkupa for the attack on their village and for Istas's capture. He supposed that Nkupa, in his ignorance, tried to return Istas to her people, and they turned against him. The thought was humorous to Gorgo. The tables had turned, and the men were out to kill the friendly giant. He hoped to see them do so. He wanted to witness the shadow of death over Nkupa's face replacing that pretentious glare in his eyes.

Gorgo followed as they chased Nkupa to his cave. Nearly pitying his stupidity, Gorgo understood that Nkupa should have never led the men to his home, endangering his family. When Nkupa climbed inside, he was joined by his brother, Kafnu, who was larger and more ferocious in appearance. He had a terrified fear in his eyes when he saw the men emerging from the forest and lining up against the bank of the lake.

Gorgo climbed a tree for an unobstructed view as he watched Kafnu surveying the field of battle from the mouth of the cave. They were trapped by the lake, and any attempt to escape through the lake would have been daring and perhaps ineffective. Gorgo imagined that the family could climb the mountain to avoid the spears, but instead, he called for his mother. She came to the cave to see the danger. She was old and moved slowly. It was obvious that the mother would fall victim to the warriors even if Nkupa and Kafnu put up a flight. Gorgo imagined that they would have to fight; his lips parted into a smile of anticipation.

The mother turned away. Kafnu followed, and then he returned with a large boulder that he placed in front of the entrance to the cave. He went and returned with another. Gorgo understood that the giants were building a barricade, but he questioned the logic behind such a task. If there was an exit from inside of the cave, they should have simply escaped from it. Why barricade the escape?

Two spears were sent sailing into the cave, and one struck the ground just a foot's width from Kafnu. The Paiutes moved closer each time Kafnu disappeared into the cave. He returned the third time and found that his enemies were too close. A spear passed over his head and into the cave. He squawked as he lifted the huge stone over his head. With a loud yell, he hurled the boulder at them. Only one warrior fell victim to Kafnu's rage. The Paiutes were not intimidated. Kafnu stepped inside and returned with another rock. With it, he successfully sealed the cave from the bottom to his knees. Gorgo imagined that the giants were desperately trying to dig a tunnel inside the cave and used the loose rocks to seal the mouth.

Men with archery equipment climbed trees and sat uncomfortably on branches, ready to attack. The cave was officially under siege with Kafnu's family sealed inside. Gorgo watched, hoping for more action, but the Paiutes just waited. He did not know why, but they watched as the sun began its descent. They seemed to be waiting for something, although no one approached the cave. No spears were thrown. Some men and an elderly woman arrived. She was dressed in warm animal skins. Her head was covered, and she walked with the aid of a stick. Two girls, new to their second decade of life, preceded the woman and unrolled a white blanket. They laid it flat on the ground at the bank; a brown colored circle was stitched into the fabric. The woman sat in the center of the circle, folded her legs, and—using a beaded string—started to chant.

Four men drove stakes into the ground, perfectly placed to the north, south, east, and west of her. On the stakes, they mounted flaming torches.

The female assistants gathered water from the lake with wooden cups. They placed the cups next to the stakes. The woman continued her chanting as the people busied themselves around her.

Gorgo continued to watch, wishing he could hear the words she mumbled. He heard another commotion and turned his attention to witness six men emerging from the forest. They pulled the strange contraption from the Paiutes' armory. Slowly they approached with it and positioned it to the left of the elderly woman.

Gorgo was more than curious as to the weapon's capability. The old woman's chants grew louder for one quick moment, and then she went silent. Everyone around her remained so quiet and motionless that Gorgo was afraid to breathe in fear that they would discover his presence. The sun was now gone, and darkness enveloped them, save for the torches.

Kafnu had the cave sealed to his head, and for a time, it appeared that he had successfully saved the lives of his family.

Gorgo suddenly heard the wooden handle on the weapon turning. A lever was controlled by a rope and pulley that pulled the lever back as the men turned. The lever applied pressure to a cord, and as the cord moved, Gorgo could see what looked like the manifestation of an arrow. The flames on the torches flickered and dimmed in tandem with the contraption as if heat energy was pulled from the fire to produce the arrow that materialized.

The arrow was bright and radiant, and it seemed to have suddenly appeared as if emerging from thin air. It grew brighter as the men cranked the handle. Gorgo was astonished and frightened.

When the arrow was discharged, a trail of light followed behind it. The rocky barricade that Kafnu concocted was no defense against the force of the arrow. The collision penetrated the barricade, and the explosion caused the rocks to crumble. The Paiutes, in celebration, took to their attack. They used the torches to light their spears and arrows, sending them flying inside the cave. Gorgo watched, feeling no empathy for Nkupa's family.

The three giants burned as the Paiutes celebrated their victory.

*****

Now Talib knew how the dream ended. He was drenched in perspiration when he awoke from his unconscious state. The dream seemed real to him. He had seen the giants in many dreams before, and in each of them, Gorgo was terrifying in both his appearance and actions.

Talib felt his heart rate slowing as he gained control of his breathing. For him, the visions were purely dreams, but when Fiona came to, she pulled herself to a sitting position. Without a word, she folded her legs, pulled a coin from a pocket in the hooded robe, closed her eyes, and fell into a deep meditation as she toyed with the coin. Talib knew that she felt his apprehension and adrenaline rush. He imagined that she felt the urge to save Nkupa.

Talib's being was comprised of two parts—one was innocent and sensitive, respectful of human life—and he could see the goodness in the gentle giants. The second part was old and elusive. It was as old as human existence. It was very different from Talib's temperament, but it had adapted and changed into something different from him. No one besides Fiona had ever noticed it.

THE DREAM OF THE
COMMITTEE OF NATIONS

For the first time in months, Talib slept in perfect peace. When he opened his eyes and read the digital clock on the nightstand, he realized that he had slept well into the midmorning hours. He climbed out of bed and immediately realized how fresh his legs felt. Talib had lived with so much tension in his shoulders for so long that he'd thought, up until then, that tight muscles in his trapeziums were normal. Suddenly, there was no more tautness; the tension had dissipated, and Talib felt anew.

After he showered and dressed, Talib went downstairs to the dining area. The cook was sitting at the glass table. The windows were opened, and a gentle spring breeze entered from the garden. The imported annuals were beginning to blossom, and the green trees were growing thick. The view from the wide window made Talib stand for a moment and admire the garden. He was curious to know where the sisters were; when he inquired of their whereabouts from the cook, he received no definite answer.

Breakfast was offered, but Talib declined the special treatment it would require to make a meal specifically for him. The cook promised to prepare a large meal for lunchtime. Talib thanked him and left, entering the garden to cross into the next wing of the mansion. He walked up the stairs slowly, hoping to make no obvious noises. He intended to spy on whoever he saw in the rooms. He was curious to know more about the things he had witnessed so far. Why did people practice yoga in one room? Why did they meditate in another? What were they trying to learn or find in the search room? More importantly, how did it all work?

When he reached the arts and crafts room at the top of the stairs, he saw Fiona. He suspected that she had already felt his presence. He stopped at the door and watched her at work. She seemed peaceful. Talib did not want to disturb her, but she invited him inside. Talib was curious about her art and assumed that her inspiration was stimulated by their session the day before. His assumptions were correct; Fiona was recreating an image of seven Paiute warriors on the edge of the river. An elderly lady was seated on the center of a blanket with a circle printed in the middle. In front of her was the weapon that Talib could scarcely identify.

"It's the weapon," she answered. "Kate says it is the bow of Artemis."

"Artemis?"

"Ancient people thought she was a goddess. They say the goddess of the hunt. When she was born, she helped her mother deliver Apollo—her twin brother."

"Is Artemis a spirit or fantasy?"

"The stories our parents tell us are part real and part fantasy. What you just discovered is that part of the story is real."

"What do you mean?"

"You found a weapon that can be used by spirits and by people." Fiona smiled. "People have searched for these types of weapons for centuries. You have its location somewhere inside of you. Kate was right. I already knew it. I had wished it weren't within you, but now I think I'm okay with it. You're a good person, Talib." She turned to her painting and continued.

Talib remained puzzled by her words. What was Kate right about? On the day he arrived, Kate had hinted that she or her family were responsible for his arrival. She suggested that fate played a role in their inevitable encounter. With all he had learned in the past three weeks, he could not help but wonder if some hex or spell had been placed upon him. Talib wanted to know why

Kate felt remorseful when she spoke to him that day. Why did she feel somewhat responsible for his misery?

Fiona stopped painting and turned to him. He could see her eyes searching for something. She seemed slightly confused about wanting to speak but was unsure of what to say. "It was Umar," she eventually said softly. "He was my grandfather."

"Umar?" Talib questioned. "How did he get a Muslim name?"

"He was Egyptian ... half-Egyptian." She stood and turned to the door. "Come. Kate will tell you."

They exited the room and walked down the hallway, away from the stairs, until they arrived at the library door. Fiona knocked gently and waited. No one answered right away, and she knocked again.

Talib tried to sort it all out. He believed that he understood how Daniel and the sisters were so fluent in Arabic and why they were so knowledgeable about Islamic culture, including the Quran. It was in their blood; they were a special group of people, genetically varied and spiritually inclined. Before Talib could question anything more concerning his religious teachings and its influences, the library door opened.

Kate was in the doorway, blankly staring into her sister's expression.

They entered the library and walked to the tables opposite from the paintings on the wall.

Kate pointed to a portrait near the end of the row.

Talib looked upon the image of a man in his thirties. He wore his black hair in a short, wavy cut. His eyes were gray, and his skin was not at all as pale as the others in their pictures. He bore the same Greek nose, but his chin, jawbone, and eyes were distinctly Semitic. The artist painted the image with Umar sitting at a desk with a book in his hand that was entitled *The Prince*. Behind his chair, in the background over his left shoulder, was a second person. The image was faint but clear enough for Talib to see that it was a woman. She was not much older than Umar—perhaps in her late fifties. She wore a black hijab and a long white garment. Talib was thunderstruck. All the other paintings were made with one single subject—all male. Umar's portrait was the sole exception. "Who is the woman?" he asked.

"She was my great-grandmother. He insisted that she was in the painting with him. She worked here as a servant, left when she was pregnant, and returned with him. It was after Umar was ten years old and after Alex, our great-grandfather, died. He would have killed her."

Using her eyes, she directed Talib's attention to the painting to the left of Umar's. There was a man in his early twenties, the youngest depiction of all the paintings. His steel-gray eyes bore a countenance of contempt and anger. It was evident that he resented the idea of posing for the painting.

Kate began to share more information. "Umar had the same gift that Alex had, but whereas Alex hated the Brotherhood, Umar embraced it. He had some idea about establishing a one-world government, so he started a war to make it happen."

Talib did not understand or see the connection. Kate, in her attempt to maintain his trust, wanted to explain her grandfather's ambitious goal. It was based on the idea that he called "New World Order" where men were to replace murder and tyranny with new ideas called humanism and globalism. The Brotherhood had attempted—for centuries—to rid the world of religious wars and create an international tolerance of all political fads, even the ones they imposed, but it was not until Umar's induction that the notion of one government and one religion seemed plausible.

He gave a new definition to the word Liberty, he defined it as a religion and concluded that it was the only religion that the world would accept. It was a belief that could easily infuse with every religion, leaving men free from institutional practices and allowing pacification for all those who needed the security blanket of a church, mosque, or synagogue. Under the freedoms of liberty, he imagined an eventual phasing out of traditional religious practices and men who defined their sinfulness by their efforts to achieve universal completeness and not by the number of prayers they made each day. Failure to achieve one's individual greatness would be the only real sin.

Before there could be one global faith, however, a single global government was needed to mandate the tolerances and protect the faith. This would require a sole governing body to set laws for the world. She needed to have her own police force and a mobilized military with the capability of resolving disputes between nations—by force if necessary. She could ostracize a nation from the global economic community and force any rebellious leader to comply with the terms or watch its people suffer from hunger or sickness. With a one-world government, there would eventually be no wars between nations. Every nation would give up her military personnel to the world government. All armies would disarm, and the one-world government would control global military actions.

Finally, a government of this kind could effectively administer the economics of the world and end world hunger, famine, and sickness. The concept of the central bank that was already implemented in six nations could be consolidated into one centralized banking system for the world. Every country on each continent would share the same currency; this single form of legal tender would be allocated to protect the wealth distribution of the world. In doing this, the end result would be a cessation of international suffering.

"Surely, you don't believe we can just ask kings and parliaments to simply surrender their governments and armies to us?" John Astor said during one gathering of the Brotherhood. He was very influential in the brotherhood, but Umar was patient and smarter. He surreptitiously organized a support group and waited. After John Astor's death, his son, William, inherited his seat on the governing board. By the time Umar and his support group manipulated and gaslighted Serbian nationalists. William, who lived in New York, was already primed and waiting for the green light from Umar. His mission was to fan the flames of nationalism inside the United States.

But before Umar could use his American friend, he needed to make waves in Europe. That idea came from Munemori. "You need to create a massive catastrophe in Europe," Munemori said. "Europeans have many conflicts in their histories; all you need to do is light the match, place it in the right spot, and watch the continent burn."

Umar liked the idea. Munemori was a scholar from a long line of the most intelligent families in Japan. He was the first Asian member to gain a seat on the governing board.

Roderick, Umar's cousin, suggested Germany. "Germany is a good choice, but it is too predictable. Perhaps we should consider another area in the old Holy Roman Empire."

"The Slavs," Umar said.

Munemori nodded and smiled. "Perfect. We will not have to do much. There are eleven major ethnic groups in Austria-Hungary. One group has a lot of national pride—the Serbs. Many of them have returned to Serbia where they have as much of a government as they can hope for, considering they will be Ottoman puppets for quite a while."

"If we were to promote that sense of nationalism among the young, college-aged Serbs, we could stimulate rash and ill-witted behavior," Conrad Brownstein said. He was not a member of the governing body, but he was the highly intelligent son of a major banking investor and had recently been inducted into the Brotherhood. Umar trusted his judgment. Born to an Ashkenazi family, Conrad seemingly held no loyalties to any Jewish tradition. He took his vows seriously, and shedding his loyalties to ethnicities and religions, he developed an affinity for power. Umar knew it was true. At that time, there were nearly four hundred members in the highly diverse Enlightened Titans. Its chapters were active on four continents.

Munemori said, "We contrast this by creating fears in the Habsburg House."

Umar said, "If we somehow have them believe the Russians are influencing the young Serbians with their nationalist beliefs, with a little luck, it will come across as an outside threat. Then we get people to influence the Hungarians to isolate the Serbs." He turned to Conrad. "You know people who can help us?"

Conrad nodded.

"That is your charge," Munemori said. "The Serbian, Austrian, Hungarian, and Russian conflicts have been building for fifty years now. We've taken advantage because we were able to build railroads with very little monetary investment."

Conrad smiled and said, "The pieces of this puzzle were already set before we even knew."

Umar left the next day with his fiancée for a trip to Constantinople where he would carry out the next part of his plan. It was to activate the mercenaries. He met secretly with Ivan Dagtekin, the new coleader of the mercenary gang founded by his father. Under Ivan's leadership, the gang had virtually become a private army, financed in large part by the Brotherhood. Ivan was often referred to as the Apis Bull. He was a highly-educated man with brown eyes and short black hair. He had two basic divisions to his militia. One faction, the Black Hand, conducted covert actions in the shadows while the Wind Storm instigated overt destruction and mayhem.

Umar understood that Ivan preferred straightforward conversations, but he nonetheless toyed with him, appealing to his vanity. "We have a mission for the Black Hand," he said.

"Who is the target?"

"This may challenge you," Umar said with a smile. He felt the yearning for adventure and danger inside his employee. "A Slav has to do it—or at least be the fall guy for it."

"Go on," Ivan said softly.

"The target is Franz Ferdinand."

Ivan raised an eyebrow but saw in Umar's eyes that there was more to say.

"It gets tougher," Umar hesitated. "It has to be carried out on July 28."

Umar did his homework. He studied his victim and understood that he had to consider every angle—tangible and intangible, earthly and spiritual. July 28 was the day that Saturn would move into Gemini, midheaven. What this meant to Umar was that on that day, the hierarchical structure of the Old World Order reached a zenith that would not happen again for a thousand years. It was no coincidence that Umar's astrological analysis and calculations placed the orb in perfect position with Franz Ferdinand's natal sun chart. Such an alignment suggested a mystical cause of an abrupt ending to a life. He also considered the energy of the Pandora asteroid belt—an energy that he expected would, given the right catalyst, unleash ill-advised spiritual energies capable of subjecting men to unpredictable terrors, inevitably leading to the death of thousands if not millions.

Such destruction was what he needed in order to establish the foundation of his ideal one-world government. With one shot of a bullet, Umar expected the Old World Order to decline and a new one to emerge that would last for the next thousand years.

He was at a restaurant in Alexandria when he received the news of a successful assassination. Soon afterward, he had his war. As time wore on, however, Umar became frustrated and disappointed at the apparent outmatched Triple Entente forces. He arose from bed late one day, knowing that the planetary positions of Mercury and Neptune were not in his favor. It was not a good day to receive news, yet he attempted to feign happiness for breakfast with Helen, his soon-to-be wife.

They dined on the patio in the garden, Helen's favorite spot to eat under a warm morning sun with the scent of lilac embracing her. Her eyes, shaded by glasses, followed Umar as he crossed the pavement to take his seat. His olive skin, to her envy, never needed a tan and never burned from the sunlight. He was not well inspired today; his shoulders slumped slightly forward as he approached.

"Is something wrong?" she asked, interpreting his body language.

Umar walked past his chair toward her and gently placed a kiss just under the bar of her glasses, close to her ear, and sat. "Today is not a good day for news." His eyes dropped to the newspaper on the table. The headlines told of the British surrender to the Turks at Kut in Mesopotamia. The news was discouraging. Just five days prior, the Germans had bombarded Great Britain at Yarmouth and Lowestoft. A month earlier, the Russian offensive against the Germans was stopped suddenly in Vilna, and the casualties were very heavy. The Germans had tremendous success in Verdun, and their U-boats were unstoppable in the seas.

Helen expressed her hopes that the war would soon come to an end. She did not like the way that it dampened her travel plans.

While she spoke, Umar barely listened. His thoughts were far away at a future meeting to take place with the Brotherhood's governing body. He was of the mind that the German capture of Fort Douaumont was a clear sign that the sides of power were unbalanced. He was in awe of the Germans having less than six decades of existence as a legitimate nation, yet it had become the most powerful force in Europe. However, Umar was disappointed in the French and the British because of their inability to prolong the war. The Russians were so occupied with marching on German soil that the Turks had a free pass in the south. The bitter cold was needed to slow down the Germans in the north, so the Russians could move into their southern border to be sacked by the Turks. It was clear to him that his plan of forming a Committee of Nations would falter unless the Americans joined the war.

He spent the rest of breakfast attempting, for Helen's sake, to be in good spirits, but when he finally sat among his brothers of the Enlightened Titans, he encouraged them to brainstorm ways to draw the Americans to the battlefield.

"It's an election year for them. The American president believes that his only chance of reelection is to keep his country neutral."

"But he is not neutral, considering his under-the-table agreement with Russia."

"Well, publicly, he didn't involve himself in the war at his front steps, so from a political standpoint, it makes no sense to send troops here."

"If we are successful, what side would they join?" asked Roderick.

"It doesn't matter what side. We just need them involved."

"Well, we need to choose. They have reason to declare war against the British. We can promote anti-British sentiment in America. We could springboard off the North Sea conflict."

Umar tapped a pen on the table top as he often did when he was on to a brilliant idea.

"As fast as the Germans are cutting up Western Europe, it won't be long before both the British and the French surrender," Thomas Walsh added.

"Don't forget about the conflicts in Russia," Munemori Murakmi said. He had arrived that morning with six other members from Japan to discuss the involvement of Asian nations in the war. Under their influence, Japan declared war against Germany and took over German territories in Asia. More importantly, Munemori had made himself an expert in understanding the Communist movements in Russia.

"I wouldn't worry about that," Roderick interjected. "That communism bullshit is just a fad. It'll never take over an entire nation, especially Russia."

"The tsar loses support every day," Munemori said. "Don't underestimate the mob."

Few people thought much of Munemori's statement. Umar, however, felt the sincerity in his colleague's heart. Munemori had a serious concern. He believed that the communist movement had a strong possibility of succeeding. There was also the risk that a growing movement against unpopular tsars would cause enough of a distraction that the support for the Russian army could falter. Even worse, the military giant could turn and head home to defend the tsar. With this thought, Umar felt a strange admiration for the communist members who chose a giant like Russia to compel. He understood that the movement was a locomotion picking up steam, and at some point, the Brotherhood needed to take a more active role in the inevitable revolution or risk the possibility of being blocked out of the Russian economy. But that was a matter for another time. Communist supporters were trying to change the world. Their numbers were small, but they were able—and perhaps likely—to conquer a giant. Umar also wanted to change the world.

He introduced his idea of a single world government to the governing board five years preceding the war. Umar was just nineteen years old at the time. The board rejected his idea, but he was persistent. He understood persistence and believed that the endurance of the communists would pose a threat to the tsar and to the idea of a one-world government. Still, he admired them for their attempts to conquer a giant like Russia. While the other men debated around him, he heard nothing outside his own thoughts. He was thinking about moments in history where little warriors unexpectedly defeated mighty giants. He thought about Muslims and Meccans, Haitians and the French, the Americans and the British—all rivals. Then he thought about the old Jewish tale of David and Goliath.

With that, Umar had come full circle, and it occurred to him that Jewish people had a history of fighting for terra firma, trying to occupy land, or defending their homeland. He reminded himself about Zionism, a popular movement among the Jews in Greece. Initially, Umar thought about how the modern-day Jewish people were so far removed from the Middle East in both genetic makeup and through intermarriages and cultures that they had no legitimate claim to any part of Palestine.

Then there were the Khazars to consider. Genetically, they held no rights to Palestine. However, due to their historical decision to convert, they—a non-Semitic group of Jews—had over the centuries assumed all "benefits" of Jewish people. Furthermore, the Turks laid claim to the entire area, and they were not giving up any land for the sake of a Jewish settlement—at least not without a fight. At the time, the Turks were on the winning side. It appeared that the British and French would submit any day— and the Enlightened Titans would have to work faster to cement the foundation of Umar's one-world government. He realized that one or two weeks would not be enough. The war needed to last one or two years longer. It occurred to him, at that moment, that the only way to prolong the war was by bringing in the Americans on the side of the Allied forces.

Connect the dots, he told himself. Find the connection. Jews, Americans, Turks, Committee of Nations, Britain, France ... it all has to fit together some way. There was something about the Jewish people, he thought. They were key in the equation, and the sentiment, although it was no more than a gentle whisper on the tongues of few Jews, was certainly a springboard for something inspirational. Zionism was a motivation, a sales pitch to give to all Jewish people. It was also a pathway to a soft spot found in all the Christian-minded Europeans who remained bitter about their losses from the Crusades. If Zionism could be sold to the Jewish—an easy sale—and if Palestine could be wrested from the Turks, then Jewish support for the Germans in Germany could be bartered, compromised, and wrestled away from the Germans. The idea seemed very plausible; however, unless the Americans were pulled into the war, neither a Jewish state nor a Committee of Nations would ever manifest.

He looked up from his tapping pencil and across the table to William Balfour, who was married to a woman said to be a Jewish

Khazar. William was a plump soul with a thick brown mustache that had hints of gray. Umar remembered him as an excellent shot on the polo field. From all appearances, he seemed unable to properly guide a horse, but in the emotion of competition, William was unstoppable.

At that moment, the dots connected. The Zionist movement was not only something talked about in Greece by a small band of Jewish citizens. It was also discussed in small crowds in Britain, and Umar assumed, the same for America as well. This idea of a Jewish state was the line that he needed to connect the dots. He smiled at the satisfaction of figuring out the answer. At that moment, he needed to convince his colleagues to take the action he wanted them to take. "I have a question," he said. He was barely aware of what was being discussed. His voice was louder than usual and carried a ringing of intellectual energy. "What are Wilson's chances of winning?"

The room hushed to a silence. Their conversation had long since changed from the American involvement in the war, and it was concluded that there was no way to pull them in. Carl James had convinced everyone that if the Americans joined, they would enter on the German side since there was no other way for them to get past the U-boat barricade.

Thomas Walsh was the most connected to information on the American political culture and answered Umar's question. "He has a slight chance. It's difficult to say with the country so divided."

"What if we could guarantee his victory? Would he join on the side of the British?"

Thomas Walsh pondered the idea momentarily until he heard Carl James repeat the crux of his previous argument. "They won't get beyond the barricade." Thomas wanted to side with Carl and discuss how impractical the question was. "It makes more sense for them to join the winning side and then represent our voice in the peace talks and treaties."

Umar could feel Thomas's conflicting emotions. "Thomas?"

Thomas cleared his throat. "He may join on the British side if we could guarantee his reelection. The Americans always have a predisposition to the British. With the proper motivation, help from the brothers in America, and a strategic election plan, he just may do it."

Roderick leaned back in his seat and watched the wheels turning in his cousin's mind. "Umar, what are you thinking?"

"I'm thinking about our good friend Lionel. He is a baron in the British government, isn't he?"

Thomas Walsh laughed at the notion that such a man could play a role in cajoling the Americans into a war. He smiled patronizingly. "Umar, Baron de Rothschild is a banker. He's practically in charge of our banks."

"Wars need money," Roderick muttered in support of his cousin.

"He is more than a banker. He is our brother, and he is also a leader of the Jewish community in Britain. Is he not an influential voice among them?"

A collective nod gave Umar encouragement.

"Good. I am totally convinced that he has a major influence in the Jewish voice. Tell me, William, is there any Jewish organization supportive of Zionism in Britain?"

William thought for a slight moment. "There is the Zion Federation of Great Britain and Ireland."

"And would it not be sensible to think that he has or can easily get the ears of the leaders, in this organization?"

"Perhaps," Roderick answered.

"Then we ask him to influence the European Zionists to explain to the American Zionists that Britain favors the establishment ... no call it the reestablishment of a Jewish state in Palestine. If the Americans joined the war to defend Britain against the Germans, they would one day, very soon, have rights to that Jewish state. We'll employ one or two antics. Let's say the Germans sank an

American ship or something similar that we can use to strike up public support ... then we could get the States involved."

The room was silent as the men sat back in their chairs to contemplate the idea.

Carl James said, "In order for that to have a chance, you'll need a guarantee from the British that they could establish a Jewish state ... and that they are willing to do so."

"So, we give him a guarantee. We even sweeten the deal and let him bring the Committee of Nations idea to the table when the war ends. He will look like a hero."

There was silence. Roderick was in opposition. "Umar, are you sure you want to give this up to someone else?"

"We are a brotherhood. We live in the background. The world needs not know from where the ideas come—it only needs to know the ideas. Furthermore, we owe him a good gesture for signing into law the use and operation of our bank. Let him have the credit for creating the Committee of Nations while we will run and operate it."

Roderick submitted to Umar's logic and focused his thoughts to the scheme. "If this works, it may create a divide in the Jewish sectors in Germany."

Umar shook his head. "There won't be a divide. Once the Jews hear about the intent of the Americans and British to create a Jewish state in Palestine, they will turn their backs on the Germans in one united front. The German Jews will come to see Germany as an obstacle in the way of creating a Jewish state. They would trade away all support for the Germans and turn it to the British. Who knows ... they may even support the Russians."

Roderick glanced at William Balfour. "William, your uncle is the foreign secretary in Britain ... is he not?"

"He is," William answered.

"Perhaps you can convince him."

"Perhaps." William's eyes rolled upward, revealing his

thoughts—he was on board with Umar's idea. "I'll meet with him, and we can discuss it."

"This sounds like a possible plan, but how will we get past the negative Jewish sentiment against Russia?" Munemori Murakmi said. "They were not too long ago kicked out of Russia."

Roderick said, "There is still a large Jewish population in Russia and in Poland. If we promote Zionism ... I mean make it a big deal ... a religious movement, it will catch fire everywhere. It will make it easier for the Marxist movement to take hold. The tsars will have too many interior problems."

Umar smiled. "Then it is settled. The Jews have no love for the Russians. Their support for the Germans is fickle and will go away. We will target them internationally with the idea of a return to Palestine and the rebirth of Israel. They will turn their backs on the Germans, the war will prolong, the Jewish support of the American President will guarantee his victory, the Americans will save the British and the French, we will run the Turks out of Palestine, make our Committee of Nations, and create our first set of international laws that will establish British control over Palestine to make a Jewish state."

Carl James said, "We can even get Christian groups on board in Britain."

"This may work with the Communist movement. Many of the Jewish people in Russia will want to flee, and they'll have somewhere to go," Munemori Murakmi said, making his approval for the plan obvious.

Umar looked at William and smiled. "It's all up to you now. You work on your uncle. Roderick, I'd like you to speak with Rothschild."

Thomas smiled. "This is very ambitious," he said. "It just may work."

When the meeting disbanded, Umar remained seated as the twenty-one members filed out into the garden.

Roderick, watching Umar in deep contemplation, waited for

the others to leave before closing the door and joining Umar at the table. He didn't say a word at first, he only stared at Umar.

"Not to worry," Umar said. "Some would say we just released the devil himself into the world."

Roderick smiled. "Don't be silly, cousin. You must crack eggs to make a cake. Besides, when the Americans join the war, it will come to a quick end. They are rested, young, and wealthy. There's no way the Germans will stop them."

"That's not what I mean." Umar sighed and then gave a slight smile. The concern remained on his face. "Imagine this: the Germans are winning the war, and the Turks are winning. The British cannot guarantee a Jewish state unless they defeat both the Germans and the Turks. You must have forgotten that Palestine is controlled by the Ottomans."

"Without the Germans, the Italians and Ottomans will falter."

"Yes, I know, but the Germans will look for a scapegoat."

"And that will be the Zionists," Roderick said.

"Exactly." He paused and walked to the window. The sun fell between the spaces in the blinds and shined across his face. "Can't you see how we just turned one of the most powerful nations in history against the most defenseless people in the modern world?"

"Potential genocide?" Roderick whispered.

Umar nodded.

"But wouldn't the danger in Germany cause them to flee for Palestine—their homeland?"

"Not all Jews are Zionist," Umar said. "Some of them do well in Germany. Not all Zionists are Jews. When or if Germany loses this war, the Allied forces will demand payment. The economic stress placed on this young German nation will cause a national collapse. They will probably, however unlikely, resort to socialism in order to survive. They will hate the Jews for their betrayal. That hatred will spread to Poland, Austria, Turkey, and only God knows where else. Millions will flee. Millions will stay and be killed. It could very well be international genocide."

"I think you're overreacting. These people have a history full of betrayal. Keep in mind that when the Persians set them free from Babylon, they returned them to their land—and they turned around and betrayed the Persians in favor of Greece. We educated them and civilized them in ways that advanced their culture by centuries, and they betrayed us for the Romans. Then they fought against the Romans. They will betray the Germans today or tomorrow. At some point, they'll turn on the British— the same people who gave them a homeland. Don't worry—their fate or blood is not on our hands. They will survive. Don't forget who these people really are. They are Jewish by faith and political advantage—not by ancestry."

"Some of them, I know. My dad wrote about it."

"He did? Oh, what did he write about Khaziers?"

"Come now, don't patronize me. You are not ignorant to their Khazier history."

"So, then, you understand my point. History has shown that Jews and Khazier Jews alike are not on your side or mine—they are only on their side. You need not ever pity them." He paused and walked to the window to look out into the garden. "You're a smart man, cousin," Roderick complimented. "Juxtapose this to our decision. Jacob, the father of Israel, had seventy children; only twelve of them lived in Egypt and became slaves. When they were emancipated, Moses had the daunting task of uniting the Hebrew slaves from Egypt with those who were already free and living in the desert. He was able to do this very simply. He appealed to the fact that they all had the same dream—a homeland. Now we are uniting them again with that same dream."

Umar laughed. "Are you really going to lecture me on a historically inaccurate religious book?"

"Of course not." Roderick moved closer and placed a hand on Umar's shoulder. "It doesn't matter if the Bible is accurate or completely false. The message is all that matters."

Umar nodded. "I understand."

"Khazars, Jews, Semitic or not—who cares. We'll get the Americans involved. We'll kick the shit out of the Turks, rebuild an ancient society, and rule the world. The way I see it, putting those Jews in Palestine with all those Muslims will only make our Committee of Nations more imperative. If they survive the British, they will attack the Muslims or the Muslims will attack them, maybe both. The Middle East will need our committee to keep the peace." Roderick smiled. "It's a brilliant plan."

Umar nodded. He understood a variety of things after speaking with Roderick. He understood that his vision of world government was far different from Roderick's and the sad truth was that there were more members of the Enlightened Titans who felt the same way as his cousin than those who felt opposite. This was, in Roderick's words, a chance to "rule the world."

TARTARUS: THE BLEEDING MOUNTAIN

Talib enjoyed his first night of restful sleep in months—since his nightmare about the tragedy at the cave. Now, after learning about Umar's ambition and the impact his dream had on so many lives, Talib found it very difficult to drift off into a restful slumber. He could not help but assume that the meeting Umar held with his fellow members was the same meeting the sheik spoke about. It was the meeting where the fate of Palestine was decided without Palestinian representation.

Talib was thunderstruck to discover that everything the sheik experienced was literally planned and predicted for the sake of achieving centralized banks and governments. In fairness, he tried not to make Umar out to be an evil man. He tried, at Kate's behest, to see the world from Umar's point of view. Perhaps he was not fully aware that the Jews would transform from the helpless victims of German enmity into merciless killers and oppressors in Palestine. Umar was great at many things, but he was not fortune-teller.

His cousin Roderick, however, had already calculated the possibilities, and his predictions were spot on. Since then Umar's Committee of Nations had evolved into the United Nations, and there had yet to be a reprimand against Israel for their crimes. The Palestinians still had not been represented in their counsels.

Talib had spent many years listening to older men speak about the crimes against them and their families. He witnessed the violence endured by worshipers who wished, like his father, to simply enter Jerusalem to pray.

Talib was angry. He did not want to be angry, and as he attempted to see Umar as a visionary, he could only conclude that he was, in fact, evil. What made it worse, he was Egyptian—or at least partly. It was as if he betrayed his own Arab people. He could have been the voice for Palestinians and made a better deal for them. With these thoughts racing through his mind, Talib drifted into a fit of sleep. He expected to have an uncomfortable night as he noticed that, when he became upset during the day, such patterns inevitably led to nightmares.

That night proved to be no different from the others. Whereas his dream was definitely frightful, there were no visions of Gorgo. Still, withstanding, Talib found himself inside of a dark, enclosed place, and he did not like the way it felt. He seemed to have arrived there by walking through a door. He was isolated and surrounded by wooden walls held together with tar. A rat scurried about the dozen or so wooden barrels that were scattered around the room.

It took him a moment to realize he was inside the cargo area of a ship that was docked near a beach. He had never personally set eyes on a beach, save for his dreams. He walked up the steps to the ship's deck and saw the bright yellow sands of a South American coastline. The trees were a bright display of full, green summer leaves that, at first sight, presented a tranquil vibration to his soul.

The serene vibration was soiled by a creature that Talib would have described to be an angel, at least upon first sight. It had folded wings similar to those of a raven. The back of its head was covered in gray feathers to match the wings. It stood as tall as two men. As Talib approached, he could see that the being had yellow-hued, humanlike skin. Its large appendages covered most of its back, and as Talib got closer, he noticed that the creature wore no clothing and bore no genitalia. By apparent physical structure, it resembled the likeness of a man—strong, fit, and capable of committing whatever catastrophe it wished. It had a face like a raven. Its eyes were as blue as the sea. His left hand hung by his side with a saber in its clutch. His right hand lovingly stroked the head of a black wolf, sitting beside him and peering ahead with great attentiveness. The creature noticed Talib coming forth and turned its head to face him. He spoke in a tongue unfamiliar to Talib—at least consciously—but somehow, he conveyed his feelings and subconscious with ease. "Behold my masterpiece," it said.

Talib looked past the creature and the wolf and noticed a crowd of people gathered around. The overwhelming majority of them appeared to be Spanish sailors, clothed in colonial garments. They mingled among a smaller audience of giants, not so much as savage and fearsome as Gorgo's clan, but equally strong and powerful. Their hair was dark, skin brown, and one of them—a female—had bright eyes the color of the evening sun. They were no different from Gorgo's eyes. She held an ax and stood in front of a man tied to a tree. Above his head was a firebrand engraved into the tree. It was a symbol that made no sense to Talib. The brand was made of horizontal lines with a triangle at the bottom and nine small circles at the end of each line. It also had three crosses—one that extended from the top of the isosceles triangle— and two hooks, like the letter J placed in perfect symmetry. A circle was made around the sigil, and the sight of it caused Talib's heart to tremble.

The winged creature watched in anticipation for the sudden strike of the ax against the roped man's arm. It fell to the ground at his feet. The victim's agonizing wail was frightening, and before Talib was startled from his sleep, he was in another place on the ship. The men were cold. He could see the white fog of their exhales rising above them into an overcast sky. The ship moved through the water, pushing aside floating ice. The landscape in every direction was blanketed white as far as one could see. It would have been expected that, with such cold and desolate surroundings, the sailors' spirits would mirror the ambience, but they were fascinated by the sight in front of them. They all stared in awe at a mountain covered in ice; from it, an endless trail of blood flowed into the water at its base.

The captain of the ship called for his men to fetch him a straw basket. They moved as if their lives depended on the speed of their obedience. Talib watched as the sailors opened the basket for the captain. The captain reached inside and wrapped his pale fingers around a metal sphere. Talib became tremendously frightened while watching the captain hold the sphere. He felt an undying need to escape. He was not certain that the sphere posed danger to him, but his psyche in his dream threw chaotic images of pandemonium.

Talib saw a man with copper skin and a ring of the same color and presumed it to be the same material as the sphere. He stood in the center of a multitude of creatures that fled from him in a panic in every direction. He wore a breastplate of armor that was engraved with the Star of David. Despite their hideous features, he did not fear the creatures. When he lifted the hand bearing the ring, one of the creatures suddenly became motionless. The thing was shaped like a man from the waist to the neck. He carried a bow like a skilled archer or hunter. His ears were at the top of his head. The skin on them was loose, the tips were pointed, and they flapped at the sides. The tops of his brow were two horned stubs. He had a long, pointed nose. His eyes were invisible, and from waist down, his figure was a cloud of black smoke. His arms flailed as if trying to escape the power of the ring. Escape, however, was impossible, and the owner of the ring called to his captured slave, saying, "Barbatos, you will teach me the speech of the animals."

At that moment, it was clear to Talib that the ring master was none other than King Sulemon. He watched on as the djinni turned helplessly to Talib.

"Yaron, free me!" Barbatos screamed with the panic of a hundred sheep just moments away from slaughter. The sound of its voice frightened Talib, and he felt as if he would soon face the same fate as the djinni. Talib was spooked and suddenly jolted awake, covered in perspiration.

The next morning, Talib was sitting in the garden in

admiration of the vegetation. Fiona inquired about his sleep, and he admitted that the nightmares had returned. "Will you paint them?" he asked.

"No," she said. "Your energy is mixed up."

"Mixed up?"

"Yes ... like a radio when it cannot find the station."

Hearing what Fiona said as she joined them, Kate interjected with a solution to Talib's scrambled energy. "You need to meditate," she said. "It's time you learn about your Kundalini."

Talib had not heard the word before that day. Kate explained that Kundalini was an energy obtained by him while he was an embryo—a biochemical energy that stimulated cell growth and organ production. "When you develop a spine, the energy becomes static and coils at the bottom of the spine until the body calls upon it."

"But your mind can call it too," Fiona added.

Kate said, "When you experience tragedy, the body—and maybe your mind—calls for the Kundalini to awaken and rise into the lowest energy center, the root."

When Talib joined the sisters inside the meditation room, Kate pointed out the images painted on the ceiling. In all, there were thirty-six. She explained how the images represented doorways to different levels of consciousness. She pointed out one that was painted red. It depicted a square, a circle, and a triangle. "When you need to survive, the body calls for the Kundalini. It is the energy and power of creation inside of you that finds a way when there is no conscious way to achieve something." She smiled, and her voice became warm. "It is kind of like making it all the way here from Palestine without money or food."

Talib admitted to himself that, under any other circumstances, he might have failed to reach Israel—let alone travel by cargo train for days. There was some power, which he had no clue existed, that pushed him forward and enabled him to endure.

Kate asked him to lie still on his back and stare at the ceiling.

She asked him to burn the symbols in his mind, and when he was successful, to close his eyes and focus all thoughts on his breathing and the feeling of his body sinking into the floor. She spoke softly in his ear and encouraged Talib to channel his feelings to the small of his back. "Imagine everything you felt—your hunger, thirst for water, your need for safety—was all one red ball of energy. Remember each feeling. Force those feeling into the red ball."

Kate walked counterclockwise circles around Talib, and he attempted to follow her instructions.

"Now take the ball and force it into the small of your back. Place it there and let it simply exist. Now feed it the energy of the air you breathe. Take in the red air and send it into that spot, the small of your back. Let the ball grow heavy and sink into the floor underneath you."

They spent twenty minutes in meditation. When it ended, Talib sat on the floor mat and smiled. He felt different. He felt lighter, and his mind was clear. He was less concerned about his nightmare and Umar's ambition.

Kate encouraged him to meditate each night before sleeping. She promised that his dreams would eventually change. "Instead of fearing them, you will use them as tools."

"Tools for what?"

"Tools to discover things."

"What things?"

"Whatever you want. Whoever you want."

She suggested that he and Fiona meet that evening for another session. There were things about his nightmare that required understanding. She called them clues.

He remained willing to accommodate Kate and to allow Fiona to look inside the secret corridors of his mind to find whatever was needed with the hope that there was an answer that would accomplish their mission.

When they met, dressed in hooded robes, Kate asked Talib to look at the clay tablet again. He readily obeyed, and after partaking of the libation that caused drowsiness, he lay inside the circle, submitting to the shadows of his unconsciousness again. Fiona lay beside him.

What they saw was a group of seven men gathered around a fire. Trees surrounded them like an unimposing army of terracotta soldiers. Crickets chirped incessantly as if the seven men were part of their choir. A pale moon spied from a black sky among thousands of stars. The firelight danced against their faces, and the wood crackled underneath the flames. Two men were seated on boulders beside an older man who sat on a chopped trunk of a tree. The others sat cross-legged on the dry ground. They all had black hair and eyes similar in shape to the Paiutes from Talib's last dream. One would suppose that they were descendants from the small band of nomads, but the shapes and sizes of their bodies were notably different. Their shoulders were broad, and their heads were large and elongated. They had hands that were far larger than any regular person. Perhaps they were descendants from Gorgo and his clan—minus the red hair, the barbaric decorum, and the jagged teeth. Although they were larger than typical men, they were smaller than Gorgo's clan. It was as though evolution had reduced them in stature, making them slightly more civil and organized.

They were engaged in a meeting, and the eldest folded his brow as he stared into the fire. "It is now three full moons since the Spaniards arrived," he said. "We still have no plan to rid them from our land."

"I think we should consider Belair's idea," said one who sat on a rock. He was older than the others, an obvious adviser to the elder. "There are too many of them to fight, and they have weapons that are far better than ours."

"Have you seen these weapons? Do you know how they work?"

"Belair has."

The elder turned to one of the four who sat near the fire. Everybody's eyes focused on Belair. He was no less than three decades younger than the leaders. Not at all a boy, he had his vigor still with him. He had developed a reputation for his wily ways. He had golden-shaded eyes that illuminated and danced with the fire before him. "It is true. They have a stick with a hole in the center of it. It is made with metal at the end of it. They pour a powder inside the hole, and then they place a ball. Then they smash it together with another stick. They make a spark on top of it, and when it makes a loud noise, the ball comes out and kills what it hits."

"You suggest we do not fight them—but have them fight against each other. How is this possible?"

"I know their words. I know they believe in a woman. They pray to her and put her image on their huts. They drink the firewater, and they become angry with each other every night. They look the same to us, but they are not the same and they do not like each other. I only need to cause them to fight among themselves. I will cause them to kill eachother."

The elder moved his large fingers through his white beard and then gave his permission to Belair. "Their commander will return in three days. Make sure he returns to a war."

Although three days was a short time, Belair was confident he would succeed. He rose from his slumber, walked to the beach, and looked upon the blue ocean. A yellow sun climbed in an azure eastern sky that was spotted with cumulus clouds—puffy, white, and suspended over the ocean whereupon five sail ships rested. The flagship bore its name, *Trinidad*, and carried upon it the flag with the name of the Spanish king, Charles V. In the company of the large ship were four others bearing the names *Victoria, Concepcion, Santiago,* and *San Antonio.*

The admiral was not among the men who sailed the ships. He had been gone for thirty days, escorted by the elder's only son through the thick jungle in search of a water passage that would allow the sailors to travel through the giant's land to the west of it. As he and his small crew of men searched, the larger company of sailors waited on the beach.

Belair was the first of his kind the sailors met. He danced naked on the beach to attract their attention. He felt responsible for their arrival and feared—just as the elders did—that if the sailors did not find their way to the west, they would stay and wage war against the natives. Belair brought this problem to his clan to discuss ways to eradicate the foreigners just the same.

There were many weaknesses that Belair could explore. One of the most obvious was Juan Elcano, a former merchant who wanted to find profit in his friendship with Belair and often inquired about Belair's knowledge of gold. Now was the perfect time for Belair to offer Juan a golden bracelet. Although Juan was warned by another sailor that the admiral did not favor the exploitation of the natives, he aspired to keep the jewelry.

"The commander does not need to know about this, does he?"

"My knowledge makes me involved and guilty as well," the sailor responded.

"Well, then, that gives you more the reason to shut up."

Unaware that Belair was already knowledgeable enough about their language to understand them, the sailors continued speaking in his presence. Belair absorbed all they said and did. He took in their notions, mannerisms, and tendencies. He noticed the fluctuations in their voices whether they were excited or concealing their intentions. Of all the men, Juan Elcano was easiest to read. His motivation was simple: he wanted gold.

Juan de Cartagena was nearly as easy to read as Juan Elcano: he wanted to be commander. When one sailor explained that he was from Portugal and that Juan de Cartagena was from Spain, Belair understood more than what the sailor intended. "And your chief? He is Portugal?"

"No," said the sailor. "Our king is a Spaniard."

When Belair departed from the sailor, he was prepared to play his cards. He had a multistep plan; the first was to approach Juan Elcano with gold and to supply him with more each day. He wanted to feed the greed of the merchant sailor. The second part was to wedge a knife in Juan de Caragena's pride and envy and twist it until it was excruciating and unbearable.

He cheered as he approached the captain. "Portugal, great! Mighty men, yes?"

Juan de Cartagena was instantly insulted. "No!" he yelled. Then he turned to his officers and said, "Get this fool out of my sight."

There was laughter from others, and some sailors called for Belair to join them. They offered him rum, and he accepted. Belair, to their low wit, had watered the seed of rebellion in the captain. He waited for his next opportunity to twist the knife. It came shortly after the captain gave a name to their settlement. He called it Puerto San Julian. In their short time on the beach, the foreigners built six wooden structures—one being a place for the sailors to pray and make confession before Padre Sanchez de la Reina, who took to the belief that he should convince Belair to accept the Catholic faith.

Belair laughed at the priest and the idea of an immaculate conception. "The bird, the fish, the monkey, everything. One male, one female make baby." He laughed. "Everything born comes from two. Even a simple idea comes from two: knowledge and situation. One is a female, and one is a male ... together they make idea." He looked away from the priest, observing the priest's eyes shifted to the approach of Juan de Cartagena. He was suddenly aware that it was an opportunity to twist the knife.

He did this with an apology and pleaded for the captain's clemency for his statement regarding Portuguese superiority. In any other circumstance, the captain would have dismissed the oversized juvenile, but in that the priest was present, and Easter Sunday approached, Juan de Cartagena decided to exercise good Christian decorum and show humility.

"You are forgiven," he said. His voice was agitated as he sidestepped the giant to continue his approach now four steps from the priest.

Belair, however, had more to say of the matter and turned to walk slightly behind the captain. "Please forgive me, but I try to understand."

"Understand what?" asked the priest. "I do not understand the commander of all these men. Is he Portugal, no?"

"Yes, he is Portuguese," the priest corrected.

"But you are Espain, no?"

"Yes, we are Spanish."

"But you follow Portuguese. Why, if Spain is so great, you follow the weak? Mighty men should not follow weak men."

"Well, there is much you do not understand," Juan de Cartagena said.

"He has one ship. You have one ship. Maybe you take his ship—and you have the big one," Belair said. "Many men here are Espain. They will appreciate to follow a strong man from Espain—not a weak man of Portugal."

With that, Belair hoped to plant the seeds of mutiny. Whenever he was not nurturing his seeds, he was engaged with Juan Elcano who had asked the giant to travel with the crew on their voyage. From what he learned, there was no man in Spain who was as tall as Belair. The citizens would have treated him like a king.

Belair said, "This sounds very nice, but I have responsibility here with my people. Maybe I will send with you my daughter."

"Daughter? I did not know you had a daughter. I will take her to our king. He is a personal friend."

"Oh, she would like that. She would like to see your boat and float on it all around the great ocean." He hesitated and his eyes turned down to meet Juan Elcano's eyes. Belair had a serious glare of concern. "But you must promise to take good care of her. You must feed her."

Juan Elcano said, "By the Holy Mother, I swear it. She will not go hungry."

"And I will give you more gold to take care of her and to give some to your king, yes?"

"Absolutely," Juan Elcano said. If nothing else, he was an opportunist.

Belair continued to spin his web, using his daughter as bait for his trap. If he had known, however, that the men aboard Captain Luis Mendoza's ship, *Victoria*, would bind and rape his daughter, he might have thought differently. If he knew that she would later give birth to a bastard who was fathered by one of the sailors, he would have planned differently. But Belair was no fortune-teller. He was, however, extremely focused and concerned with the outcomes. He did not think his daughter would be in any grave danger. By his estimates, the commander of the fleet would return within a day, which meant that, at the very worst, his daughter would be discomforted for just a short while before he rescued her.

Unfortunately for Belair and for his daughter, the commander's return was delayed due to a heavy rain that trapped them in the jungle. Belair realized that, with the extra time, he needed to ensure the success of his scheme. When the commander returned, Belair wanted the flames of mutiny to consume them all. This led him to the captain of the *Victoria*, who had just one day ago given permission for the giant female to board the ship.

"She is a beautiful girl," Luis Mendoza said.

Belair was appreciative of the compliment. "I am worried that some of your men believe it is wrong for her to come."

"Nonsense," he said.

"I don't want to cause trouble with your men. You are very kind."

"There will be no trouble," Luis Mendoza said. "And she will be protected."

"Thank you for your promise. It is just that I hear many bad things about your commander. He is a very stern and unfair man, no? I hear that he will punish you."

Belair laughed. "I hear that, and I laugh because he is Portuguese—and Portuguese are weak men to Espain. I do not understand how a weak man can punish strong men. I think that maybe Captain Juan de Cartagena will be leader—and you will be happy to follow him, no?"

"You make good observations," Luis Mendoza said. His eyes shifted, and he fidgeted as Belair had previously noted to be the captain's mannerism whenever he wanted to conceal his thoughts.

It was already too late. Belair had already heard about Luis Mendoza's secret meeting with Juan de Cartagena and the priest. Belair had already tested Gasper de Quesada and suspected that he had joined the coup. By Belair's suspicion, there was only one captain loyal to the commander—Juan Serrano.

Belair whispered, "I must say to you Senor Juan Serrano that, while your commander is away, I fear that the other captains plan to kill you."

His words were frightening to the captain. Belair carefully read the captain's reaction. He was touched by Serrano's fear with a unique vibration reaching him. Serrano was gullible, and being the only Portuguese leader, aside from the commander, put him in obvious danger. Belair was strategic to point out the many dangers that Juan Serrano should have considered. Aside from the fact that the other captains were Spanish, it was a strategic advantage for them to overtake him before the admiral returned from his expedition. With Juan Serrano conquered, the Spanish captains would have four ships to launch an assault against the *Trinidad*.

"Watch them carefully," Belair continued. "Sometimes the men forget that I understand their words, and I hear them speak very angrily against Portuguese men. One of them said that the tongue of Duarte Barbosa should come from his mouth."

"They said as much?"

"Yes, I heard it with my own ears from the padre. He said it to Juan de Cartagena. They created a list of men, and I hear them say the names Antonio Pigufetta and Enrique of Malacea and your name."

Juan Serrano was convinced of the giant's credibility. "Keep this to yourself," he said. "If you hear more, let me know."

"I will," Belair said. "I have just one question and favor of you?"

"What is that?"

"As I understand, your men were told by your kind commander that they must obey certain provisions."

"Yes," Juan Serrano answered, dumbfound at how Belair would know the commander's orders as well as articulate the words with such efficiency. Hearing such use of language convinced him even more that Belair had indeed overheard a conversation from the Spanish. He felt himself indebted to the giant.

"I have seen with my own eyes that Juan Elcano has many gold pieces of jewelry, and what concerns me is that they seem to be the same as those I made and gave to my daughter."

"I didn't know you had a daughter. I've yet to see any women of your race."

"I do have a daughter, and as a father, I am very worried that she has been missing for two days."

"Are you to claim that Juan Elcano has taken you daughter?"

"No, but I ask that you investigate. I will inform you of the plans that the other captains have against your life."

"When Admiral Magellan returns, I will have an audience with him. I will tell him of these plans. If they have your daughter aboard one of these ships, you will have her back. I swear it."

Belair returned to his village in a clearing near a river that snaked as far north and south as any of the giants had roamed. They had built homes for themselves by using trees and thick leaves from surrounding plants. The rain had ended, and dusk fell upon them.

Despite the cool air and the mud-covered landscape, the champion of medicine—an elderly lady affectionately called "the Mother," was busy with a cauldron mounted on a bed of rocks set above a fire. Belair did not know what she made, but she said her concoction had been brewing for two days already and was now close to completion.

Belair enjoyed his visits with her. She was wise and had served as midwife for more than half their clan. Her energy was different from the others. She understood the jungle, the air around it, and the energies within. It was she who originally advised Belair that the visitors—if they intended to bring danger—could only defeat themselves in battle. Accordingly, the Mother's words spawned his notion to plant seeds of mutiny.

"What you must do is cultivate their greed, pride, envy, and all the wickedness they possess. When you do, the wolf will come, and no one can resist or defeat the wolf."

"I've done it," Belair said. "They are consumed with hatred. Call your wolf—and let us be rid of these men."

She tilted her head to the sky. The clouds continued to loom, and the sky was clear of the stars and moon. She seemed undisturbed. "This is a good night for chaos. Go and sleep. When you awake, prepare for war. The wolf will visit them. If you were successful, his visit will be short."

Belair followed her instructions and was awakened early the next morning by a thundering of cannon fire. He rushed to the beach, pushing limbs and branches aside as he tore through the jungle. When he arrived, he noticed that the ships were out at sea. Five men on the beach watched as the attack unfolded. The *Trinidad* chased four men in a rowboat who were heading for the *Victoria*. Belair walked slowly to the edge of ocean, letting the water crawl to his feet. He watched as the *Trinidad* gave chase. Turning to the sailors behind him, he asked about the course of events.

"The commander was suspicious of insubordination. At dusk, he sent men to the *Victoria*. Despite the admiral's order, they were not allowed to board. Shortly afterward, Captain Cartagena's men boarded our ship and took Quesada's command. Many of us who are loyal to the admiral were taken prisoner. We, alone, escaped in the night. We have been here since."

"Will you not help your admiral? Will you fight with him?"

"He may not know that those loyal to him are prisoners. He

may assume that every man on our ship has risen in mutiny. He will kill us immediately."

Belair was proud that his plot had unfolded and that the wolf had come to make war among the foreigners. He had little time to bask, however, as his thoughts moved suddenly to his daughter. He feared that she was perhaps in greater danger now that the ships fired upon each other. He pointed at the *Victoria*. "You must take me to that ship."

"This we cannot do," one sailor said. "It is too dangerous."

"Danger?" Belair turned, and his eyes burned with a furious desperation. "You have not seen danger. I will take you by your heads to our village. There, you will hang by your feet while we cut one small part of your body, piece by piece, each day until you die." As he spoke to them, he approached, his voice saturated with hatred. "And that is just the beginning. Our women will think of more ways to cause suffering."

"Okay," the second sailor said. "We will take you there, but then we will leave you."

Belair agreed and boarded their rowboat. His thoughts were centered on his daughter, and the guilt of endangering her life swelled inside of him. The cannon smoke and maneuvering ships disrupted the otherwise peaceful ocean waters. It was as if nature had somehow turned a blind eye to the fighting men, and Belair remembered that in such apparent serenity, the wolf did his most effective work.

When the sailors reached the *Victoria*, Belair noticed that war had already taken over the ship. Fernandez, one of the admiral's most trusted men and valiant warrior, had already used his cunning mind to hoodwink the crew and board the ship with just a few men. He provided a distravtion just long enough for Belair to climb the ropes dangling on the side of the ship and center himself in the commotion.

Belair did not hesitate in his attack against the sailors. He threw one man over the side of the ship; a second was charged and lifted from his feet by Belair's massive hands. Then, with a force so great and foreign to the sailor, Belair crushed his body against the ship's railing. A third sailor witnessed the assault and attempted to aid his fallen mate when Belair took him by his arms, and with the long reach of his legs, planted a foot in the sailor's chest. His golden eyes bore the fury of a thousand years as he gritted his teeth and extended his leg, pushing back on the sailor until his arms separated from their sockets. Afterward, he searched freely for an opening that led below deck. From hearing the conversations, he knew that prisoners were kept there, and there was an entrance somewhere.

Fighting went on all around him; cannon fire and harquebus smoke filled the air, but Belair held his focus, intent on locating his daughter. Suddenly, it occurred to him that escape would be impossible if he found her. Belair had boarded the ship with no plan for escaping, and it occurred to him that he must fight with Fernandez. He had only once laid eyes on Fernandez, but he remembered him to be rather short man of high position. His cannonball shoulders extended into a set of large forearms. A black beard hung from his chin, and the hair atop his head was black and curled like lamb's wool. He had olive skin and bore the phenotype of his Moorish ancestors.

Belair, in his disorganized rage, killed twelve men that day and did not know if they were for or against the admiral. In the end, the ship was captured, and he looked upon Fernandez almost as a friend. They battled for a common cause and won. As a result, the prisoners were marched below deck to the brig, and Belair saw his daughter released. A green flag was lifted high above the ship to signal to the *Trinidad* that the *Victoria* was captured, and although very damaged, the ship, upon Fernandez's order, moved forth to attack Cartagena.

The fighting lasted the entire day. Belair saw the *San Antonio* captured by the admiral shortly after the *Victoria* was retaken. The boat that Belair earlier saw and assumed to be in flight of the *Trinidad* was just another of Fernandez's ploys. The sailors, loyal to the admiral, feigned flight and defection to board the *San Antonio*. Their battle was a short one in comparison to the fight over the *Victoria*. Outnumbered, Juan de Cartagena was eventually taken from his quarters and stripped of all clothing to stand trial for his deeds the next day.

When dawn called forth the sunlight, the admiral patiently ate his breakfast. He waited for the giants to return to the camp sight. Belair and his daughter showed up with the entire village—twenty-one in all—to watch the trial and hear the sentencing. The admiral was reputed to be a fair and consenting man among his peers. He sought the advice of his closest comrades and was advised by Fernandez that any sign of clemency would encourage a second mutiny. Furthermore, the clan of giants in the audience meant they were potentially prepared to execute their own justice—if they were unsatisfied with the admiral's sentence. The punishment for mutiny was death, and since he needed to repair his ships using supplies furnished by the natives, the admiral decided to act in opposition to his merciful notions. The natives had never witnessed such wanton cruelty.

Fifty men in all were captured and sentenced that day. Thirty were imprisoned to the *Trinidad* until the time came for them to pump the ship when needed. The priest was sentenced to a life of isolation—marooned on a small island—and given a handgun and one bullet to use as he saw fit. Those who were guilty of advising the mutinous captain were sentenced to hanging by the neck. They were stripped naked and hung high in the boat's mast so the birds would feed on their corpses when the ship sailed.

When all the other sentences were given—and Juan de Cartagena fully understood the consequences of his actions—the admiral turned to him and said, "Juan de Cartagena, my only fault in your eyes is that I was not born a Spaniard. Such disdain in your heart makes you guilty of an unpardonable crime. You are fully aware that the royal sovereign of Spain gave me command of this fleet, and therefore your actions against me are simultaneously against the king. Without the king's blessing, you have used bloodshed to attempt to assume command of this fleet in an unquestionable rebellion. You deserve no pity. You are thereby sentenced to be quartered at the hands of our merciful hosts. They had every right to slaughter us, yet they spared our lives. Because of your actions, one of their own has been violated and defiled for life. To her, you must answer."

Fernandez carried a medieval ax with a smooth ebony handle. As the nature of the punishment was explained to Belair, it was the admiral's request that Belair's daughter carry out the punishment of the traitorous captain, and she was instructed to use the weapon against him. Juan de Cartagena was tied to a tree with his arms behind him and his legs fixed with a tight rope. Her charge was to ax him into four parts by first separating his torso from his arms and then cutting the remaining part in half at the hip. The last was to behead him.

Although the punishment was cruel, she did not hesitate. The admiral hoped that the violent aggression against the traitor would assuage the natives' anger against his crew. He watched without any remorse as she swung the head of the ax with a force he never imagined possible for any female of any race. He saw her as fierce and monstrous—as if she were the spawn of Satan—and for a moment, he imagined that she enjoyed what she did. At any rate, he hoped that she and all the other natives were satisfied.

By all appearances, they seemed content, if not for the administered justice, then for promise that the foreigners would leave. As the crew made repairs to the ships to prepare for their departure, Admiral Magellan explained to the natives that he had ventured off on their long voyage to see the entire world. "To go in one direction and return to the starting point," he said.

The Mother understood and explained to him, via an interpreter, that his suspicions were correct. "The earth is no different from the other orbs in the sky. It is round, and it moves in an orbit, just like the crew of adventurers who move in one direction to eventually return to its starting point. "When you doubt that you will return, you will have reached the farthest point away from your home. It will be cold—and the ice may destroy your ships—but you will find hope when you see the dungeon of torment. Spirits find torture in the bleeding ice mountain." She turned to wave at a child who stood behind them.

The little girl approached with a straw basket. She seemed frightened by the foreigners, but she sheepishly obeyed the Mother and offered her basket to the sailor. Inside was a silver metal ball, a hand's width in diameter.

She cautioned him against taking it out until it cooled since it was still hot from her pot. She recounted how the ball was a special metal made of matter taken from both the earth and the spirit world. She called it *pazloa*. "It will be your protection as you draw nearer to the mountain. The angels cannot harm you if you have this. Evil spirits will run away."

When he left them, the admiral pondered the Mother's figurative language. There was no place to his knowledge where spirits were tortured except for the fiery pit of hell, but that sounded nothing like the Mother's description. However, her words rang true when his men had exhausted their rum and there was nothing more to keep them warm.

Magellan could see their hope for survival diminishing. He saw the desperation in their eyes as the men hunted rats aboard the ship for food. When Fernandez yelled from the doorway of his chamber, awakening him from his sleep, the admiral saw sudden enlightenment in the Mother's predictions. He rushed to the deck and saw the bleeding ice mountain with his own eyes. He was astonished at the blood running down the mountain to the icy water and the idea that the Mother, having never laid eyes on it, was aware of the mountain's existence. He remembered what she told him and ordered the two men closest to him to fetch the basket.

As the men scurried for the goods, Magellan noticed a drop in the ship's sails. The dense air was remarkably warm, and he sensed an evil apparition among them—just as in the Mother's premonition. He and his men had microscopic knowledge about spirits and their intentions, and he was not aware that they numbered in the thousands. Since leaving the giants, the admiral's quest was by now reduced by two ships one was wrecked, and the other was lost to desertion. Rumors spread that the men aboard the *San Antonio* were stricken with sudden delirium and that Captain Gomez had abandoned the mission and returned to Spain.

The admiral took the sphere in his hand, walked to the bowsprit of the ship, and held it high above his head. In an instant, it seemed as if a curtain was pulled aside to unveil a new, mystical world that merged with his tangible reality.

This netherworld was void of sunlight and air. The mountains and rocks on either side of his ship radiated light of their own—an aura that illuminated this dark, seemingly lifeless universe. Magellan's ship continued forth at a snail's pace in waters that seemed motionless.

Straight ahead, a multitude of creatures sprinted toward him in inevitable assault. The creatures ran along the surface of the motionless waters like it was as solid as the wooden floor of the ship. They had the faces of bats and bared hideous teeth from their snarling jowls. Their clawed hands and feet didn't even make a sound as they trampled across the water. A pale red, fiery glow radiated from their bodies. It was obvious to the commander that the creatures had no intentions of having a friendly encounter. They had come to wreak havoc and drive his men insane.

Standing firm, the admiral bravely and curiously kept the sphere raised over his head as the demons approached. When they laid eyes on the sphere and its material, they dispersed in full retreat, scattering frantically in multiple directions. None of the men were aware of what the admiral witnessed; to them, demons were of no consequence.

The creatures scampered right into the ice on the mountainside, intentionally avoiding the bleeding section at the summit where two tall figures stood in observation. They seemed to stand guard over the mountain, holding flaming swords in front of their winged bodies. They seemed immovable and showed no regard for the passing ships. There was no care or concern for the survival or the destruction of the crew. They seemed undisturbed by the scattering creatures or the calamity that they intended. It was obvious that the two large figures were angels.

TALIB'S REALIZATION

Kate sat in the library and wrote in her journal. It was an electronic journal that she saved on a hard disk. She, like her ancestors, took pride in updating the family's progress of their search, and she adamantly recorded a journal of her discoveries. She sat at the computer for three hours, writing in as much detail as she could, the things Fiona claimed to have seen through Talib's dreams.

> After today, there is no doubt that Talib's dreams are evidence of lucid dreaming and the detachment of his soul—or at least part of his soul—from his body. Belair was the second creature we found to have hosted the gabamnoteh. He had similar tendencies to Gorgo. Despite his primitive behavior, he possessed an uncanny ability to manipulate his superiors. He did not voluntarily follow the status quo or conform to the norms of his clan. Like Gorgo, Belair possessed incredible strength and had eyes that were noticeably different from the others. It is my belief that the eyes hold the key to beings who are possible hosts to gabamnoteh. In addition, a second clue relates to the possibility of merging objects between spiritual and physical planes. This was evident in Talib's dream when a native referred to as "the Mother" made a magical sphere; she did this by using both elements common to men and a

separate substance with origins from a spiritual realm. When I compare that story to the use of the bow by the natives in the Gorgo dream, there are at least two elements or weapons on this earth that are linked to powers in the spiritual plane.

What is also apparent from Talib's dream is that there are other spirits invested in the search for the hidden gabamnoteh. It is as if the spirits want to reincarnate the Nephilim as much as do we. It is unclear as to what type of spirits they are and what their intentions are, but Talib did identify a sigil in one of his dreams. After Fiona recreated an image of that the spirit burned into a tree trunk, my research discovered it to be the mark of the demon Andras—the same as mentioned in the scroll. I speculate that a band of unfriendly energies seek to use the Nephilim for unknown reasons.

Kate was interrupted by an Ethiopian servant who often busied herself inside the family library. Kate always thought she did a remarkable job with the cleaning and polishing. She loved the way the servant made the library feel as if a serene spell had been cast over it. The servant brought tea, placed on a silver tray with a porcelain bowl of honey and teacup, and set it near Kate. At Kate's request, she filled the cup. Kate was pleased. It seemed to her that this Ethiopian was born to service others; her decorum was always peaceful, and even the tea seemed to taste better when she served it.

Returning to her thoughts, Kate realized that she needed to speak to Talib about her discoveries and suspicions. She feared that, as the reoccurring nightmares diminished, his desire to stay and assist them would go away as well. Kate concluded that the secrecy of his function would endure for only a short time. She needed another way to hook him. She knew that Talib's complete cooperation and conscious commitment were the most important ingredients for their success. She was certain that her uncle, Daniel, had already disclosed their very significant discovery to members of the Brotherhood and that they believed that, at some point in the very near future, they would reclaim the missing scroll.

She decided to break the news to Talib after his second lesson of meditation so he would have full disclosure. Two months had passed since Talib first arrived, and Kate hoped she had won enough of his trust to allow her the privilege of guiding him as she guided Fiona. She had become extremely happy and proud of the many things Fiona could do. Kate was certain that they would both make extraordinary accomplishments with Talib's help and partnership.

The second meditation lesson began with a focus on the second energy center. "You will need to raise the Kundalini a little higher," Kate said. "When you have mastered ... or at least are able to open the energy center at the root, you allow the Kundalini to flow through it into the second center and strengthen your spirit."

Talib followed her instructions and peered at the painted image on the ceiling. It was designed with an orange hue. The image bore a crescent centered within three circles; attached to one circle were six petals. Kate explained that the second energy center was the swadhisthama. "It is the center that radiates your emotional energy. Without this, you become emotionally imbalanced. Without healthy emotional energy, there is little hope of freedom and spiritual autonomy." She hesitated. "Do you know what spiritual autonomy is?"

"No," Talib said.

"When one obtains spiritual autonomy, he or she gains the ability to give and receive positive energy from others into the world. It was the freedom of spiritual mobility that allowed great men and women to endure persecution and—despite their unbearable trials—influence and inspire the world. There is a change to this world that I am sure you wish to make. That cannot happen if you are ruled by hatred from those who caused you misery."

She watched Talib's eyes fall as if to admit his shame, and she understood that his emotional cup was indeed filled with hatred and remorse. Kate knew that it was important for him to release and control the flow of his emotional energy, and she explained the necessary meditation sequence to heal the damaged chakra.

She asked him to sit with folded legs, and when he was comfortable, she placed a cardboard box in front of him. It was no larger than the area of his palm. Following Kate's instructions, Talib removed the lid to find small slips of paper that were varied in color. Kate asked him to think of something that caused him grief as it related to guilt. "When something comes to mind, take a blue one and place it in the box."

Talib pondered for a moment and then placed a blue slip of paper in the box. Yellow, as Kate explained, represented things that embarrassed him. Red stood for anger, and green was for remorse. When Talib had thoughts of any of these emotions, he took a paper strip and placed it inside the box as instructed. He closed his eyes and imagined, by Kate's command, a tunnel of water.

She told him to breathe deeply and release the air slowly. "Expand your chest," she said. Her voice was low, almost a whisper. "Tell yourself that you see yourself as water."

As the meditation went on, two other people gravitated toward Talib. They took a seat on either side of him. One was an older man who was starting to gray at the edges. The second was just barely older than Talib. He was Kate's cousin, a college student home on holiday. They each brought a box that they placed in front of their legs.

Kate continued. "Say to yourself, 'I reflect things as they are. I am like water. I see myself as water. I am calm. I am cool. I reflect things as they are.'"

Kate invited the group of three to repeat the statements inwardly. She explained that air was like water. It flowed through their veins, destined to cleanse every cell in their bodies and fill them with orange passion and love. The water represented a flow of passionate energy that traveled up the sacrum to gather into the lower abdomen—just above the genitals. "There is where life begins; there is where creation flourishes." Kate implored them all to concentrate on the flow of their love and creativity. She explained that the energy would elevate to their chests and into their facial features until the musculature generated a smile. "Fill that area with your love and your joy."

She turned their attention to the cubes in front of them. "Don't forget about the box. That box is inside your tunnel—the tunnel of happiness, creativity, and love. You must smash the box."

Kate watched as Talib obeyed. He kept his eyes closed as he reached out and placed an opened palm atop the box.

"Smash it," Kate commanded. "Destroy the obstacles in front of you. Allow the orange water wash away the obstacles."

It was the longest session she and Talib had together. She was impressed with his tenacity and willingness.

When he opened his eyes, he felt a tingling sensation somewhere deep behind his navel. As Talib explained that feeling to Kate, he smiled.

She was satisfied with his headway into understanding the flow of energy within him. "Come," Kate said. "This is the perfect time to chat."

When Talib stood, Kate noticed the charm under his shirt. She was pleased to see that he had not lost his attachment to it. They left the meditation room and joined Fiona inside the arts-and-crafts room where she was busy painting the bleeding ice mountain in much the same way that Talib had dreamt it.

"It's Tartarus," she said. "Do you like it?"

Talib admitted that he liked the painting, but he confessed to knowing nothing about Tartarus.

"It is a prison," Fiona said. "We used to hear stories about a great battle long ago between the gods and the titans. The gods were born to the Titan of Time, Chronis, but he was afraid that his children would grow more powerful than he and rule the universe in his place. Since he wanted to prevent them from taking over, he ate four of them. He was as greedy and selfishness as he was afraid. In all, he had six children. The two who survived were Poseidon and Zeus. When they grew into older and stronger gods, they rescued their three sisters and brother from Chronis's belly and became a united force. This started a war between the gods and titans. The gods had help from the Cyclopes who made weapons for them to battle the powerful titans. When the gods made their victory, they imprisoned the titans in Tartarus."

"Children were told that story all throughout history," Kate said. "The truth is that Tartarus is actually a real place. Beings are trapped there. I think they are imprisoned because they made pacts with men—human beings stood to benefit from the knowledge these creatures have. We were told a story about a titan called Prometheus who was kind to the men; he was their friend and ally. The world was young, and people lived like barbarians and cavemen. The world was cold, and they had to scramble for heat to survive. Most of the immortals had no care about suffering men, but Prometheus was different. He had a heart for helping mankind, and he threw a lightning bolt against a tree, causing it to burn with fire. From then on, men learned to use the heat for cooking food and keeping their babies warm. Prometheus, however, was punished by the gods. By day, birds were summoned to eat at his liver, and by night, his body healed—only to be eaten the next day. These tales make nice bedtime stories, but they exist to tell us about real spirits: the merciless ones, the helpful ones, and even those that are dangerous.

"Talib, I want you to know that our mission is to connect

all of mankind, including ourselves, to those spirits who were punished or unjustly trapped in Tartarus—just like Prometheus." She hesitated and chose her words carefully to avoid frightening or offending him. Kate was completely aware of Talib's continued connection to his Islamic faith. "Not all people support us. Our very own great grandfather, Alex, did everything he could to prevent my birth—and Fiona's—because he did not believe in our mission."

Talib had heard many stories about Kate and Fiona's ancestors, and each of them seemed mutually accepting of the global influence and spiritual pursuits of the coming generations, but to learn of a rogue—an ancestor who did not approve—was interesting to him.

Kate reminded him about Adam, who was recommended to the Brotherhood by Charles. Adam lived a long life. He survived to mourn the deaths of his dear friend Charles, his son Marcus, and his grandson Antonios. He was around long enough to see four generations of Charles's offspring become members of the Brotherhood. During that time, the Enlightened Titans' membership reached far across the globe, spanning five continents. They devised chapters and ranks of varying degrees, which depended on a member's loyalty, wealth, and knowledge. When a member "learned his craft," he was promoted or at least given the chance to advance in his entitlement within the organization. Dividends of brotherhood investments were allotted and increased based on a formula between what was invested and the member's level of rank. When an affiliate was promoted to a higher level, he was made privy to esoteric knowledge as well as the Brotherhood's political, spiritual, and financial involvement. In some cases, that member was charged with assignments, called orders, which in many cases involved access to parliamentary or congressional proceedings. Some of their members were appointed presidents of large corporations, banks, and nations. All of their "successes" came under the tutelage of Adam who, in

time, became senior governor of the Brotherhood. He passed on
the tradition of rituals and ceremonies to other members to carry
on after he had passed away. Through these rituals, the barrier that
existed between the realms of men and spirits had been breached.
Consequently, Adam believed there were many other spirits who
had access to the world of men.

One year before Adam died, he offered his leadership position
to Alexander who, uncontested, became the youngest member
since Charles to take such a pivotal role. Adam saw something
special in Alexander that reminded him of Charles—his great-
grandfather. It was something that seemed to go undetected in
Alexander's predecessors. Unlike Adonis and Antonios, Alexander
had the same gray hue to his eyes that Charles had. His hair was
black and slightly straighter than his father's. He had a knack for
understanding things right away, especially the wording of the
scrolls. By this time, the Brotherhood had completely deciphered
the two scrolls, but they had not completely understood their
meanings.

Adam explained that the minds of men were "problems" that
caused interference and prevented them from fully understanding
many things. The scrolls told stories about the lives of different
men, stemming all the way back to the first man and boy—killed
in his youth for being able to cross the barriers between man and
spirit.

"That boy could have been a great man," Adam said. "He
was able to see the spirits, talk to them freely, and interact with
them just the same as he did with men. For him, the two were
not different from each other. Even though the young lad could
cross into their world without meditation, when he did meditate,
he could project his consciousness into the deepest corners of the
spirit world and the realm of two types of spirts for that matter—
not just one. But he was murdered. It was such a travesty, with his
death, thousands of secrets went to the universe. The true power
of men, the essence and nature of the universe, and the book of

life disappeared with his death. But the third scroll suggested that he could return according to the will of men. It suggested that the soul of the once-enlightened man was hidden in the world. If men persisted, they could reincarnate the soul of the enlightened man, embodied by a child naturally brought into this world."

Adam lay in bed with ninety decades behind him. He was compelled to submit to death, being tired and without energy for most of the time in the fall of his life. Proud of his work, Adam still felt the urge to do more and learn more, but his feeble body imposed despondent limits on him. He felt, sadly enough, that the least he could do was put Alexander on the path to carry on with his work. There was something in addition to the second scroll that begged to be found. He hoped that his words were inspirational enough to Alexander to invoke a relentless search.

"We could lean the cures to every sickness the world will ever know. A universe without war is in our grasp. Please take care to read the scrolls a third, fourth, and fifth time. They hint at the resurrection of that boy's soul. There are two spirits hiding in the world; one is the interpreter, and the other is a seeker. The seeker is the key. He will know how to locate the third scroll. It does not give random information about landscapes and prisons, although it might appear that way. It tells us of particular spirits that are trapped and imprisoned because they wished to aid and assist mankind."

"Aid us in what?"

"Christian teachings—both Catholic and Protestant—that angels were cast out of heaven. This may all be false information. Do you recall the story of the titan Prometheus?"

"Yes. He used a lightning bolt to make fire for men. Zeus punished him by binding him in a mountain, and Zeus sent an eagle every day to eat his liver."

Adam paused. He was proud that Alexander remembered the bedtime stories. At that point, Adam regretted waiting so long to explain the deeper truth behind the myths. He hoped that his approaching darkness—the winter of his life—would stay for just a short while. He smiled at Alexander.

"It's a nice story," he said and breathed deeply to calm his racing heart. "It's more than a story; it's a message. We've heard these stories and taught them to our children, but they are not for mere entertainment. The scrolls confirm these messages to be true. Prometheus represents the kindness that spirits bestow upon men. Zeus represents authoritative and dominating spirits that control men and make us eternally dependent. In all the stories, Zeus was a tyrant and rapist; as such, he represents the pending darkness that will eclipse the world if the brotherhood fails. In this story, men were cold and had little to protect them from the elements. The bitter cold symbolizes mankind's dependency on one group of spirits based on their overall lack of knowledge. The first man, Adam, was in the garden with no knowledge of himself or his true power. When that knowledge was made available to him, both he and the spirits who opened his eyes were punished. That knowledge and Prometheus's lightning bolt are one and the same. He provided man the greatest tool for survival that ever existed at that time: fire. For that, he was punished. Now, other spirits wish to liberate and empower us just as Prometheus did, and they are forever imprisoned. As it is written, the wisest of all spirits was imprisoned when it tried to teach men to seek out the Book of Life.

"Now this is important. The boy was killed in a ritual. His soul was splintered into many parts and hidden throughout the world. These segments, torn and separated, are parts of his soul that the scroll refers to as the gabamnoteh. These gabamnoteh are nothing more than energy. If energy can be separated, it can also be reunited. I believe we are able to recreate this child. That child can be born right here and trained by the Brotherhood. He can learn his true power and purpose. Through the Brotherhood, that child can bring order to the universe and teach all mankind his true ability."

Adam asked for water for his parched throat. Alexander watched the old man drink and patiently waited for him to continue. He could barely keep his eyes open. Sleep was heavy on them, but he had more to say and felt that if he did not speak to his heart's desires, he would not get a second chance.

"There are other clues," he continued. "Stories apart from the scrolls give us information as well. I did not know until very recently, but the Orpheus myth, it is a clue. Orpheus is the boy, he is Yaron." He laughed slightly then started to cough from his dry throat. After drinking more water, he spoke again. "Our ancestors have been trying to tell us about this for a thousand years. We are all so very blind. Find the seeker and the reader, and then we can resurrect Orpheus—the savior of the universe."

That was the last conversation Alexander had with Adam before he died. If he had known better, he would have refused a trip to the Far East with John Caradoc, a member of the Brotherhood who served as a diplomat for the British Parliament. John had recently married the highly sought-after Catherine Bargration and cut his postmarital enjoyments short to serve both his government and the Brotherhood's interests. Alexander joined him, hoping that his involvement would expedite John's trip and assist him with a more important mission: extending the idea of a central bank in China.

The Chinese were tough negotiators, and many members of the Brotherhood did not believe that diplomacy would work. They preferred war. Alexander, convinced that he could find a window of opportunity did not expect that, in doing so, he would find himself in a moral dilemma. In the end, cognitive dissonance prevailed allowing him to reason that, since the Chinese showed no concern about how the influx of Chinese goods into Western Europe affected the economy and the Brotherhood's money flow, he should hold the same amount of concern about the Chinese people suffering from an inevitable opium epidemic that was about to be inflicted upon them. He reached this conclusion while sitting in a discussion with John and Emperor Daoguang.

Alexander, John, and the emperor met in a remarkable garden at the perfect time of day when a mixture of lilac and rose scents gently wafted through the air. Alexander, so impressed with the emperor's landscape, later had an imitation of it recreated at his mansion. Guards surrounded them. The three gentlemen sipped tea while Emperor Daoguang reiterated to John everything that had previously been disclosed to the Chinese diplomat. John insisted that the emperor consider a proposal to allow balanced trade, but Daoguang was firm in his position. According to him, the Chinese people were at utter peace and tranquility. His nation had no need for the imports offered by the Europeans, excepting the silver he had accepted from the British as a "courtesy."

Alexander studied the emperor. There was something he kept hidden, a dark embarrassment—a vice of the Chinese people that he wished not to publicly acknowledge. Understanding this, Alexander leaned over to John and whispered. "Ask him about the opium imports."

"My people do not want the opium in large supply," he answered.

Alexander detected an uneasiness in the emperor's false statement and centered his thoughts on Daoguang's next move. He took notice of his feet, the movement of his hands, and the shifting of his eyes. As Alexander concentrated, his senses became acute, and images of chaos reflected in his mind—people rebelling in the streets, soldiers using opium and being brutally punished. He could sense Daoguang's heart racing in his chest, and Alexander knew that there was considerable concern about Chinese addiction to the drug. That addiction, Alexander understood, was the window of opportunity for the Brotherhood.

Alexander was well versed in politics, and he understood clearly that the Chinese state was extremely self-sufficient. The people had very little need or desire for products from the West, and as long as they remained behind the Great Wall, they would know little of the world outside of it. But war would seize China. The Brotherhood was not about to allow their position in the world to weaken because the scales of trade tilted in Chinese favor. Alexander decided that the Enlightened Titans should manipulate their assets in Russia to instigate tensions against the Chinese emperor. Such an action was not foreign to the organization's members, and the Enlightened Titans had become very good at invoking wars. Alexander, on the other hand, was not a proponent of military strikes. His proposal to smuggle an overwhelming supply of opium into China was an acceptable solution.

"It appears that opium and similarly addictive drugs are a better weapon than cannons," he said to the board upon his return to Bavaria. "I recommend an increase in opium farming and investments. Secondly, we'll have to discover ways to smuggle opium into China and disperse it to the population free of charge. When the people are thoroughly addicted and the demand for the drug increases, the sale and trade of it to the Chinese will be inevitable."

John added that British-controlled India was close enough to both the opium farms in Afghanistan and the Chinese border to create a protected route of transport under the British military command. "Alexander has seen the future," John said. "If we can weaken China from the inside, we can gain access to her economy. I never thought that opium would become our greatest weapon."

John was placed in charge of the special mission and collaborated with politicians in Britain and with naval policymakers. Alexander suggested that John employ a network of spies for the sake of research and information. "We need to know exactly how the people are taking to the drug and if there are any problems with distribution."

Taking Alexander's advice, John employed Eldred Pottinger, a recently elected member of second degree within the Enlightened Titans. Eldred was charged with acting as an Islamic holy man while operating the network. Aside from gaining important information to disseminate to the British at a hefty price, the network uncovered a joint Russo-Islamic plot to destroy the opium farms in Afghanistan. John was concerned, and as always, he relied on Alexander's advice.

"This is no problem," Alexander said. "In fact, it is a blessing. Since we already sell information to the British, we simply tell them that the Russians are planning to invade India. The great king won't dare lose the diamond on his finger. When they send troops, we will have an entire military fleet protecting our opium farms. And if by chance Daoguang tries to cut off trade, the threat of British presence in India and Afghanistan will deter him."

"It is as if we are gods," Pierre Rensselaer said. He was a guest at Alexander's home in Paris where he and his first cousin Henry joined Alexander to report on the American chapter.

From Pierre's limited perspective, it seemed that all was well with Alexander and the Brotherhood, and in some cases, he was correct.

Alexander had many domestic problems that he could never resolve. Unfortunately for Alexander, Olivia heard what Pierre said. Alexander's marriage to Olivia was an arrangement between his father and a man who owed him a big debt. Olivia was an extremely attractive seventeen-year-old girl. At first, she was struck by the lavish lifestyle that Alexander offered, but as he soon learned, his wife's Orthodox Christian upbringing was incredibly problematic for his endeavors. Pierre's declarations only reinforced rumors that Alexander and the Brotherhood had made a pact with the devil and often performed Satanic rituals.

After Pierre said what he did, the distance between them grew, and although Alexander was aware of her thoughts and fears, he had no power to change them. Instead, he resolved to endure her diatribes and accusations of his evil affairs while holding his torn family together by a mutual love for his son. Alex's birth made Alexander realize he was no longer able to read people as he once could. He assumed at first that the ability faded with stress and age. He waited nearly fifty years to become a father; but then he learned that the reality of his dulled ability was that he passed the gift onto his son while somehow losing it within himself. Alexander was plagued by this fact.

As one might guess, the strain of conflicting ideas between the in-laws had its effect on young Alex. He often heard his mother protesting the presence of a visitor from time to time. She refused to accompany him at certain gathering, and at times, she spent nights with the young Alex, sharing his bed, crying when she thought that he was asleep. Alexander was often gone away from home. The Brotherhood's business was increasingly demanding on him as the American Civil War seemed to have no end in sight and the betrayal of Bismarck against the Brotherhood to push for an annexation of the duchies to Prussia threatened to alter the balance of power in Europe. Then there was a strong sentiment against the Brotherhood in France as the young revolutionary minds sought to expose any and all secret societies

With such heavy involvement, Alexander saw very little of his son during his formative years. As a result, the child, through no desire of his own, he was heavily indoctrinated by the church dogma. He spent much of his time learning about God and the Virgin Mary while his father's symbols were in plain sight at home. Some of the symbols were so obvious that his mother covered them, but others were left exposed—like the owl centered on their dinner table, a pyramid engraved on a door, a butterfly on a ring, or a flamed torch that symbolized the Brotherhood.

Despite her objections, Alex never stirred his attention away from his father's stories about the scrolls and his ancestors on those rare occasions where he actually saw his father. As a teen, he won just enough of his father's trust to gain access to the family's library and the journals of his ancestors. He was incredibly intrigued and did not hesitate to read and absorb the adventures in the journals. Despite his intrigue, the gray-eyed youth chose not to join the Brotherhood. With all he learned and with all the benefits at his fingertips, Alex could not help but feel ashamed of his father's associations.

Alex did not take well to his gift. Experiencing the thoughts and feelings of others was not a thrill for him. It taunted him with nightmares. At times, when he sat among members of the Brotherhood, he would envision the malice of their intentions. In his dreams, he lived the consequences of war. People suffered from hunger, disease, cold weather, and homelessness. He witnessed the disregard for them in the eyes of the Brotherhood members and felt their pain.

As Alex grew older, he wished to spend more time apart from Titan affiliates, his father, and—at times—his mother. Oddly, he never lost his passion for reading and studying. When his father asked about his fixation on the journals, Alex said, "I want to know how evil I am."

One day, not many years after making that remark, Alex's father tried to convince him to consider marriage.

Alex replied, "I've thought about your proposal very long, and although I love you, I will disappoint you."

Alexander was indeed disappointed. As an only child, the legacy of a long history of family tradition rested in the loins of his rebellious son.

Alex said, "I learned something from the scrolls. Well, at least I made some connections."

"What connections?" Alexander asked.

They were alone in the family library, a place where Alex was commonly found. The boy was brilliant and had an acute sense of insight. He understood the writing between the lines, and sense he could read into a person's thoughts, there was very little that escaped him.

Alex endured emotional conflict for his entire life, and at the ripe age of twenty-three, he chose to learn the truth behind that conflict. He was curious about why his mother insisted on having no decorations on his bedroom walls—they were all painted a single color. He wanted to know why his father's associates were the kindest and most gentle people he knew, yet they harbored sinister greed and thirst for power over other men. His mother's influence would suggest that what he noticed in those kind men was their tendency toward evilness due to their opposition to the love of Jesus Christ. When he found the same gloom and disposition in the clergymen, his bewilderment increased. These "men of God" looked only for the evil in men with intent to exploit their weaknesses for what they believed was the only way to save a man's soul. Ironically, his father's associates looked for the good things, the talents, and the skills of men. They encouraged him to read and learn the sciences and attend the more prestigious universities. What was so evil about that?

Alex resolved to attend Oxford, and the question of man's origin dominated his four years of study there. In June of his first year, he attended a debate between devout Christian intellectuals and scientists who adopted Charles Darwin's explanation of mankind's origins. Thomas Henry Huxley a friend to the Brotherhood, Alexander's close friend took the young Alex under his wing and often talked about the nature of men. He once had a prestigious debate at that very school with an equally intelligent man, Benjamin Brodie, and Oxford continued to buzz from that debate, many years later. He spoke of another member of the Brotherhood who wrote Alex's letter of recommendation to Oxford, before Alex grew his first tooth. Robert FitzRoy died, before Alex was a full year old, but the letter of recommendation, held for nearly two decades continued to hold weight at Oxford. He was naturally curious of FitzRoy and spent many hours reading his methods of predicting weather. He had some interesting conclusions and theories regarding astronomy, something that Alex was cautioned against by his mother, but Alex considered that Robert was not a bad guy, sense he openly acknowledged the saints and the authority of God in his writings. He was not a member of the Brotherhood, but he did use their money to conduct research. At any rate, Alex felt obligated to learn about Mr. FitzRoy and he came to admire him.

When it was nearly time to graduate from Oxford, Alex disclosed to Huxley that he would not join the Brotherhood. His experiences at Oxford inclined Alex to consider the flaws in his parents and compelled him to learn about the conflicting sides. This progressed into relentless study of the Orthodox Church— the religious lessons as well as its history. Although not a member of the Brotherhood, he had access to the interpretations of the scrolls and the journals left behind by his grandfather and his grandfather's grandfather. The journals dated all the way back to Joseph Konstantinos.

He had not completed his self-discovery or understood his place in the universe and doubted that he ever would as one subject or school of thought inevitably led him to another, which required even more study. Alex had arrived at that conclusion that, in the end, he was inherently evil.

Alexander said "Son, we've been through this before—"

"No! I am inherently evil. This is what I've learned. It's no one's fault. No one is to blame. Do you remember teaching me about the seeker and the interpreter?"

Alex had been twelve years old at the time.

"Well, my study of the scrolls, the journals, and what people wrote about what is in the scrolls explained that there are spirits hiding in the world. They use humans to survive, taking their energy from the souls of their hosts as if they were spiritual leaches. The interpreter spirit has the ability to read the dreams of men and understand them. It invades the thoughts and emotions of people and manipulates them. They call it the helper of the Nephilim. Your great-grandfather Charles wrote about a spirit being a conscious force of energy that can compel men to act—if that man so allowed. This is how the third scroll begins. It speaks of the ability of a spirit to compel men, so when people claim that the devil made them do things, they are partly correct. I know you refute that there is a devil, one supreme evil spirit, and I agree with you to a point. However, what name we give a spirit is irrelevant, and if these spirits are no more than energy with consciousness, how do you explain my own amplified conscious energy that allows me to see and feel what others think or feel? Something inside Charles allowed him to absorb or connect with the conscious energy of other people. The same was once with you. When you chose to concentrate enough on someone, you were able to see much about them. Is that not true?"

"That was a long time ago ... before you were born," Alexander said. "It was a gift, son."

"I doubt that it has all left you. Nothing can stay with a man so long and leave nothing behind. Did you not use that gift to advance the missions of the Brotherhood? Was it not because of your gift that the British now control the world? Better yet, the Brotherhood controls the world—and Great Britain is the face of the Brotherhood. Wasn't it Charles who used his gift to create the American Policy of Stability? When will that take effect? When will the Brotherhood rip that country in half? 'To stabilize America, we only need to take away their slaves.' Well, that is happening now, is it not?"

Alex was aware that the Brotherhood had long since calculated the growth progression of the Americas—it was written in Antonios's journal. They had already become the best of cotton-producing nations. They created a very effective navy and had already sharpened their skills of war against Muslim pirates in the Mediterranean. The hands and support of the Brotherhood amplified their growth, and Adam Weis once described it as their favor with the spirits who gladly accepted the American offerings of blood and sacrifice. The process of slowing American growth had already taken affect. Laws were passed, and the British navy had run interferences against the transport of slaves across the Atlantic for nearly one hundred years. The policy of balancing

American lands between free and slave-holding states had been in effect for some time, and it effectively slowed the growth of the nation which allowed the Brotherhood to invest in the development of industry and factory work. It was inevitable that the Brotherhood would disallow free labor to interfere with the growth of the American economy.

"'In order for industry to explode, slavery must eventually phase out,'" Alex repeated the words of another brother—an American who predicted that the nation would fall into a civil war. It was only through war that the opportunity would present itself to shape the production of goods in America to follow the model that was already used in Europe.

"This gift is not a gift." Alex continued. "Nor is it a curse. It is the energy of the spirit 'interpreter' that is in me. It became part of me when you fertilized your wife at my conception. It is a part of my entire existence, and the only way to destroy it is for me to have no offspring."

As Alex expected, Alexander did not refute what his son said. Instead, he suggested that Alex continue his research, saying, "Perhaps you'll discover something to make the world a better place."

"A better place for whom?" Alex asked.

"I don't know," his father replied. "Perhaps that will also be for you to decide."

Alex spent the remainder of his life in constant turmoil. His father died a few years later, and Olivia—choosing total separation from the family—packed her bags and left for a life of seclusion in Milan. Alex visited from time to time when he needed to clear his head, but Olivia did not allow that to happen with her constant insistence that he leave his life behind and join her in the safe boundaries of a peaceful city.

Alex, however, felt safe inside the mansion that was his inheritance. When Alexander died, he passed his seat on the governing board to his cousin's son, Randel, who—according to

Alex—was a sinister man who wished to rule the world. This did not stop Alex from loving his cousin dearly. If nothing else, he was humored by his cousin's fixation on Russia. From time to time, Alex entertained Randel with thoughts of undermining the tsars for the sake of an egalitarian model.

Alex despised any involvement with the political and tyrannical undertakings of the Brotherhood. With three relatives serving as governing members, it was very difficult to have visits without them questioning his special insights. He was fully aware of their motivations every time they arrived at the mansion, but Alex was torn between his love for his cousins and his moral convictions. He often submitted an ear to their questions. He once explained to Randel that the world in no way would become a safer place with the consolidation of the German states, a political move that Randal often celebrated. "The Marxist government that you like was perhaps the best model for them. However, the Marxist were undermined and outwitted. Georg Graf and the counts of Caprivi, Caprera, and Montecucoli all supported Bismarck. Even now, after all these years, their ideas are the strongest and their supporters remain as strong as they are wealthy. If there will be a Marxist government, it will not start in Germany. The people will not accept it unless it is forced down their throats."

That was the last conversation Alex had with his cousin. As time passed, he spent more time in isolation. He designed a separate wing to his home that was accessible by one long hallway and a single door. The hallway led to a section at the far east side of the property, giving him access to a garden that he learned to enjoy in place of traveling to Milan. Alex created a pond that he filled with koi; it reminded him of his father. This garden was his haven for resting and reading. Often, he fell asleep beside the water. In his garden, Alex decided to conduct a private ceremony to reach outside of himself and into the multiverse to make a connection or call to something that he knew existed but could not identify. In his understanding, the ceremony was like a distress call. He hoped for a response, but he was not certain he would live long enough to know if the call was heard.

Alex believed that there was some spirit, a gabamnoteh, hiding inside of him, hoping to escape some divine punishment, and somehow imprinted or sealed to his soul. The spirit and his soul were inseparable. As long as the gabamnoteh chose to remain within him and part of him, he was able to use its intellectual energy to read and understand the thoughts, feelings, and intentions of others. Upon marriage and conception, the spirit would detach from him and harness onto the unborn baby. Alex believed that there was another spirit dormant, waiting to be found — or at least waiting for a specific time when to find him and entice him to work as a companion for some grand scheme - perhaps to resurrect Orpheus.

There was more information to gather than what Alex believed could be gathered in a single lifetime. Whatever secrets the spirits hid, he believed that he could foil their plan. He would summon them; perhaps the one identified in the scrolls as the seeker would get the message and seek him out. When that happened, Alex believed that a simple murder—homicide—would damn his soul but save humanity.

When he first set out to perform the spiritual ritual, he was ashamed by the idea that his mother would be disappointed in him. However, he believed he was infected with evil, and as such, it was to no fault of his own that he would summon the evil outside of him by performing an evil act. When he completed the ritual, Alex had little concern for the slit in his palm from the voluntary, self-inflicted cut used to personalize his spell. He buried the knife and the cloth it was wrapped in beside the pond. There was blood on both. Then he searched for liquor. He wanted to drink himself into a stupor, become madly intoxicated, and lose himself in pity until sleep took over him.

He spent many nights after his father's death drinking wine. He tried unsuccessfully to empty every bottle within his chamber, but sleep fell over him before he could finish the second bottle. Alex was slouched in a chair, leaning over the glass table where he often ate breakfast. He would have perhaps bled to death if not for the chambermaid—the only person with access to his quarters—who arrived just before midnight to offer him tea. Alex often kept himself busy until late hours with his studies and research. He had become accustomed to a cup of tea that revived his study energy.

On that day, Alex needed no tea. He required medical care. The chambermaid, Aida, noticed the light from the lamps casting a glow on droplets of blood on the floor. She saw Alex in his slouched position and spied the wine bottles and shards of glass that were scattered across the floor and the table. Alex's arm hung at his side, allowing the blood to flow endlessly from his hand. Aida immediately came to his aid, cleaned the wound, and wrapped his hand in cloth bandages. His eyes opened as she tended to him, and he called her name.

"Yes, my lord?"

"You are the only one who cares for me."

"I think I am the only one who is given a chance," she replied. She tried to help him to bed, but he was too heavy. She asked him to give a little more effort.

Alex stood, propping himself against her for the sake of keeping balance. His eyes were barely opened, but he saw Aida clearly. She had full lips, dark eyes, and long, dark hair. Although she was Egyptian, Aida's skin was pale. Alex often asked her how she got that way. She insisted her father was dark and that her mother was partly Macedonian. Alex joked that the Macedonian in her caused him to adore her so. The truth was that he could see her purity. Aida had a clean soul, and her every thought was an offering of service to him. She was young and on that night, she appeared more beautiful than he could remember.

"Why do you treat me so well?" Alex staggered to the bed. "Why don't you look at me as if I am a creature, some animal, or perverse imp?"

She did not answer.

"Why don't you?" he asked again.

"Because you are not as such. You are a kind and gentle man."

"No." Alex shook his head. "No, I am not. You don't believe that. I can see your thoughts, but you cannot see mine." They reached the bed, and he fell to it, pulling her of top of him. "I've lusted over you." He did not hold her against her will.

Aida quickly rolled off him and stood next to the bed.

"I am evil!" he yelled, and then he started to cry.

Aida pitied him, but Alex did not want her pity. He wanted love—pure and simple. He tugged at his shirt but was unable to pull it over his head.

Aida moved closer to him and assisted. When she removed his shirt, his hands fell at her waist. He sobbed and leaned over to rest his head in her bosom. "Why are you so kind to me?"

Alex was not in control of his actions, but he was very aware of what he did. There was something compelling him to hold Aida tightly and kiss her belly. Perhaps it was the smell of her slightly scented hair or the touch of her hand when she bandaged him. Her embrace around his waist was arousing when she helped him to the bed, and despite his promise that he would not engage in a sexual experience, his entire body yearned for her. Aida was a spring shower in his desert of despair. She was soft, tender, and pure—in stark contrast of what he believed himself to be.

He knew that Aida wanted no part of his advances, yet he persisted. In his persistence, he reconciled himself to be as evil as he imagined himself to be. He knew that Aida did not want to jeopardize her employment, but despite her desire to resist, she wanted to protect his pride. He knew she would not reject him, and in that, he felt permitted to indulge himself in her flesh—an act that he had never before committed.

Aida lay motionless under Alex's will and power. She cried gentle tears as she—without objection—allowed him to steal her innocence.

When Alex had fallen asleep, Aida crawled from his bed and quietly left the room. That was the last time he saw her. Aida did not just simply escape the shame of his bed; she escaped the mansion and the island as well. Alex asked about her when he noticed that Louis, his cousin and caretaker of the mansion and its affairs, had replaced Aida with a different servant. Louis admitted that Aida had returned to Egypt. She was to attend a school in Cairo. Alex tried to read his cousin to determine the credibility of his statements, but he failed. Something had happened, and it seemed as if he had lost his gift. The thought frightened him. Alex realized that he had betrayed himself that night. He knew that he had passed his seed onto the servant girl—and the gabamnoteh inside of him was no longer there.

Upon such realization, Alex flew into a rage. He threw chairs, broke the glass table, and cursed his life. He once believed he had the opportunity to save the world, but now he understood that he had wasted it. "The evil inside me has been unleashed, and it was done in my moment of weakness."

For three days, Alex could barely eat. He concluded that he did not wish to live any longer. He contemplated suicide, but he did not want to die in pain. He tried to drink himself to his death, but he merely fell into a deep sleep. It was not often that an intoxicated man is aware of his dreams and far less normal that he remembers them, but one night, Alex was fully aware of what he dreamt. The memory brought warm feelings as it involved his mother and him as a young boy. They had gone to a fair where she allowed him to ride a dobby. Alex was excited to see it and most anxious to ride. He chose the black horse for his riding pleasure. His mother stood on the side, just outside of the ropes that were used to direct the flow of traffic to a single point of entry. A man in a black top hat sat on a real horse that pulled the dobby in its rotation. Around and around, Alex moved up and down, while watching his mother smile each time he passed. She was worried that, despite smiling and waving at him, he would fall due to his

unwillingness to hold onto the straps. The wooden horse slid up
and down a pole that extended from the center of its back. It was
an extra safety measure, but Alex had no intention of riding safely.
He wanted to increase his adventure by using no hands. Then, just
as his mother feared, he fell. He dreamt he heard her scream, but
instead of hitting the platform, something else happened.

Instead, the bottom of the platform opened. Alex saw himself
walking through the opened doors of an amphitheater. It was an
old, dark place, and the walls were made of rocks. Just front and
center, there was a stage with strange markings on the platform; a
play was about to begin. He quietly took a seat behind two others
who, besides himself, were the only ones present. The two people,
one male and the other female, were very similar in appearance,
and Alex instantly understood that they were twins.

"Are you ready?" the male asked her.

She said yes.

They stood, without taking notice of Alex, and walked down
the steps to the platform. As they walked, Alex heard a commotion
behind him. The door he passed through was closed shut, and
the noises behind it grew louder. It was the sound of fighting—
something like war.

Alex was not comfortable sitting alone and walked down the
steps toward the platform. At the far side was a door—and to the
right was another.

The boy escorted his sister to the door on the right, reached
for a paintbrush that seemed to come from nowhere, and painted
a symbol on the door. "This was our father's mark," he said. "Now
it is mine."

His sister looked at him. Her gray eyes were electric. "How is
it that you are not afraid?"

"When you see the mark, you will know that I am with you,"
he said. While he reached out to embrace her, the door opened.
A man in a hooded robe walked through it. In his hand, he held

a dagger. Without any word or warning, he stabbed the dagger into the boy's back.

The girl, in fear, released her brother. He fell lifelessly to the platform. She raced across the platform to another other door. There was a mark on it, but Alex could not see it clearly. She opened the door, and it swung in toward her. Inside was another door and another and another, each door slightly smaller than the previous one—and each bearing the symbol that Alex could not readily identify. When she seemed to realize that there was no escape from the approaching man in the hooded robe, she turned to see him getting closer to her. She inhaled and allowed her emotions to fade into numbness. Alex could feel her calming into a meditation. He could feel her emotions as if they were his. She accepted her fate—she was going to die. Rather than fearing the inevitable, she resolved to accept it. "Kabeir, please find me," she said.

Alex watched the hooded figure thrust his dagger forward to slaughter her. His motions were heartless and void of any emotion. Alex was terrified. His eyes shifted to the right, but the body of the male victim was no longer there. He looked to the left, and the girl had also instantaneously disappeared. The hooded man was with her. Alex was alone in the amphitheater. He could clearly see the symbol on the door where the male died. It was a square and a shape like the letter Y underneath it, off-centered to the right. Alex understood the symbol's meaning. He did not know how, as it was foreign to him, but he knew that it was an abstract image of Atlas holding the world above his head. Inside the square representation of the world, thirteen circles were interlocked. They represented the fruit of life.

The door to the left was now closed, and there was nothing to obstruct the view of the symbol carved into it. Alex walked toward the door. He could see that the symbol was shaped like the letter sigma, turned backward. It was slightly disfigured in that some of the edges were rounded so that it appeared to take on the form of an Egyptian cobra. Alex recognized the symbol. He walked closer and saw that it was indeed what he suspected—a reverse image of his family seal. When Alex saw this, he was startled out of his sleep with the awareness that the symbol on the door was the mirrored reflection of his family's sigil as created by Charles Stannis, his gray-eyed ancestor.

Alex startled from his sleep, sat up in his bed, and looked into the dining area of his chamber. He could see no beams of sunlight falling through the window; dawn was far away. Climbing out of bed, he expected to be wary and hungover, but it seemed that he had no lingering side effects from the night's intoxication. He walked to the dining area and sat at the glass table, a similar design to the one he destroyed. He thought for a moment about the irony that Louis loved to provide him with transparent tables when his life was far from transparency. For a moment, he simply stared out the window – another transparent object. Then he moved to it. He wanted to see the sky. There were times when he could see Venus in the horizon—but not so on that day. He contemplated one glass more wine or a cup of tea. A cup of tea meant that he needed to leave his private section of the mansion and enter the common areas. It had been over a year since he had seen the kitchen, and he doubted that he would remember where to find a teacup.

As he hesitated with his indifference, the thoughts and visions of the dream became stronger. He could remember very visibly the terrified glare in the twins' gray eyes. He promised to find her. Was he the seeker? Alex began to piece together the events of the dream. He left the window to retrieve paper, ink, and a pen. If his theory was correct, and he was at one time the interpreter, he would be able to understand the dream. He wrote down the details: his mother, the fair, the dobby, the black horse, the man in the top hat, the amphitheater, the twins, the dagger, the man in the hooded robe, and the two doors marked with symbols. The male said that the symbol was his father's symbol, and now it was his symbol. Alex drew the symbol of what he remembered. The square is the symbol of earth, yes; that was the earth, and the figure below it was Atlas. Were the twins two separate spirits who descended from Atlas? Then there was the second door where the girl died. It was his family's sigil on the door as if it was reflected in a mirror.

Charles Stannis had taught his children that the Egyptian cobra was a symbol of royalty and since the family was not members of any royalty class, they could rule the noble lords. His father's statement became their family's moto: It is better to be a kingmaker than to be a king.

After he sketched everything that he could remember from his dream, he explained their perceived meanings and made connections to the scrolls that were his family's treasure. He explained that his spiritual teachings from the Orthodox Church were incorrect; there was never a war in heaven between God and his angels. He wrote that God created angels and other spirits that were known as demons. These demons were not necessarily evil; they had willpower the same as men, and because of this, men and demon were separated by a barrier. He believed that the demons reached out to mankind and asked for help in removing the barrier between them. "Man," he wrote, "has the ultimate power to remove and pass through the barrier for he has the authority on earth."

He wrote that the two doors in his dreams represented the realms that separated men from demons. The symbols on each door were gateways that, if properly manipulated by men, would give him access to cross the threshold into another dimension of reality. He believed and wrote that the threshold should not be crossed. Mankind can do unspeakable things in the universe—both good and bad—but nothing without consequence. *In that we are unable to comprehend our existence through observation as we simultaneously exist in it, we have no way of fully understanding the consequences of our actions. Therefore, when it comes to mergers or pacts between men and spirits—whether they be demon or angel—responsibility suggests that we should differ.*

He explained, in his writings, that the twins were demons that were sacrificed for some unknown reason. He did not believe that the spirits were killed, but they transformed into a lower energy and could hide inside the mortal shell of men while interacting with the spirit world, which he called the astral plane. Having the ability to interact in the physical plane of men and the astral plane of the spirits, these twins were able to track and protect the divided soul of the youth—the Nephilim. If a person, having the energy of these twins, learned to empower it to communicate and travel the earth freely, the locations of every such human host could be located. It is then that the separated soul of the youth can, through sexual reproduction, of those who bear parts of the whole, can recreate the whole. *We must be prudent not to practice such rituals, for if the soul of the child is reborn, it will unlock energies that are currently bound by the commands of angels.*

The most important proponent to the spirits' plan is the seeker. Note the sigil written on this parchment. It is the seeker's sigil. It is important for the survival of mankind to destroy the one who carries this symbol.

He spent three years writing the theories and discoveries that led him to complete his study of the scrolls. More than four thousand parchments were hidden behind a trapdoor under his bed. After his affair with Aida, he hired Francisco Dagtekin, an Ottoman, who promised that he could deploy his gang of mercenaries to find and eliminate any target at any time. Alex wanted him to find Aida, and if she had given birth to a child, Francisco was ordered to assassinate that child. Little did he know, and he never learned that Louis had betrayed him, calling off the mercenaries and employing them for other missions designated by the Brotherhood.

When Talib learned these things, he concluded that there was much that he did not know regarding the universe and the supernatural. For what seemed his entire life, Talib was curious about the spirit world of djinn and angels. He loved to hear stories about Solomon who, according to his Islamic teachings, ruled the kingdoms of men, djinn, and angels. It was those same Islamic teachings that cautioned him against people who interacted with the unseen. He stood in a house with a history of sorcery and magic usage. At times, he thought he had no place there. At other times, he felt himself growing and becoming aware of an intangible world that, as elusive as it seemed, obeyed a set of laws that allowed him and any other man to influence and possibly control his fate therein.

"I know this is all overbearing," Kate said. Her voice was very empathetic. "We need you. The entire universe needs you."

"And what do you think I am or have that you need?"

"We've tested you, and you've passed all of the tests. You never get ill. The shade of your eyes. Aside from your father, have you ever seen an Arab with eyes like yours? You've grown taller since you've been here. Your clothes no longer fit. You speak the angels' language when you sleep. You have an affinity for the supernatural. You dream of spirits. Your dreams are not all dreams. They are messages—messages and memories that come from something deep inside of you. Something ancient is trying to communicate with you. When you reveal them, the reoccurring dream ends. When you saw the scroll, you did not read it, but you knew what it says. You know because you've experienced it. I believe you even remember it. I believe you were there. Not you in the physical sense, but a part of your soul was there. It is attached to you."

"What's attached to me?"

"A gabamnoteh," Kate answered.

Talib shook his head.

"Talib, you found powerful spiritual weapons. You found the hosts of the gabamnoteh that we were searching for. We've searched for centuries, but we were nowhere closer three hundred years later. You've taught me more in two weeks than four hundred years of research could do; if that doesn't convince you, there is one more thing I must show you."

She stood and asked him to join her. He followed with Fiona behind him. They walked to the library, and Kate, using her key, entered. She walked faster than usual. She was determined to convince him of what she had known for some time. She led them to the far end of the library, past the bookshelves to a large iron safe with a combination dial. She barely needed to squat to turn the dial. Talib watched as she moved it right, then left, right, then left again. His heart pounded against his chest when he saw the metal door open. He did not know what to expect, and the fact that what Kate sought to show him was locked away in a safe made him anxious.

"My family has searched many years for the Seeker. The spell that Alex made worked. It did not work right away; things had to happen to make it work. This is how the universe was made. It has its own time frame. For the spirts and the universe, a year is like a minute; a hundred years is like an hour. But my great-grandfather's message did reach Kabeir, and Kabeir came to join his sister. You may not believe me yet, but it is a fact that you have his mark around your neck."

Talib felt a jolt of energy in his chest, and his heart trembled as he continued to deny his connections to the djinni.

Kate stood, turned to him, and held out a laminated piece of parchment. She turned it so Talib could see the sketch that Alex made after his dream. "Is this the charm that you wear around your neck?"

Talib hesitated. He turned and walked away from them. He felt his legs growing weak, and he retreated to a table that bore the carved imaged of the butterfly. Placing the parchment on the table, he reached for his charm and removed it. He had not shown them the charm around his neck—only Theodore had seen it. His words came to Talib again, and Talib finally understood what Theodore meant. There was indeed a connection between the charm, the dreams, and—from what Talib learned in the past weeks—five hundred years of world history.

Seeing his charm sketched on the paper in front of him caused his heart to tremble as he questioned himself and searched for an explanation. Was he the victim of a djinni's trick? Such things, he could accept, but to think that Fiona and the power she possessed was real, and even more a part of him, was frightening.

Kate and Fiona approached him cautiously. The charm he placed beside the sketch was a near-perfect match. They understood that the part of the charm that was shaped like the letter Y was a representation of the titan Atlas. The square shape represented the world, and the gems were perfectly arranged to represent the Fruit of Life.

Kate said, "Each gem made to honor the thirteen sisters."

Fiona said their names as she pointed to each stone, "Aesyle, Ambrosia, Cleeia, Coronis, Eudora, Pedile, Cardie, Phaeote, Phyto, Polyxo, Synecho, Baccho, and Niseis." She pointed to each gem as she said their names.

Kate said, "They were the daughters of Atlas and were all murdered. This is their family seal, their mark, and it belongs to you. You are part of them."

Talib was lost in his fears and unable to deny that the sketch before him was the same as the charm that had been in his family for decades. He, like those who had passed the charm from one generation to the next, was oblivious to the fact that it was the mark of an immortal spirit.

Kate called to him as his mind spun desperately. "Talib, there are others in the world who are like you. We are trying to find them. Before you, we had all the knowledge and the know-how, but we were missing one thing and that was you. There are others like you and Fiona who need your help."

"How can I help them? I can't help myself."

"You can help us find them and train them to protect themselves from ..."

"From what?" Talib asked.

"Danger. There are spirits ... energies that have an agenda that is very dangerous to the entire universe. If they get these people who have a gabamnoteh, they could influence many terrible outcomes."

Talib thought about Umar and the tragedies that were caused by him. "My grandfather was the first to use his gift that way."

Fiona said, "We can make it all right and better for the world. Think of your mother and brother. They stand to gain if you help us."

Talib hung his head. He did not completely understand how finding someone would help save the world. He did, however, want to believe Kate. He thought for a moment that if he had a gift or ability that could benefit the world or put an end to the tragedies he faced, it was only right to use it. With that thought in mind, Talib agreed to help them.

THE REVOLUTION

Now that Talib, through his voluntary commitment, had joined them, Kate was free to give him all the information he needed. She informed him that, according to the scroll, there were two major types of spirits characterized by angel types and demon types. "Inside each type are different species. Now, popular Christian belief is that some angels rebelled against God and were kicked out of heaven after a big war. This is false information. The demons were never angels ... they were what you call djinn. The Christian faith makes no mention of djinn, and as such, that leaves this energy force to move freely through our universe without any confrontation in the Christian societies." She hesitated to give Talib a chance to digest her words.

They sat in the Search Room, dressed in their hooded robes. Talib was outside of the circle and leaned against the trough built at the base of the wall and made into a pool and fountain where the koi swam. He remembered from his religious teachings that there were material differences between angels and djinn.

"At some point, the djinn rebelled, and they fought to take over one level of heaven. They were opposed by the strongest of djinn and thus condemned to our universe. Now it gets complicated. When mankind was made, he was given complete authority of his universe. This means that, to some degree, any djinni or angel that enters our universe is bound by laws that makes it subservient to us. Think about it in the sense where, if you are in the sky, the rules of gravity function differently than if you were in a pool of water. Some djinn accepted these laws, whereas others do not. Those who reject have vowed to destroy all of mankind, but they have a problem. A djinni cannot destroy anything. Destruction only comes by the hands of men. A djinni can cause man to destroy himself or his universe, and if he does, not even an angel will prevent it. The angels are bound to the same laws of our universe."

Talib was fascinated. "You learned all of this from the scroll?"

"Yes," Kate answered. "When you have raised your Kundalini to the fourth level, you will be ready to experience the scrolls for yourself. In the meantime, we need you to help us find those djinn who do not wish or plan for the destruction of men. They are those who we wish to teach us how to defeat those who bring destruction."

Talib finally understood the importance of his work. When Fiona entered, she stood beside the circle without a word. Her eyes told her story of apprehension as she waited for Talib to join her. When he did, and when the candles were lit, Kate passed the libation to Talib. He drank and stared at the image on the clay tablet until sleep overtook him.

Kate stood over them and watched as Talib's dreams took him away to an island tucked away in a gulf just west of the Atlantic. It was adorned with green mountains and wild flowers. It appeared, from a distance, to be a tranquil sanctuary, but nothing was further from the truth. A man with dark skin and black hair climbed out of a small boat and pulled on a chain that was attached to his neck. The sun blinded him. He had spent the entire voyage in the dark cargo area. His hands were also bound, and he tried to cover his almond-shaded eyes to allow the adjustment, but he had no such luck. He needed his hands to keep balance as the Frenchman pulled at his neck with the chain until finally coming to a stop to stand before his new slave master.

"My god, you are tall," the slave master marveled.

"What should I do with him?"

"Thistlewood said his name is Dutty." He stood back so that he could examine the slave from head to foot. "Can you believe he's only about eighteen years old? They say he's a book man. He can read. That means he's a fast learner." He stopped and turned, standing seven paces away from his slave. "We have no need for reading here, boy." He spoke French, and Dutty did not understand. Knowing this, the master ordered that the slave be taken, bathed, and taught how to care for the horses.

Just as expected, it did not take him long to adjust and become functional in speaking the language. There were many slaves on the plantation, and the brutality seemed less severe to Dutty when compared to what he previously experienced on the Thistlewood plantation. However, the merciless slave driver was equally brutal as the one he left in Jamaica. The humidity was equally cruel, but the increased leisure time seemed to make his servitude more bearable.

With his obvious accelerated physical growth was his high aptitude for language and mathematics. It was also recognized that Dutty was extremely gifted in understanding directions and maps. He knew the stars and constellations. For most slave masters, such knowledge and aptitudes would have been intimating, but on the Frenchman's plantation, it was assumed that no such danger existed from a boy as young as Dutty.

With Dutty's size and strength, it was a wise choice to have him care for the horses and the carriages. He learned to cut and shape wood and to repair the carriages and polish them. It was expected that the seats and the interiors of the carriages were spotless. It was rumored that the last coach driver, before he was retired, once failed to ensure the cleanliness of a carriage. When it was discovered that the master's daughter had a smear of mud on her Sunday dress, the chauffer was whipped until his back was like jelly. Dutty was determined to not endure such a fate. He spent hours cleaning the carriages and received many accolades for his efforts.

Driving the plantation master and his family to Sunday Mass services was often the highlight of his week. He would drive along the road in a long train of coaches driven by slaves from various plantations. The steeple reached into the blue sky and became a symbol of rest, leisure, and frivolous conversation for the chauffeurs. For Dutty, however, it symbolized entertainment.

While waiting for their masters and families to exit the church, the slaves were required to enter a staging area, giving them up to two hours of casual conversation time. With one exception, the chauffeurs were male. Cecil, the one female, seldom participated in conversations. She often slept. Her mind always seemed focused on something far away. There were times, however, that Dutty noticed her watching him. He never seemed to have anything to add to the conversations, although there were times when he joined in laughter. Most of the conversations were frivolous and filled with rumors and information bearing little substance. Often their conversations ended with insults and angered diatribes.

"Now, we got this boy who tells a lot of stories, just came from some plantation over there in the Dutch islands," Arceneaux said. "He said that, while he was young, he was taken on a trip to the mainland ... to Louisiana. He said he spent some two years there before coming to Saint Dominique. I have it firsthand from him ... the words were straight from his mouth ... he said that the place is beautiful. The women there are called Creole. They have that Indian blood in them. He said that the hair and the skin is like somethin' made straight from God. And they have the most beautiful eyes—blue, green, golden. He said it was something amazing to see."

"What does that have to do with the God damned bighting mosquitos?" Benoit asked, and then he laughed. His laughter echoed from the waiting area into the church.

Frasier joined in the laughter and commented on Arceneaux's customary divergence from the subject at hand.

Arceneaux said, "If you give me a minute, I was getting to the goddamned mosquitos. The boy's name is Germain, and he says that the mosquitos there are the size of a man's finger."

"You don't say?" Frasier said.

"He says they are brutal, but I tell you they're not as bad as those white people there. Those whites there in Louisiana got so many slaves that they have no need for them. They use the babies to catch the alligators."

"Catch alligators?"

"Yeah?" He paused. "I swear to you. The goddamned whites on the mainland will take a newborn baby, sit 'em up nice, and secure them well in these little pens like the fuckin' chicken coops. They go down to the swamp at nighttime with the baby and tie 'em up with a rope around the neck and around the stomach. The baby be cryin' and kickin'. Then the alligators would come, bite them big jaws on the baby, and get his ass caught in the trap. That's how they make them nice shoes and purses for the women. They got so many slaves on the mainland they make bait of the babies."

"That's too much," Francois said. "I don't believe it." He turned to Dutty as if to invite him to share his opinion.

Dutty, however, reserved his opinion as to whether Arceneaux was honest or not. When their eyes, met, however, Arceneaux smiled arrogantly at him. "You'd never guess that the white man was so evil, hum?" He laughed lightly. "You just a young boy. You big as hell, but you young, maybe not even twenty summers. You better be careful around these whites."

Dutty was insulted. "You don't need to tell me to be careful, old man."

Francois laughed, and Cecile smiled. It was the first time they had heard Dutty speak.

"You know, you sure right about that," Frasier said.

"You know you have to be careful about them quiet blacks," Arceneaux said, his eyes focused on Dutty. "Those be the ones who run back and tell the white man everything you said. He pulled at the reins on his horse and moved closer to Duty's carriage. "What's your name, boy?"

"Dutty."

"Dutty? What kind of name is Dutty? That's not French, is it?"

"It's my name."

Receiving Arceneaux's isolated attention caused Dutty to inherit the attention from the other slaves.

Benoit said, "Where he get them eyes?"

"Is he one of those Creoles?"

"You got some Indian in you?" Arceneaux asked. "Don't you?"

"He has more than that in him," Cecile said.

Hearing her voice was equally surprising to them. She was perhaps only three or four summers older than Dutty. She had inherited the job of chauffer after the untimely sickness and death of her father. Rumor had it that she had been trained extensively in the voodoo religion by her mother and was initiated when she was young. Since then, she had allowed the possession of her body to three different spirits. As such, the men gave her very little grief.

"Oh, Cecile." Frasier, the eldest in the group, smiled. "You know I give you all the respect in the world, but you might be a little sweet on this boy. I see the way you look at him."

Cecile, without a word, dismissed the old man's comment and continued to allow the slaves to entertain her.

"What else you got in you?" Arceneaux asked, turning the attention to Dutty again. "A little white blood?"

Dutty resolved not to answer any questions about his past, but Arceneaux persisted.

"You're not gonna go tell your ole master what we talk about, are you?"

Dutty did not respond.

"You know the white man cares nothin' about a loyal slave. You see you're a young boy. You haven't seen nothin' yet. I could tell you stories, boy, that would make you stay awake at night."

"Leave the boy alone," Benoit said.

Arceneaux said, "I could tell you stories about what blacks do to those who go and tell. Then you won't sleep at all."

By then, Dutty could tolerate the sound of Arceneaux's voice no longer. "Let me tell you a story, old man. Let me tell you a story about a man—twice the man you will ever be. A man big and strong ... strong enough to lift a carriage with his bare hand and change its wheel with the other. This is not what I heard—it is what I saw my daddy do. This man was loved by the master. Master wanted all his slaves like him. He made my daddy give babies to nearly every woman on that plantation. Then they took him, and they throw fire on him while he was alive. They tied both his legs and arms to two horses, and they made me watch them horses run in two different directions when they saw that fire. You never got to know your daddy, but I seen mine. I seen mine ripped up and burned right there before my eyes." There was a long pause. "There is nothing you can tell me about what a white man will do." His anger boiled inside of him, and he envisioned himself springing from the driver's seat of the coach and upon the old man. He could imagine himself unleashing every ounce of caged anger upon slaves and whites alike. Instead, he prompted his horse to move away from them.

Arceneaux was speechless.

Cecile gave an angry eye to Arceneaux and drove her coach toward Dutty, joining him for a kind word. "You were wise not to kill them." She spoke warmly.

It was the first thing she had ever directly said to him. Her words were gentle, and with them came a feeling that was very familiar. Dutty could not remember having any friends aside from his two students who learned to read by his tutelage. It had been a year since he had seen them, and he knew that he would never see them again. The same was true for his mother. His father taught him to read, and he taught other slaves. For that, he was punished and sold away. The reality of slavery crashed upon him suddenly and without remorse or clemency. He loathed everyone—whites and slave alike.

"They are foolish men," she said. "There is something very different about you."

"Everybody says that. I know, my eyes, right?"

She shook her head, fixed her eyes on him, and studied him. "No. It's not that your eyes are different—it is the reason."

Dutty did not want her to look into his eyes, and he turned away. He felt something from her—a vibration or an energy that reached out toward him and pulled at something inside of him. He was not naïve to what she pulled at, but he knew that he did not want to release it.

She said, "How is your relationship with the Rada?"

"I have no problems with the Rada, and I believe it is pleased with me, but my love is for the Petro."

"Petro? Usually when a man says he loves the Petro, "It is because he is afraid of his master—and he wants protection."

"I am not afraid of my master."

"Why not?"

"He is weak. His god is weak. I don't believe that his god is a real god. The white man only do what he do to us because we let him."

Cecile smiled. "I always encourage slaves to do right by their masters and to obey them—to make them happy. Do you know why?"

Dutty sighed and shook his head.

"Because they give them pass and free time to come learn about the real gods—real spirits." She hesitated and read his expression. It was obvious by the shifting in his eyes, which tried to avoid her, that he was interested in what she had to say. "We meet Sunday nights at Bois Caimen. I would invite you for lessons, but I think you already know. You ever petition one?"

"Yes," Dutty said.

"What happened?"

"They threw me in the hot box just before I came here. They kept me there ... did not feed me. The box was so small that I could not turn or stretch my legs. It was hot, and I could not breathe—so I did a meditation. I called to the Petro, and I saw a vision. Mr.

Dewey put me in the box. I imagined that he would be dead in the morning, and in my vision, I saw him lying in bed, asleep. A little knee-high man with a child's body and a man's face came into the room, climbed on the bed, and sat on the white man's chest. When Mr. Dewey woke, he saw the little man and tried to move him, but the little man got heavy. Every time he tried to move him off his chest, the little man got heavier and heavier until he crushed Mr. Dewey's chest. When they took me out of that box, they told me that Mr. Dewey was dead."

She did not seem surprised or startled. She nodded. "It was an alp," she said. "Who did you call? Was it Papa Ghede?"

"Yes."

She smiled. "You see, there is something special about you. Papa Ghede is not so easily helpful. He sent a servant to grant your wish and allowed you to see it happen." She hesitated and waited for him to turn his face to her. "I want you to come tonight. I will teach you to appreciate the Rada loa."

Cecile had pale green eyes, ebony skin, and unusually white teeth. Her head was covered in a green wrap that made her eyes noticeable. She was thin and seemed too small to control the horses, but she managed just as well as any man. Dutty liked to look at her, and he did not want to stop. As such, it was nearly impossible for him to deny her. He agreed to seek permission to join her at the gathering.

The sun painted the sky a remarkable orange color in the west, and in the east, a pale moon made its way over the mountain peaks as Dutty found his way to Bois Caimen by help of an escort. Dutty had not witnessed such a large gathering of slaves, nearly three dozen in all and no white faces among them. He was certain that there were those who would report back to their masters if anything happened worthy of concern, but at that moment, he was content with the simple enjoyment of the emancipated feeling that fell over him.

When he arrived, he did not see Cecile right away. The slaves gathered in a circle around a tall wooden stick that was placed vertically in the ground. All around the stick were designs made on the ground with white powdered flour. Inside the circle, an older man with receding hair was dancing. He waved and twirled a wooden sword as he danced. To his right and left, two young dancers held sticks with towels connected to the top, transforming the sticks into flags. Beside the long pole in the ground, Cecile danced slowly. The other three knelt and kissed the ground at her feet.

That day, Dutty learned more about their religion than he had learned before leaving Jamaica. Every move of the dance had a meaning that contributed to a larger story—a story of struggle between men, coupled with his interpersonal struggles and those struggles against the spirits, which were called loa. Every design on the ground held spiritual meaning. The designs told a story of energy and the flow of energy from the temporal realms to the nontemporal. They told a story of the gatekeepers: the spirits that guarded the flow of energy. Those spirits deserved recognition and appease. They could open doors and gateways between the worlds and made it possible for physical relationships to develop between men and spirts. Those gateways were the crossroads that were symbolically drawn on the ground with the flour.

Cecile drew a circle in the dry black dirt. "The crossroads is the juncture between the physical world that we see and touch." She drew a second circle with lines intersecting at two points.

He looked down at two intersecting circles—one to represent the tangible world and the other to represent a spiritual realm.

She pointed to a point where the two circles intersected. "Here is the crossroad. Here is where the energies of both worlds collide. Legba controls this. Legba is the first loa that we must salute."

He learned that Cecile was a Hungon, a leader who was very well connected to the spirit world. Cecile surrendered her energy to Erzule Freda whose sigil was painted on a white blanket. She sat on the edge of the blanket, her body fell limp, and her eyes opened widely. Her pupils dilated as if she stared into another realm of existence. She did not blink or shift her eyes. She spoke gently in a tone and pitch that was different from her normal one. No one understood what she said save the one interpreter.

"The day for freedom is close," the interpreter announced. "The fire has arrived, and he is in our presence. He will light the fuse, and the land will burn."

It did not take long for many people who heard the interpreter to infer that Dutty may have been the fire. He was taller than any of them, and his eyes were so unusual that they had to be evidence of something divine. He had not come to their gatherings before that day, and no one seemed to know much about him other than he had come as a slave from Jamaica. He spoke few words, and he seemed to have no fear of his masters or care for their power. Other slaves believed that the fire was symbolic of their desire to win their freedom and that it would take a lot more than one slave with a large frame to break the chains of slavery.

When the ceremony ended, Cecile informed him that she intended for him to be her apprentice. "Something is brewing in the air," she said. "I want you to feel it. It is freedom. I can feel it in the air just as clearly as I can feel the rain before it arrives."

Dutty was open to her ideas, and he was excited to learn from her as long as it allowed him to be near her. He enjoyed being in her presence. She was a very good instructor, and he was fast to learn the sigils of each spirit. She called the markings veves and explained that it was important for him to make every mark perfectly to maximize the effect. The sigils had the ability to absorb the creator's energy, and that energy played a major part in attracting the loa. She taught him the heart-shaped veve that was associated with Erzule. Next, she taught him to make the veve for Damballa. "He is the father of all things," she explained. "He created the cosmos and the stars with his seven thousand coils. He was there at the beginning of creation, and it was he who gave men the knowledge of good and evil." She wanted him to experience a possession of his personal loa. "It will open your eyes. You will understand the balance of the universe—the connection between men and the loa. You will find your power."

He was hesitant at first, but one Sunday night, Dutty lingered behind after the ceremony. Cecile asked him to meditate, and he called the names of the spirits as he sat with folded legs inside the circle of white flour. Around the circle were different veves. Four small fires burned in large iron bowls. They were placed perfectly in the four directions of the planet. He called the names of the spirits again and again. He called them rapidly and focused his thoughts on the names until he was no longer aware that his lips moved.

As he meditated, she made tributes to the proper spirits. When she finished, he was calm and unaware that he was sitting on the cool earth. He felt something tightening in his chest in much the same way that a mother might cuddle her infant. It was a warm and safe feeling that took over him. He was certain that he felt a presence. He had not before reached out to his personal spirit, so he did not know for certain how it felt to have it reach back at him, but the presence he felt did not feel personal at all. In fact, he felt crowded. Whatever it was that had come to the opening had come with a multitude. He could almost hear them as if flapping wings had passed by his ears. He did not move. He was not afraid. He allowed his ears to tune in to the sound, and as he concentrated, he could hear voices. The many voices seemed to speak to him all at once, but he could not understand them. He attempted to deepen his focus, but he could not understand the words.

When the sounds disappeared, he opened his eyes.

Cecile was standing away from him. He did not see her clearly, but he knew that something was not right. She was startled and amazed. She did not answer him when he inquired of her state. In her twenty-three years, she had witnessed many people falling under possession, but she had never witness anything as remarkable as the flashes of light that circled around him like fireflies. She was hesitant to approach him because she did not know if the loa would allow it. She said, "You are ready. The gods are with you." She smiled and walked to him. "I knew you were the one."

She reached out to him, gently took his hands, and disclosed a far-fetched plan where she and her followers were committed to solicit the help of the gods to aid them in their rebellion against the slave masters. She explained the ceremony that she had organized. During the ceremony, she would introduce him as her assistant and partner. "You will then give a speech. Your voice will be the spark to start the fire. It will happen in five days ... when the stars are just right. I beg you to spend more time meditating and reaching out to the gods. I hope they direct you."

Dutty followed her instructions, and he meditated each night before the arranged ceremony at Bois Caimen. When he arrived, there were already more than one hundred men and women there; the emancipated and the slaves danced to the rhythm of the drums. There was a familiarity in that place for him. The worn grass, scattered trees, and dusty ground were familiar to him. It was as if he had been there in that moment before. It was almost as if he remembered a dream, a vision, or a prophecy. He remembered the circle of people around the platform made with boxes and crates. Outside of the circle, a man on a crate sang the Song of Seven Stabs. He had a strong voice. It was not at all deep, but it projected well over the drums.

Set koud kouto
Set koud pwenyad ...

Under their feet was a dusty floor of gravel and dust. The circle formed by the dancers had worn away the grass. Approaching from the west were clouds heavy with water, and they seemed to sag and lower as they approached the island.

Prete'm dedin a pou n'al vomi sang mwen sang ape koule

Pike yo sept fwa
Manmam Ezeli Danto O

Away from the music and dancing, Dutty heard the cry of a goat
and shifted his eyes in that direction. Even that was familiar. The
animal was flat on the ground, and it struggled to free itself from
the ropes that bound its front legs. Its back legs were also tied
together, and the rope extended from its hind legs to a tree. Dutty's
eyes followed the path of the rope. It was thrown over a thick
branch. On the other side of the branch, three men were sipping
rum. Dutty knew that they were to hang the goat by his hind legs.
All of this was familiar to him; the animal would be their sacrifice
and seal to the spirits.

Map Pike ke yo
Mache ak kouto-m mwen
Ago mwen mache ak pwenya nam men mwen jou ledmi
bare-m o map
Mup pike ke yo

There was an elderly lady among them. She sat on a goatskin rug
perhaps twenty steps away from the goat and the tree. She had
folded her legs, and her body swayed to the left and to the right
and then in a circular motion. Dutty knew that she was preparing
her body for the possession of a spirit. He knew that she was
surrounded by sigils, but he did not know which ones. There were
two rugs by her sides. He remembered the elderly lady, and in his
vision, Cecile sat to her left. This thought reminded him that he
should find Cecile, but there was no need. She had already found
him, greeting him with an affectionate hug.

Cecile took him by the hand and led him past the dancing
and singing people. They approached a group of four men. Two
were dressed in military-style clothing, and one held a flintlock
pistol at his side. He rested on one knee as the others gathered

around a large map. When they noticed Dutty, they stopped their conversation. One of them folded the map. Dutty suspected that they did not trust him to see what they were doing or hear what they discussed.

Cecile smiled and introduced Dutty to them. "This is Jeannot," she said as he folded the map.

Jeannot also seemed familiar. Dutty had seen him the night before in a separate vision. It was a terrible vision, and Jeannot was a nightmare. In that vision, he saw burning homes and men running with discharged guns into the forests. He saw slaves in the mountains, racing into the valley armed with farm tools converted into weapons for their merciless attack on the group of white men, women, and children.

She introduced the others, but their faces were hidden from his visions. "This is Biassou."

Dutty smiled politely at him. He had the sidearm.

"And this is Jean Francois."

Dutty greeted the man with a nod. An older gentleman joined their group. He stood erect, and his chest appeared to swell as he looked around the men. "Is everyone here?" His eyes fell on Dutty. "This must be Dutty Boukman?"

"Yes," Cecile answered. Her eyes remained fixed on him.

"It's nice to meet you." He stepped in front of her as if to place a shield between them. He reached out his hand, and Dutty cautiously accepted the handshake. "I am Louis Michel Pierrot. You may have heard them speak of me."

Dutty had heard the name before—but not in a respectful manner.

"Have you been briefed on your responsibilities?" he asked.

Dutty was not aware of any additional responsibilities. "I am here to speak," he answered. He felt an insecurity in Louis that made him uncomfortable. It was as if Louis searched for some type of accolades or respect that was not given to him by the men who apparently respected his authority and military knowledge—but not his person.

"Good."

Cecile moved to the side, and Dutty's eyes adjusted to see her. She said, "I was just telling my fiancé here that wars need men who are willing to die if need be for the freedom of his people?"

"Shall I assume you are such a man?" Dutty asked.

Louis smiled patronizingly. "I am a career general. War is my business."

Dutty nodded. He did not want to speak to Louis any longer. His eyes shifted to the others who were gathered there. Many of the men from his vision were already there. One, however, who was very important was missing. Dutty knew his name and his reputation, but he had not met him. He was a slave owner, but he was black like his slaves. He had a regal presence, and Dutty imagined that he would rule the island when the revolution ended.

Dutty felt a vibration in his heart. He supposed that Louis wanted to be the president of the island. He also supposed that Louis was afraid of something. Dutty did not know why he would be afraid—save for any suspicion that Louis feared Dutty's popularity among the people would threaten his ambitions.

Dutty, hearing the singing behind him, turned away from Louis. The people were singing a special song of praise for their goddess, Erzule Freda, and calling for her to hear their words. Dutty knew that the song was a signal for his prayer. It was set for the perfect moment when the moon crossed the cusp and entered Aries. That moment was close upon them, and Dutty knew that by the song's end, he was to make his prayer.

"It's time," Cecile said to Louis.

She motioned to step away from him when he took her by the arm gently and smiled. "I have good news for you," he said. "Tomorrow, I make the payment. This is the last night you will ever be a slave."

Cecile did not share his enthusiasm. "We are all slaves to something."

She moved to walk away, but he did not release her arm. "When this war begins, I will send you to the mainland, Florida, until the war is over."

"We should speak of this later."

His grip tightened. "I do not like how he looks at you."

"We cannot change that."

"I do not like how you look at him."

"If you have your way, I won't look at him at all." She pulled away and walked to Dutty. They heard the singing grow louder as the sun fell below the mountain peaks, giving way to the night and the approaching clouds in the west.

Avan yo touye mwen fo'im jije yo sept fwa
Avan yo touye mwen fo'im jije yo sept fwa
Avan yo touye mwen
Map mande Bondye sa'm fe yo

Cecile took him by the hand. "It's time," she said as she prodded him toward the platform. The drummers stopped the music when they arrived at the platform, and silence fell over them. Cecile told them that she felt the spirits and that there was no god who wanted slavery for them. "Our gods did not make us slaves! If the will and desire of a slave is to become free, his loa, his god will free him." She told them that their minds must become free—and the desire would grant freedom. "The gods will open the door. Each of you must run through it." Then she introduced Dutty to them. She called him Houngan. "I was his teacher. I wanted to teach him our religion, but I discovered that he did not need my teaching. His ti bon ange is strong ... stronger than any I have ever seen. The gods are with him as if he come from the loins of a spirit."

When Dutty stood in the center of the circle, he felt a surge of energy generating from his stomach and spreading throughout his body. His arms tingled from it, and his head became hot. It was as if he was connected to the burning fire around him.

Everyone was motionless, and their ears tuned in for every word from the towering man. He was inspired by the fire. When he spoke, the flames from all around him seemed to reflect in his bright eyes. "The fire will burn," he said. "Saint Dominque will burn. I have seen the vision. I have heard the words of the spirts. Jean Francois will rise and lead the slaves to freedom. Jeannot and Biassou will strike down our white enemies. We will kill them in their sleep. Their children will burn for the crimes of their fathers. Louverture will join our side, and the whole world will feel the vibration of the slave anger against the white devils.

"This is the future of the island. Slavery ends tonight. Today, we must make a covenant with the goddess that we will love our freedom more than we hate our slavery. With this love, we will not concern ourselves with what happens when we fight. We will concern ourselves with what happens if we do not fight."

As he spoke to them in a fiery voice, his words were supplemented by the distant thunder of an approaching rainstorm. The rumbling skies were timely evidence to those who listened to him. His words were validated by the sounds and the changing environment around them. The wind moved between them, gradually increasing in strength.

Cecile circled around Dutty with a curved knife above her head. When Dutty completed his speech, she moved to the tree where the animal was hanging by its hind legs. The crowd followed her, and the singing started again as they approached. She waved her hand and waited for Dutty to complete his prayer before she slit the animal's throat. Dutty prayed—the Creole words rolled from his lips and sank into the souls of those around him. As he prayed, the storm grew closer and louder.

"The God who created the earth, who created the sun that gives us light. The god who holds up the ocean, who makes the thunder roar. Our god who has ears to hear. You who are hidden in the clouds, who watch us from where you are. You see all that the white man has made me suffer. The white man's god asks him to commit crimes, but the god within us wants to do good. Our god, who is so good, so just, he orders us to avenge our wrongs. He will direct our arms and bring us victory. It is he who will assist us. We all should throw away the image of the white men's pitiless god. God, listen to the voice for liberty that sings in all our hearts."

The animal kicked and struggled for a moment, and then its body fell limp. Blood poured from its throat, and Cecile reached her free hand under it to catch it. She spoke in French and smeared the blood over her face. There was a celebration. The drums started to beat again, and the rain started to fall.

Dutty was the first to walk under the stream of blood. The blood poured over his head, his forehead, and the sides of his face. Others followed him and washed their hands in the animal's blood.

Jeannot and Biassou were among those who drank the blood. As they celebrated the sacrifice, the chants of song gradually grew louder. More men and women joined, and the rain fell. The gentle rain was dense enough to wet their clothes and muddy the soil beneath their feet, but it did not douse the flames around the circle.

Erzule Freda walked among them. Spirits marching from the mountains searched for those who were bathed in blood and open to the energy of the warrior spirits.

As the men and spirits prepared for war, Dutty escaped with Cecile. There was more work to do, more pacts and spells to create. She understood that rebellions were won in the hearts of men—through the bullets in their guns.

When Cecile visited Dutty at his one-room shack, she explained the magnitude of his speech and prayer. "We were joined by more than just mere men," she said. "The spirits were with us. I felt the loa. I felt the energy of something stronger than the life force inside my body. It called to me when I cut the animal's throat." She opened a cloth sack that was placed around her shoulders. She walked around the room as she spoke. She inspected his quarters, and Dutty knew that her visit was more than to inform him. She wanted something else. She placed candles in the corners and burned fragranced oil in small tin cups. The aroma was quick to overtake the air in his shack. She reached in her sack and found a silk cloth, white and smooth to the touch. She placed it in his hand and opened it.

He looked upon the design made with blood, old blood, and he did not know if it was animal blood or human blood.

"I've held on to this for a long time," she said. "'Bout twelve years now. I was saving it for a special day … a special moment. It is a very powerful spell, and now I want to activate it."

She dropped to her knees and created a sigil with the flour. "There is something else inside of you that must come out. It spoke to me when I spread the blood over my face. Tonight, we will bring it out of you."

She began to chant as she made the markings on the floor of Dutty's cabin. Her chant became a song, and Dutty felt compelled to sing with her. Their voices were soft, and the sound of rain falling against the tin roof was like the music for their song. The rain was perfect for her spell. The dust, the candle, and the air absorbed the energy that was trapped in the silk cloth until she set it on fire. There was no better time to cast her spell.

She asked Dutty to undress as she placed seven chicken's feet strategically around the room. He stood naked before her and understood what she had done. She wanted him to make love to her, but it was not her that he would have—it was her loa. He knew that, as she sighed from his touch, she had already opened the shell that was her body to the spirit who would make love to him. When she mounted him, her passion was unmatched. She was in a frenzy—lost in emotion and overtaken by the spirit until she climaxed. Then, wet with perspiration, fatigued to the point where she could hardly move, and her mouth dry, she dismounted Dutty, burned the cloth with fire from a candle and took its ashes out into the rain. There, holding the ashes in the palm of her hand, she watched as the water washed the ashes away.

She was not finished with him after their ceremonial passion. She wanted more, and after returning from washing away the ashes, she approached him. Her body was cold and wet. She led him to his straw bed, and Dutty knew that he would make love to her. She was in the moment of passion, and she would feel him, receiving her own pleasure until he surrendered his prized bounty. Afterwards, when it seemed that his strength had left him, he flopped beside her and sleep took over them both.

It was dawn when he returned her to her master's plantation. There was a carriage there that was unfamiliar to the plantation, but she knew it well. She asked Dutty to pursue no further. Dutty did not understand.

"It is Louis ... he has come to make good on his promise."

"What promise?"

"He is here to purchase me. He will buy me, send me to the mainland, and start the war. This means that there is no turning back. Your vision will come true."

She walked away from him, leaving him there to watch as she approached the carriage.

Dutty felt anger swelling inside of him. He felt as if something had been stolen from him. He watched as she entered the white master's property and saw Cecile's future husband and master exit his carriage.

The door of the master's plantation opened, and a white-haired man exited.

Dutty swore that he would start the fire. He would not allow Louis to say that he started the war. Dutty turned and walked back to his plantation, knowing that he would never call that place home again. He knew that he would attack his master's home that night, and when he had burned it and killed the master, his wife, and children, he would come to Cecile's former master's home and do the same.

Kate's Journal

Our accomplishments in the past month were, without question, remarkable. Talib is the seeker. He has Kesil's gabamnoteh and was at many times referred to as Kabeir. The gabamnoteh detached from its host, was identified, and made communications with various energies throughout history. It is loyal and adamant in keeping contact with the divided soul wherever those gabamnotehs hide. What Talib's gabamnoteh has revealed to us is beneficial and useful for the mission, and his open willingness to continue will expedite our mission. I sincerely believe that we will reincarnate the Nephilim before the next blood moon.

First, Talib's dreams are not dreams at all. They are, as Alex wrote, memories of the gabamnoteh inside its host. It is obvious that, through lucid dreaming, Talib's soul has the ability to travel into the astral plan and use gateways and portals to find the Nephilim's gabamnoteh. The first that we have confirmed is the physical influential part of the soul. It influences the energies of the human body that are connected to growth and physical abilities. Those who hosted this part of Yaron's soul were giants. Although the hosts lived among other giants, I believe that the entire tribe or race of giants was originally born from a host. The gabamnoteh is passed from one host parent to the next. The third giant that was revealed to us was a man who used his connection with the spirit world to call upon spirits for assistance. This was the first example where we saw a pure connection between the gabamnoteh and the spirit world.

The revelation now gives us names of spirits to target for our aide. Talib and Fiona will have easy and unrestricted access to these spirits. The scrolls teach the process, and once Talib is educated in ways to release his gabamnoteh, we will solicit the help from the spirits in finding the missing scroll. I will solicit help from Mumar. There is no one alive who is more aware of the processes and the strategies within the multi-planes of consciousness.

THE ADVERSARIES

Kate had many hopes. She expected that the acceleration of her experiments and searches would flow along a time frame that coincided with the astrological energies favorable to her mission. What she suspected was the resistance and interference of different conscious energies. While her suspicions rested on possible dangerous energies, like Adras, she did not know that threats came from men as well.

Far south from her island home, there was a man who would be her adversary. He was not a wealthy man, and he did not live in a mansion. He had no personal access to mercenaries or large banks. He did not have as much in material wealth as some homeless men in Athens. He also lived on an island that would be found in the waters of Lake Tana. The island had no paved roads. There were four paths that led from the lake through the vegetation, mostly shrubs, to the center. The four paths were each met with one other path that circled the island. There were huts and stone buildings dispersed over the island. Centered between a cluster of four huts was cultivated land where crops grew under the setting sun. Groups of young men were training by throwing knives at tires and practicing hand-to-hand combat. Others sat beside the paths with rifles on straps tossed over their shoulders.

The adversary was called Master Moses by the members on the island. He was the overseer of the island and commanded the training of those who learned the art of defense. His dark skin was inherited from his ancestors—the builders of the enormous obelisks and descendants of the Aksum kingdom—and remained youthful in the sense that he was dishonest by twenty years of his true age. He had a narrow frame as one might expect from a man three-quarters of a century old whose primary diet was the crops grown on the island and an occasional fish from the lake. He had not lost all of his white hair, but he kept it covered by a turban. He dressed in animal-skin clothing and walked with a stick used as a cane.

He sat on a goatskin rug inside a dark cave supplied with a torch that was fixed to the wall of the cave. His legs were folded, and the back of his hand rested on his knees. He touched the tip of his middle finger with the thumb of each hand and held that position as he meditated. His thoughts and projections had taken him far away from the cave and the island to another island where a heap of ancient rubble remained from the collapse of an amphitheater four thousand years earlier.

He did not know why the spirit that communicated with him often through his meditations implored him to visit that heap of rubble, but he followed his guide and saw a relic buried in the heap that was as ancient as the amphitheater. He was a collector of relics, and most of them were significant in Middle Eastern and Asian history. When his meditation ended, he rolled his blanket, took his stick in hand, and walked to a set of wooden stairs at the end of an underground tunnel. The stairs ascended from the tunnel through the floor of a room that appeared to be a poor example of a museum full of ancient relics. The trapdoor at the top of the stairs was marked with various Solomonic seals of Mercury and Mars that were carved in the wood and painted with fresh lamb's blood.

Closing the trapdoor, he walked to another door. It was refreshing to inhale the moist tropical air and feel it moving over the white hairs on his face. He stood outside the edifice with his back to the door and watched the dirt path in front of him appear to sink away into the earth. He was there to see a former pupil—a very reliable and disciplined man like his father. Master Moses had trained two generations of this well-respected family, and he anticipated the third generation would soon reach the island.

Bisrat Ezra walked with the swagger of a fearless warrior, but he dressed like a civilian. His chest and arms declared his valor and accomplishments as a warrior. His reputation and that of his family were well known by the men of the island, and they were eternally grateful for the family's commitment and courageous efforts against the Marxist Deg and the eventual victory for the coalition of rebel groups held together by Bisrat Ezra's team of Utatazi organizers.

Seeing Bisrat made Master Moses happy, but the circumstances did not allow for much conversation or recollection. Master Moses had a mission for his former student.

"Almost three thousand years ago, the Greek people began to tell a story of a young man who went on a search to find the fleece of a special animal. It was a ram, the same ram given to Abraham in place of Ishmael who he was to sacrifice. The fleece was eventually found and used in a ceremony of a very unnatural nature. The angels, by God's command, destroyed the amphitheater and buried an important artifact in the rubble."

Bisrat listened carefully. "Do you know where this happened?"

"It is in the Attic peninsula ... in an area called Erchia."

"So, this is real ... not a myth?"

"Some parts are myth, but what was real is that, nine days into the month of Boedromion, a ceremony of major importance was conducted and a special blade—a dagger—was used."

"Would you like me to oversee its discovery?"

"Yes. You must be cautious. Our enemies cannot suspect what we do. Go first to the council and make proper arrangements for the excavation. It must appear to be an archaeological dig."

"Of course, Master Moses."

Master Moses smiled and placed his hand on Bisrat's shoulder. "Now, walk an old man to his quarters."

Bisrat was happy to help.

"I understand that you have a son."

"Yes. He will soon be taken away for training. His name is Chanoch."

"That is a good name. A mighty good name."

"Master Moses, may I ask the significance of the dagger?"

"Yes. It is more than a dagger. It can kill a man, but it can also split and separate a man's soul. The last time it was used was during a sparagmos. I fear that the time has come in human history where it will need to be used a second time."

CPSIA information can be obtained
at www.ICGtesting.com
Printed in the USA
FSOW03n0922170118
43494FS